THE GIRL WHO COULDN'T STOP DYING

The Salazar Redwood Forest Thrillers
Book 1

LAUREN STREET

STERLING & STONE

Prologue

1993 ...

"BETH!"

She ignored the call of her name as she tore through the woods.

Tears streamed down her sweaty face as she panted, her feet crunching on dried twigs underfoot, then tripping on a root and spilling down to the forest floor — barely stopping herself from banging her chin on the ground by planting both palms in front of her.

She yelped as she scrambled back to her feet, ignoring the brush of what felt like a fern in her face and dripping blood on her right hand as she ran, on a determined flight in the darkness to reach her sister before it was too late.

The moon was full, but the canopy of branches was wide overhead, cast by an ancient family of redwoods. And the forest was a pall of darkness, blocking a full moon in a star-filled sky. The Goliath trees were gods of this forest, and it seemed like they wanted to punish her, slowing Beth from her mission, using the woods to stop her from reaching Dorothy.

She tripped on the underbrush again. And again, she quickly recovered, forcing her body to run faster than it wanted to.

"BETH!"

The voice was still behind her, louder now. She didn't know if that meant it was closer or angrier, but either way Beth felt the danger like heat on her skin, bristling with the warmth that comes before a fire.

She somehow managed to make her legs move even faster, focusing only on reaching the cabin in time. She ignored the sense of writhing danger all around her, the unreasonable yet overwhelming suspicion that the forest might swallow her whole. She also ignored the reek of gasoline in the air, telling herself that it was a different scent mingling with the slightly spicy and earthy sweet aroma of the redwoods.

"BETH!"

The voice was hoarse now.

But even if the enemy was right behind her, Beth had nearly reached her destination. She could see the cabin sitting like a portrait in the clearing ahead, illuminated by a strong wash of moonlight, no longer barred by the trees.

"BE—"

The cry was severed by a massive explosion, the sound drowned out behind her as the cabin became a fireball ahead.

And just like that, Beth lost her faith.

Salvation had been in front of her, but now all was lost.

She kept running toward the cabin, ignoring the first wave of furious heat rolling past her. Going ahead might spell the end of her, but staying back could mean something even worse.

The front door burst open and her sister came stumbling out of the cabin and onto the porch. Like a figure from a nightmare, she was a pillar of fire, screaming loudly enough to scald her lungs.

Beth looked past Dorothy, up to the second floor where a pair of burning children were pounding on the glass, begging for escape.

But Beth couldn't do anything. The cabin was already gone, and so was her sister.

She crumpled to her knees and sobbed on the ground.

ONE

Sam

"I WOULD LIKE to remind everyone that the best way to get help is to ask for it," said Meredith, the organizer of Sam's usual Narcotics Anonymous meeting. "That's not just true in this room, it's true in life."

Sam wanted to groan but managed to swallow her impulse for the third time. The next one would surely come out despite her intentions.

Meredith droned on, saying absolutely nothing that Sam needed to hear. She respected Meredith, and the process, but today everything made her feel like clenching her fist. Focus was hard, and even on those rare occasions when she could fix her attention on what Meredith was saying, Sam still wanted to roll her eyes.

It was better to keep staring at the bay; she could lose herself in its depths, even from here. The surface appeared calm, but the water would feel Siberian cold once in it, and darker than the blackest night if dragged into its depths.

The swirling mist hovering above the surface would sour the view for most people, same as the scattered buildings beyond it. Sam preferred the honesty, probably because she felt bound to suffer from the incessant reminders that everything died, from the slow corrosion of an aging town to the gurgling demise threatened by the dark water lapping at its shores.

Sam's NA meetings were held on a spit of land across the bay from the rest of Rush. She couldn't look into the heart of town from here, but it was easy to see the sea burg's weathered body. Parts of it were breaking. Abandoned businesses, boarded and shuttered. Fading paint. A district scrubbed by salty wind.

Tourists couldn't stop taking pictures of Rush. But not from here, where the water was murky and never sparkled under the sun. This was where the town showed its stains, and Sam appreciated the truth.

"Thank you, Natty." Meredith left the podium with a nod, making room for Natty.

Sam sighed. Natty was half-idiot, at least. Every minute spent listening to her blather on about her endless procession of issues, which often sounded to Sam like they were encouraged by her actions.

"…I was so high in the sky, I completely forgot about Allie…" Natty wiped her eyes. An uncomfortable percentage of her stories were about "forgetting Allie," so Sam couldn't know if this was a new one. But the pain seemed fresh on Natty's face.

"I left her in a cot watching *Daniel Tiger's Neighborhood* with some apple sauce. She loves both of those things. But then Billy came over, and I know I'd sworn off both of the Billy's, but Fireman Billy gets me doing the dumbest things…"

So this was new.

"Anyway, my mom found Allie covered in feces and screaming because she was starving…"

Sam closed her eyes. She couldn't listen to another

word. She imagined herself marching up to the podium and strangling Natty until her bulging eyes popped out of her stupid head.

Natty had fallen off the wagon. Sam hoped it ran her over.

"Thank you, Natty." Meredith was back at the podium. Probably had no idea that she might have just saved the idiot's life. "How about you, Sam? Would you care to share how you're feeling today?"

Meredith gave her a warm smile, but Sam shook her head, wishing she wasn't in such a rotten mood. Because today of all days was exactly when she should share.

She just didn't have it in her. Or anywhere close.

"I have something to share!" chirped the most annoying person in the room.

Beth wasn't an idiot like Natty, and she had no child to endanger, but the perky staple of this Narcotics Anonymous group spoke in a high-pitched tone that sounded like it had been designed to burrow right into Sam.

Beth's relentless optimism was always hard to stomach, but today Sam could already feel it curdling her insides.

"Thank you, Meredith," Beth said, taking the podium, her voice more sober than usual, but still too artificially buoyant for Sam. "I have something to share."

You already said that, Sam thought. *You don't belong in this room.*

Sam had been going to Meredith's NA for a while now. Beth had attended many of those meetings. Sam had never heard her utter a word about addiction, though she sure did love to talk about herself. Beth's poems; the pictures she painted; the "hard work she was doing to heal the little girl inside her"; the recipes she couldn't wait to try, or already had; and — perhaps the least interesting of all — what she has been watching on

TV with her old Aunt Ruthie. The old woman had terrible taste.

Point was, Beth had nothing to say, and therefore she shouldn't be in the room. She struck Sam as slightly nuts and in desperate need of company. She wondered if Meredith was so accommodating because she was being kind, or because Beth was admittedly one hell of a baker, and she always brought something better than donuts.

"I saw my sister, Dorothy!" Beth announced from up front.

The group began muttering and rolling its eyes.

"Settle down," Meredith said, standing up and patting the air with her hands. "Beth has the floor." She turned to Beth. "We want to hear about your dream."

"It wasn't a dream." Beth shook her head, her smile still bright. "I talked to Dorothy a couple days ago, but now I'm worried because I haven't been able to find her since." Her face faded from joyous to upset, like the good little actress she was. "I'm afraid I chased her away by not letting her in."

More muttering and murmuring in the room, louder now. Meredith calmed the group again, but Beth kept going, insisting that her story and theatrics were true, despite as absurd as they sounded.

The group kept grumbling irrespective of Meredith's many protests, but no one had the courage to voice the obvious.

So Sam stood and did the deed herself. "You're delusional and everyone knows it."

"I'm sorry?" Beth looked slapped. She touched her chest to continue the kabuki.

Meredith stood, but Sam kept going before she opened her mouth.

"Your sister is dead. You didn't see her or talk to her.

You might be the only one here who should be trying to get *on* pills instead of off them."

"That's enough, Sam," Meredith cut in.

"Why are you saying these things?" Beth asked, still touching her chest.

"Because no one else will."

"I said that's enough!"

She didn't need Meredith to tell her, not that time. Sam knew she'd gone too far when Beth ran away from the podium in tears.

Gary — always an asshole — started laughing and clapping up front. Meredith silenced him with a look. Hector Aguayo, who never seemed to have a problem with Sam before now, turned to her, glaring.

"That was a real bitch move, Sam."

"I know it." She nodded to the room. "I'm sorry, Meredith. And everyone. I just can't do this today. I'm late for work."

Sam was already standing.

So she left the room without another word as the mumbles returned to vibrant life behind her, thinking that all the shit still ahead of her wasn't any better than all she'd abandoned behind.

TWO

Sam

SAM ENTERED the Redwood Rings Bar, cursing the series of unfortunate events that had eventually sent her into the tourist friendly hotspot — one of the hottest in all of Rush.

The old Victorian-style restaurant and bar opened onto Main Street, and still looked like a vintage saloon for the benefit of its visitors over its citizens. Tourists rarely knew any better, and thus they typically stayed up front in the Redwood Rings. But Sam preferred the Back Bar in the rear, situated in the part of the building accessed on the Winchester Avenue side, parallel to Main.

Tourists were typically chatty, often seeing conversation with townies as part of what they were paying for, but after passing between the employee-only access door that kept the two bars distinct, Sam basked in the relative silence afforded her by the regulars.

The regulars rarely ever wanted to talk, at least not to her, seeing as she wasn't born anywhere near Rush and had skin that was several shades darker than the typical resident, so Chris couldn't bitch about how she was failing to pull her niceties off. He owned the whole building, and therefore both bars; Chris seemed to figure that gave him the right to bitch about everything.

Sam longed for the Back Bar and its relative solace, but for now she was stuck up front in the Redwood Rings, forced to hold her smile while pretending her mind wasn't circling the darkest of thoughts.

Like right now, staring at the glass of water, and imaging all of that liquid in her windpipe—

"Sam!"

She looked over at Nina, startled. Her fellow bartender was waving a hand in front of Sam's, trying to get her attention.

"Sorry. I was zoning," Sam said. No comment from Nina. "What's up?"

"Can you cover the Back Bar?" Nina asked, like it wasn't a favor that Sam had been dying to grant.

"Sure."

"I need to call Wayne. He's trying to drop Jessa off at my mom's and — you know what..." Nina smiled. "It don't matter. Wayne's a deadbeat and my mom's a bitch. You know the story."

"Sure," Sam repeated. "Tell Wayne I said *fuck you.*"

"Thanks, hon." Nina gave her a hug, ignoring the barb about her deadbeat boyfriend, same as she usually did. "I really appreciate it. Daddy just came in and I'll never get out of here if he sees me."

Sam gave her a nod.

The Redwood Rings was an inferior working experience due to its abundance of tourists, and a deficit of secrets. In Samantha Salazar's past life — before the loss of everything that ever mattered — she had served in the military police and was damn good at her job. She was an eavesdropper by nature and enjoyed listening in on the business dealings that were both birthed and nurtured in the Back Bar, the entire place plastered with pictures — from vintage sepia to modern and glossy — featuring the most famous folks who had stopped in to wet their whistle at some point in the past century.

Until recently, Sam had been assigned to the back more than the front. But then Nina got hired. It would have been easy to take the demotion personally, since Chris's decision had little if anything to do with her competence. Sam was a better server in every way. But Nina was younger and prettier, and more importantly, she was a local.

Chris claimed that Nina wasn't as good with the bigger crowds, but Sam called bullshit. It wasn't just her youth or her looks, or that she was a local while Sam was not. Nina was Ralph Colton's daughter — so not only was she nice to look at, having her around increased the odds that anyone drinking in the Back Bar might get a chance to indirectly curry favor with her old man.

In a town the size of Rush, even a slight accommodation could tip the scales.

Sam would always be an outsider, and that truth could be a cold blade warmed by her bitter blood, but most times she accepted it as the gift that it was.

Because who would ever really *want* to belong among a group of asshole locals who refused to truly accept anyone who wasn't born and raised within a twenty-mile radius of where they took their first shit?

Not to mention that an unhealthy segment of the town were clearly racists, whether they shelved their slurs in the closet or not.

Big Pete Wilder was surely the worst of them.

Sam entered the Back Bar, then closed the door behind her and saw the devil himself — Big Pete at his usual table, sitting next to Rip Graham and Nina's daddy, Chief

Colton. So, the three most powerful men in Rush all shooting the shit and probably thinking up new ways to capitalize on the unfortunate. Rip Graham was the biggest farmer around, both in size and stature. An honest man, despite his dishonesty. His particular choice of crop had only just been legalized in California, yet he had been growing it for years out under the sheltering canopy of all those redwoods.

It was a light night, with only two occupied tables in addition to Big Pete's. One older couple — Mr. and Mrs. Jacoby, married for longer than Sam's forty-one years on Earth — and another trio of buddies who were always laughing too loud and rarely up to any good: Levi, Christian, and Eddie, but since they always traveled together, Sam thought of them as Manny, Moe, and Jack.

The Rings at the front was great for people watching, seeing as she could mostly stay behind the bar and tend to requests as they came to her. But servers in the Back Bar were expected to constantly check on the patrons.

She hit Big Pete's group first. Rip offered her a friendly nod and Ralph a little wave, but Big Pete chose to ignore her. He and Ralph were both puffing on cigars. Smoking indoors was illegal, but the same was likely true for the majority of conversations among the three of them, and seeing as one offender was the chief of police, they weren't in any danger of getting arrested.

"Can I get you gentleman anything?"

"Where's Nina?" Big Pete finally stopped ignoring her.

"She'll be right back. Is there anything I can do for you?"

Big Pete took another long puff on his cigar while scowling at her, then returned to his conversation. Rip and Ralph gave her a set of matching smiles, equally brief and translucent, then Sam walked away wondering the same thing she always wondered after an encounter with Big Pete.

Did he dislike her because she looked Hispanic, or because he knew about her one-night stand with his son? Either could be true. And probably both.

Big Pete had his own table at the Back Bar, despite his lack of regularity. There was only one reason why he ever came into Chris's place, instead of staying at the Kalamack where he belonged. The members-only club — owned by Big Pete and a few of his richest buddies — was the small city's most exclusive spot.

Big Pete only came into the Back Bar when slumming it with his old buddy, Rip. Even being tight with the unofficial president of Rush himself wasn't enough to gain entry into the Kalamack — especially considering Rip's criminal past and possible present-day activities, trafficking in every level of illegality as they were rumored to be.

Sam went to check on Manny, Moe, and Jack next, numbed enough over time that she was barely surprised and only mildly offended by the end of Levi's racist joke, reaching its conclusion as she arrived at their table.

"*—that's nacho cheese!*"

Christian and Eddie had the grace to at least act uncomfortable in her presence, but their unease only made Levi laugh louder.

"Fuck you both. She don't care." Levi glanced at Sam so they knew whose emotions he was speaking for. "She's not really even Mexican, raised just as white as you and me."

"She doesn't even speak Spanish." Eddie was sincerely trying to help, but the man was dull enough to have no idea that his supposed aid was just another coat of paint on the racism.

"You don't speak Spanish?" Christian appeared baffled by the news.

"What can I get you guys?" Sam tried to smile.

"Nina already took care of us." Levi gave her a lecherous grin. "You wanna take care of us next?"

Christian sent him a hard look, then glanced across the way at Chief Colton before leaning in toward Levi with a whisper. *"Her dad is right over there."*

"I didn't say anything wrong," Levi replied, a little too loud.

"Your orders?" Sam said.

"Another three Tulls." Eddie looked at his friends for confirmation.

All of them nodded.

"Three Artemis Tulls on the rocks."

She went to check on the Jacobys next. They didn't want anything, other than for the "three young men at that table to please keep it down."

Sam promised to see what she could do, knowing that she probably wouldn't, because she couldn't really do anything. Asking Levi to "please keep it down" was like requesting that he crank it all the way up, and *telling him* to keep it down was like begging the asshole to scream.

She turned around and saw that Nina was already back at the bar. "I thought you had to leave."

"I took care of Wayne's bullshit with a phone call. I had to after Daddy texted asking where I'd gone off to. I think he wants me to make him look good in front of his friends."

"You mean Big Pete."

"Well, no one cares how they look in front of Rip." Nina laughed.

"Except maybe his entire crime ring?"

Nina laughed again like it was a joke, then nodded at Levi's table. "They want whiskeys?"

Sam nodded. "They do."

"I got them if you take care of Otis."

"Where's Otis?" Sam asked, just as the door to Winchester swung open and Old Otis sauntered inside. She turned around and gave him a wave. "Hey Otis!"

He gave her a nod and took a quiet table in the corner as she started walking over. "How are you doing, Otis?" Sam asked when she got there. "The tourists still making you thirsty?"

"I can't stand this time of summer." He shook his head and laughed. "Every year. It's the townies versus them tripper kids, each group making the other one even stupider. I'm sick of it by June, and by August I'd vote for Rush to declare a hunting season."

"On trippers?"

"On anyone being stupid," Otis clarified. "Only a matter of time before stupid gets stupider and the two sides finally start fighting."

"So, you're suggesting we hunt humans?"

"Of course not." Otis laughed again. "But out of the two of us, I'm more allowed to say it."

"I'm a minority, too."

"There's a hierarchy, and us Black folks are at the bottom, that's why we get to say whatever we want."

"I'm not sure the world agrees with you," she argued. "Dave Chapelle is always in trouble."

"That's because Dave Chapelle doesn't know when to keep his fool mouth closed."

"An Old Fashioned?"

"I've been drinking them since they were new." Otis smiled at his same old joke.

She nodded and went back to the bar, where Nina was staring hard at the closed Redwood door.

"What is it?" Sam asked.

"Not sure." Nina shook her head, still looking like she was trying to see through the door. "I heard something a minute ago … might be a fight. I guess Chris will take care of it."

"*Might be a—*" The sound of an elephant falling over onto a pool table exploded from the other side of the door. Sam was already running. "I got it."

She flung the door open, scanned the Redwood, and saw the problem immediately: a brewing skirmish between a group of trippers and townies, the teams standing toe-to-toe, or chest-to-chest was more like it, about to start brawling. Otis was a prophet in his own land.

Sam marched right over, stopping a few feet away and right in between them. "No fighting. And that goes for all of you."

"We were just explaining how things work here in Rush," said JJ, a townie piece of shit with a winning smile and a perfectly sculpted early twenties physique.

The lead tripper, the only other Black person in either bar, who clearly knew how handsome he was, grinned wide at Sam while leaning on his pool cue.

"Explain it outside," she said, ignoring him.

"Are you kicking us out?" JJ asked.

"Did you break anything?"

JJ nodded at the largest one of the trippers, six feet and a handful of inches, his eyes almost comically bloodshot. "That dumbass right there wasn't paying attention to where he was going and fell on his stupid out of town ass."

The lead tripper looked at Sam as he answered. "Actually, that asshole right there tripped my buddy because he couldn't stand to lose." He gestured at JJ.

She looked from one group to the other, then her eyes settled on JJ. "The tables are theirs for the next hour. If you don't like it, you can go."

"You can't just—"

"I mean it, JJ."

He glared at her, then turned to his sycophants. "Come on, guys."

The townies scattered like insects into the bar, then the tripper turned to her with yet another smile. "I'm Aaron. Thanks for that."

"Just watch it. JJ's fine right now, but if he drinks through this next hour of not getting his way, he might be dangerous."

"Thanks for the warning."

Sam gave him a friendly but in no way encouraging nod, then returned to the Back Bar. She expected more trouble in the Redwood and should thus stay on that side; she just needed to let Nina know.

But Chris had just returned with a fresh keg for the bar and was waiting for Sam in the Back. "Sounds like I missed something rowdy out there."

"You did. *Trippers Vs. Townies Ten: This Time It's Personal.* But not really. Just the usual bullshit, this time from JJ."

"Can you handle it?" Chris asked.

"Can *you*?"

"Absolutely. But next Friday, I want *you* to give *me* the check."

"You know it's uncool to send a damsel into distress."

"You're hardly a damsel," he replied. "And if JJ's distress, then we're all in trouble."

Sam shrugged like she could give a shit, even though she wanted to stay in the Back, then made an about face and went into the Redwood.

Near the end of his hour, JJ ambled up to the bar and

leaned lazily against it while raking Sam with his eyes. "You know you're not too old for me."

Sam ignored him.

"I'll have a Frontier in the bottle."

Sam grabbed the bottle and handed it over.

But the bottle wasn't enough. "I bet you taste like cinnamon."

"Enjoy it, JJ. That's your last one."

"I'm nowhere near drunk."

"But you're already at least one bottle past being an asshole."

JJ's face turned sour. "I'll take another bottle now."

"No, JJ." Sam shook her head.

"It's for a friend."

"Then tell your friend to get it himself."

"You can't do this to me."

"As a bartender, it is my right to refuse—"

JJ pulled a wad of cash from his pocket and started throwing bills at her. "I said I wanted another bottle!"

"Just like a baby." Sam grabbed the nearest bottle and moved it even farther away from him.

JJ jumped to grab it.

Sam pulled away, but he yanked the bottle out of her hands and took off running.

She leapt over the counter and chased him to the corner where all his friends were waiting with indecorous leers.

"Just give it back to her," grumbled one of his buddies, she couldn't see who.

JJ made the mistake of not acquiescing fast enough.

Sam grabbed the bottle, then forced him into a head-lock, making the entitled crap bag squeal like a pig just a few seconds into it.

"What the hell are you doing?" came a voice from behind her: *Chris.*

She let him go. "He stole that bottle from behind the bar."

But Chris wasn't interested in her explanation. "So you put him in a headlock?"

"And for no reason," JJ whined. "She refused to serve me, even though this is only my third beer."

Chris gave her a look and held it, just long enough to make her realize that she was the asshole here. Then he offered her his open hand and waited for her to fill it with the bottle. She did and he handed the bottle over to JJ like a gift.

"Here you go," he said.

"Shouldn't you make her tell me she's sorry?"

"I'm not sorry," Sam answered for him while walking away.

"You ever seen anyone make her do anything?" Chris asked him.

Sam didn't hear his reply. By the time he responded, Sam was outside.

THREE

Sam

THE DOOR to the Back Bar slammed shut behind Sam as she stepped down into the rear parking lot, overlooking one of the area's several crystalline lakes. A forest of trees cast the area in majesty during the daylight hours, but in the black of night, all those branches were a pall of unrelenting shadows. She stared out at the water, same as she always did, daring the dark water to someday take her.

She heard the door open again, but Sam didn't need to look. Chris had followed her outside. Her cigarette was lit and on its way to her lips before he sidled up beside her. She took a long drag without looking over, then another, and another after that.

"So, you're giving me the cold shoulder?" he finally asked.

"You're the one who came out here. If you've got something to say, then say it."

"You're pissed at me."

"Of course I'm pissed at you, Chris. I had everything under control, and you sided with JJ. That made me look weak."

"I wasn't 'siding with JJ.' I was avoiding trouble. Trying to be diplomatic."

"Fuck diplomacy!" She took another long drag. "Those spoiled shits don't deserve diplomacy."

"The townies spend a lot of money and so do their parents. We're in the service industry, so guess what? That means it's our job to serve them. And we can't do that if they don't feel safe."

"They're all a bunch of animals."

"You don't need to tell me." Chris shook his head. "I'm the one sweeping the glass when those kids decide to break a few windows."

"I'll keep watch all night … make sure that no one breaks our windows." She glanced over to her beat-to-shit Jeep parked a dozen yards away, and the glove box housing her taser, imagining JJ wriggling on the ground like a worm in the soil.

"You mind if I ask what's up with you?"

"Of course I do." But then a second later, "This is a particularly difficult night for me, and I find it hard to stay sober."

"Why didn't you ask for the night off? You know I would have—"

"Are you kidding? You think sitting in my RV all alone is better than working a shift?"

"You don't have to be alone tonight … we could even cut out of here early."

Sam shook her head. "Thanks, but I'm not in the mood."

"No sex. We can just sit together, maybe head out to Hunter's Point and look up at the stars. We can talk about the meaning of life."

"Congratulations, you just happened upon the very last thing in the world I'd want to talk about."

"I can keep my mouth shut if you want me to."

Sam didn't respond, but after a moment of lingering quiet, she looked over, only to find him looking back, his eyes vulnerable despite his strong facade.

"I appreciate it … but I think I really need to be alone tonight."

Chris kept looking at her, but this time he didn't break the silence, probably hoping that if it persisted long enough, she might be the one to finally shatter it. He played the tough guy, but her boss was a softie. She appreciated him and his efforts to console her, but right now she needed to be alone.

This was all her fault. It was a mistake to have ever gotten involved with him. Chris was her boss, and she should really break it off, sooner rather than later.

Now would probably be good.

But they weren't really even dating, so maybe the thought that she had to do *anything* was only in her head. They had hooked up a few inconsequential times and she'd been blowing him off ever since, delivering a steady stream of reasons as to why she didn't want to date.

So, no. She and Chris weren't an item, and they never would be.

She finished her cigarette and stomped the butt with her heel. "I guess that means break time is over." So much for a moment alone. "Were you serious about us both being able to leave?"

"Of course."

"Then it shouldn't matter if go by myself, right?"

Chris was trapped, but he took his defeat like a man. "Sure, Sam." But judging by his voice, it clearly did matter. And his expression wasn't exactly judgmental, but it was definitely questioning. "I'm not going to use, if that's what you're wondering."

"I wasn't accusing you."

"I'm sober a full year tomorrow. I'm not gonna fuck that up. I don't even have any pills if I *wanted* to take them." Not that it would be hard to get her hands on them in a town full of addicts.

He looked over again, chewing on his bottom lip and keeping too many thoughts to himself. But instead of saying anything, he gave her a hug and told her to take care of herself.

Same as always, the embrace made her squirm. Nothing against Chris. Hugging was always uncomfortable.

She heard the bar door slam while climbing into her Jeep. Tears were a threat as she started the engine and falling by the time she pulled out of the parking lot, already stinging as she swung a right onto Winchester.

Sam couldn't remember the last time she had felt such a hard longing to use. She nursed her regular fantasy, that she had plenty of pills waiting at home, thanks to some careless patron leaving a half-filled bottle of painkillers behind at the bar. They made their way into her pocket instead of the Redwood's lost and found. Proof that even the universe wanted her to die and was willing to give her both the tools and the courage to say goodbye for good.

A morbid thought, but that kind was always storming her mind uninvited.

She took a left on Canyon instead of a right, wanting to elongate her drive home. Pulling up in front of her Airstream now would put her a few minutes from a very wrong move. She needed to stretch her trip instead, leave enough time to talk herself out of what she absolutely should not do.

For the last year, Sam had suffered the agony of restraint. A slip tonight would mean starting over tomorrow. Back at Day One. That would lead to an epic embarrassment, having to get up in front of her group and admit to feeling as worthless as she was.

And even more humiliating to prove that Chris had been right to worry about her. It was irksome, him being able to tell that she was even *thinking* of using.

Sam couldn't afford to let anyone else into her fucked-up head.

Not now. Not ever. Not—

She yelped and started pumping the brakes, her heart pounding out of nowhere as her headlights washed atop a carcass in the road ahead.

The deer looked like it had been partially ground into the asphalt. Flattened, with its limbs akimbo in a halo of dried out guts and congealed blood.

A dead animal left to the buzzards was enough to turn her queasy, but since Sam had stopped seeing it as an animal a second after the sight hit her eyes and instead saw the roadkill as Sophie, the vomit was gurgling up from her throat before she could stop it.

The Jeep screeched to a stop as a thick dribble of puke poured from her open mouth. She snapped it shut, trapping the rest inside as the Jeep lurched back from her throwing it into *Park*.

She opened the door and spilled the rest of her liquid fear onto the road, chunky vomit like runny oatmeal hitting the ground and sticking to the corners of her mouth.

Once empty, she closed the door and leaned all the way back in her seat, breathing hard.

She wiped her mouth and curled her knuckles around the steering wheel, squeezing tighter and tighter until they were finally white, still inhaling and exhaling too hard, her whole body shaking but slowly starting to settle.

She couldn't go home. Not right now.

She might slit her wrists. Or walk into the woods and never walk out.

She started the engine and pulled onto the road, making an immediate U-turn and heading back the other way, her only destination being away from the roadkill and its brutal assault on her memory.

Though … maybe Sam did know where she was going.

Because less than ten minutes later she was pulling into the parking lot of All Bottled Up, Rush's newest and best stocked liquor store.

Why was she here? Was it because the booze gave her an easy bridge to the pills, one that would be easier to excuse or blame on something other than herself? And maybe that bridge might lead her across that final threshold.

Or maybe it was better to go inside, buy a bottle, and drink in her car until she passed out. At least then she'd still be alive in the morning.

Assuming she wanted to be.

The only thing Sam knew for sure right now was that she couldn't go home.

So she sat in the parking lot and whispered a mantra on repeat to herself.

"I'm not going to drink. I'm not going to drink. I'm not going to drink."

But no matter how many times the words left her mouth, Sam knew she was lying.

FOUR

Beth

"WAIT FOR ME!" Beth yelled after the bobbing redhead of her summertime bestie.

"Keep up!" Jenny yelled back at her, running faster.

Jenny was a tripper who came to Rush every summer with her family. For ten years now. Their families met when she and Beth were both just four years old. Dorothy had been six, and already bossy, but all three girls were a set. They all looked forward to meeting again each summer, but Beth actually counted the days. She loved playing with Jenny, but after a lifetime of feeling jealous of her older sister, it was nice to know that someone envied her life.

Jenny could never stop talking about the Garricks' gorgeous old Victorian mansion, and she ended every summer with the same exact cry: *I wish I could just stay here forever, instead of going home!*

But this summer things seemed a bit different. Jenny not only ran faster than her, she acted faster too. And she even dressed faster, if that was a thing. Jenny came to town this year in baby doll dresses and Doc Martens, while Beth was still wearing the jumpers and Keds picked out by Dorothy.

"I waited," Jenny declared when Beth finally caught up, one massive fallen log and at least a thousand pinecones away from where they'd started.

"How can you run in those things?" Beth asked, glancing down at Jenny's purple boots.

"Pretty much the same as I would run in anything else. I make sure to keep my legs moving. Like this!" Then Jenny started racing up the hiking trail again, toward Make-Out Point and away from Beth.

They had taken the long way, so no one was likely to witness the girls on their way to see what Dorothy was doing up there with none other than *Peter Wilder.*

The grownups all called him Little Pete. His daddy was Big Pete, and everyone in Rush knew who he was, not just by name but by sight. He owned a bunch of the town, but sometimes it seemed like that embarrassed Peter, even when he was bragging about it. Beth wondered if he even liked his father, considering how hard he always tried to get all of the kids at school to call him Peter instead of Little Pete. Still Little Pete was better than the occasional Petey.

Beth had been obsessed with him for as long as she could remember.

She finally caught up to Jenny again, this time at the edge of a clearing, looking tiny while pressed against the massive trunk she was hugging, peeking out from around it at a lone car looking out over Rush. A Datsun hatchback with a rusted bumper that might as well have been black in the dark.

Beth realized three things at once: Aerosmith's "Cryin'" was coming to an end inside the cabin as the Datsun rocked ever so slightly.

And that motion meant that—

"Dorothy and Peter are full on *having sex in the car!*" Jenny announced out loud and finished her thought. She looked around and nodded toward another tree, much closer to the Datsun. "Do you think we can get over there without being seen?"

"Why?" Beth was horrified by the thought.

"So we can see better! Are you kidding?"

"You want to *see better*?"

"You don't?" Jenny seemed equally shocked. "Your sister is like totally doing it with Peter right now and that's not interesting to you?"

"Cryin'" died and "Whoomp! (There It Is)" took its place. The car rocked harder, as if to prove Jenny's point.

"I'm *so jealous,*" Jenny admitted with a laugh. "I wish I was in the car with Peter right now."

No comment from a devastated Beth. She had been in love with Peter since four years ago when she saw *The Little Mermaid* and Prince Eric's thick black hair look *just like* Little Pete's. She had seen love in movies before, of course, but that was the first time Beth had ever felt it in her body. Her brain was flooded with images of Peter Wilder, and she'd been writing his name in her notebook at least a hundred times every day since. She'd also stopped calling him Little Pete, thinking that he might notice her as the only one respecting his wishes.

It hurt to know that Dorothy was in that Datsun with him. Beth didn't really think that her sister would go through with it. She and Peter had been flirting all summer, harder than ever and a lot more often than they used to, but Dorothy wasn't the sort of girl to surrender her virginity at make-out point. Even now only yards away from rocking Datsun, Beth had a hard time believing that her sister was becoming a woman.

Daddy would be furious if he knew. Not just because

his little girl was no longer his little girl, but because Peter was a Wilder. And the Wilders were strictly off limits to Garricks.

"Whoomp!" wasn't yet finished with the first verse, but the car had stopped rocking.

"I can't believe your sister just had sex!" Jenny exclaimed.

"Neither can I," Beth finally said.

"I mean, I guess it's not that early."

"What do you mean?"

"The bonfire is next week. I don't even live here and I know what that means," Jenny replied.

"What does that mean?"

"The bonfire at Scorpion Point is where all the townie *and* tripper kids go at the end of each summer, right?"

"Right…" The big bonfire on Copperhead River was only for teenagers. This would be Dorothy's third year, but Beth and Jenny's first.

"Most of the girls say goodbye to their virginity at the bonfire."

"Not most of them." Beth shook her head. But *was it* most of them? "We're too young for sex."

"Says you."

"Jenny!"

"Isn't it better to get it over with when we're young, so we can enjoy the hell out of our teenage years?"

"Sixteen is still young! We're only fourteen!" Beth was getting upset, and having a hard time believing she was having this conversation right now, even if it had been brewing all summer. "We can't have sex!"

"Do you think he was wearing a condom?"

"I don't know!" Beth exclaimed. "I hope so!"

"I heard it feels a *lot* better without one…"

Jenny kept going, but Beth couldn't hear anymore. This was all too much.

Dorothy was apparently in love with Peter enough to willingly give him her virginity. And Jenny was obviously more interested in boys than in any one of the baking projects that Beth had been suggesting all summer.

Beth wanted to go home and crawl into her bed so she could finally cry.

After suffering another hour and a long walk back down the trail, that's exactly what she did.

FIVE

Sam

Sam climbed up onto Miller Bridge, looking down over the edge into the black water below, bottle in hand, weighing her many reasons to jump against the few she had to keep both feet planted on the wooden planks below her.

For a horrible, beautiful moment, Sam lost her balance and pictured her body toppling over the railing and down into the drink. She managed to right herself, wondering why she hadn't just let herself spill over the side.

After all, a part of her had come to do exactly that.

Maybe that was proof that she wasn't really suicidal, and that she was only here on Miller Bridge to feel sorry for herself. Drunk off her ass, a failure to everyone.

She should probably just get it over with. Jumping would be easier than dealing with the growing weight of her life. Even that seemed too generous a word for what she was living.

Samantha Salazar had once enjoyed a fruitful existence, but now every new day was a bruise. She had been one of the lucky ones, adopted by a family who loved her enough to let her find her own way. A job she was good at and made her feel useful. She didn't have a man, but she sure as hell didn't need one, not once she'd had Sophie. She might have come into Sam's life as an accident, but her daughter had filled a hole that Sam didn't even know she had.

Now Sophie was gone. That hole had become a void, sucking parts of Sam in after her.

She climbed down from the railing and sat on her ass. Sam didn't really want to die — she wanted to stop hating herself. Suicidal thoughts were a garnish to her first lapse of sobriety in a year. But she couldn't really do it. Her mom had lost another child to suicide, long before Sam was born. She wasn't really a replacement for the "real" daughter her adoptive mother had lost, but Sam had always felt a responsibility to fill that void. It was her job to be the daughter that lived. And how could she ever do that to a fellow mother, after intimately understanding the agony of losing a child?

Sam would suffer a shame she couldn't sleep off. Wake in the morning as a drunk and an addict, with no one in the world left to depend on her. Sophie had been reduced to a parade of memories that she didn't know how to live with or without. Ever since losing her, Sam had been confronted with the bitter reality that no one would ever need her like Sophie used to, not ever again.

She looked out at the water, remembering her daughter's face as it had been in life. Not the bloated and ruined version that emerged from the sea. A tear fell from her face into the darkness.

"I'm so sorry," she cried. "I promise I'll be with you soon."

She raised the bottle. A momentary pause as the glass kissed her lips, then she tipped her head back and spilled another few shots down her throat.

Might as well, seeing as she was already drunk.

Sam hadn't even finished swallowing before the warmth blossomed in her stomach. *Soon.*

She took another long swallow, knowing it was too much and wondering what might come next. Did she really have the courage to say goodbye to it all like a swelling part of her so desperately wanted to, or was her cowardice only biding its time?

She stood, reaching out to grip the railing as she raised the bottle, pausing at her lips again, but this time because she wasn't alone.

Sam saw the shadow of what looked like a woman in white on the shoreline below, drifting toward like her like a ghost. A chill rippled through her as she set the bottle down and peered into the mist.

The ghost uttered a terrible wail. Something that sounded like, *"Mommy!"*

The mist was too thick, the forest too muted. The ghost kept floating closer to the bridge, its agonized cries getting louder and louder.

The voice came again, clearer this time. *"Dorothy!"*

Sam squinted, struggling to focus as the figure disappeared into a floating wall of fog. The ghost was obviously human, and likely ascending the bank to see who might be standing on the bridge.

Her heart pounded. She felt so unreasonably scared.

Maybe because she was standing on Miller Bridge around midnight, drunk enough to die more than once.

She heard a rustling, branches being moved aside somewhere nearby. She turned toward the sound as the figure emerged from the trees.

Sam wanted to laugh. Maybe cry. Seriously, dying might be her best move.

Here she was like a kite, so who else would come

drifting out of the forest wailing and moaning like a lost poltergeist finding its way?

Why, Beth Garrick, the woman she'd humiliated in NA. *Of course.*

Though she had always found her annoying, Beth struck Sam as a fellow outsider, despite her history in Rush. Quirky, but too shy or too afraid to really show it. Her reticence made sense considering some of the whispers Sam had overheard or been privy to directly. It was no wonder that Beth always seemed to be watching everyone, maybe trying to figure them out, letting her artificial wattage do the job of making it look like she was more comfortable than she actually was. But no matter the act, people still thought she was crazy.

"Sam?" Beth seemed startled to find her there, even though Sam was clearly the one who should have been asking Beth why she was wandering the woods in her nightgown and moaning like a ghost.

Sam glanced at what was left of her bottle of vodka, mercifully obscured behind a railing post, then pursed her lips in an admirable stab at an un-slurred sentence. "I was just out for a walk."

"Now?" No comment on the state of Sam's speech. "Here?"

"Songbird Park is right over there." Sam pointed to the general direction of her trailer park. "What are you doing out here?" A drop of rain fell like providence from the sky. "Looks like it might come down."

"I was looking for my sister," Beth explained.

"Your sister, huh?" Sam replied, feeling another stab of guilt over her unfortunate blunder.

Beth took a step toward the railing post and Sam darted in front of her, obscuring her most recent shame.

Beth stared into the dark without answering. Sam figured that was probably just as well.

Beth was Avon Lady friendly, chirping more than actually talking most of the time, never showing up to a meeting without a freshly baked cake or a container full of assorted cookies, and always including at least one vegan variety, of course.

But contrary to the purpose of NA, Beth never discussed her past. And being the kind of gal who thought that it was best when the goose and gander agreed, she didn't expect anyone else to spill the poison inside them.

So, if anyone from NA was to come across Sam's stumble, Beth was the ideal person, despite the general opinion that she was a few cans shy of a six-pack.

"Beth is … Beth."

"She's an unreliable narrator."

"Beth Garrick belongs in the loony bin."

But Sam didn't give a smear of shit what anyone in the group said or thought about Beth. Or anyone in all of Rush for that matter.

"Why are you looking for your sister?" Sam broke the silence with an obvious question. She wasn't sure how to ask the harder one. "I didn't mean to be cruel earlier. I just really thought she was dead?"

"Dorothy came to see me. Two nights ago."

"Oh?" Maybe people were right about Beth being an unreliable narrator — in the moonlight, she almost looked like a specter herself. "What did she want?"

"To confront Peter Wilder," Beth explained.

"About what?" Her heart skipped a beat. Something about this felt serious.

"I think he did something to my sister."

Sam winced at the memory of her laying naked with Big Pete's son, sweaty on the floor of his boat. "Why?"

"Peter is a bad man."

"Do you have a specific reason as to why he's bad? Or is this because his father is—"

"No one believes me," she scoffed. "I don't blame you for seeing it the same way everyone else does, but I'm not crazy. Or at least I'm not crazy in the way everyone thinks I am."

"I'm not saying I don't believe you," Sam assured her. "What is it you want me to believe?"

No comment from Beth. Just a long pause before she was suddenly weeping, soft at first like the drizzling sky, then heavy like a promise of what the clouds surely had in store for them.

"It's okay," Sam said, knowing she should want to hug her.

"I went to the station yesterday. Peter claimed not to have seen her, and the police won't do anything."

Of course they wouldn't. Big Pete had them all in his pocket. "Do you know where Dorothy went?"

Beth shook her head, still crying. "I didn't even let her in the front door. I thought she might be a ghost or something. She was angry and her face was all … burned." She went from sobbing to inconsolable, heaving into what seemed like it might be a panic attack.

So of course it started pouring.

Sam looked at Beth and felt an inexplicably strong yet furiously urgent desire to help. A sense that seemed to come from somewhere else. Maybe from beyond.

What if Sophie sent Beth to save her? Even if the woman was crazy, that didn't mean she wasn't an innocent. Sam hadn't been there for her daughter, but maybe she could be there for this poor woman with the oversized eyes.

"Come on." Sam took her by the hand and tugged

Beth away from the bridge, mercifully forgetting about the bottle but then kicking it due to her neglect.

Sam stopped walking as it tipped onto its side, rolling a few feet along the bridge, spilling vodka onto wood that was already wet enough to obscure how much had been swallowed from the bottle.

"I swear, I only had a drink."

Beth raised a hand to stop her from making any more of the lie. "Did you take any pills?"

"No." Sam shook her head, ashamed. "Just the drink … it's the anniversary of my daughter's death. She died two years ago today. While I was in Afghanistan."

"Oh. My … how did she die?"

"Let's get you home." Sam gave her the best smile she could manage.

Beth looked embarrassed. "I sort of slipped myself. More than the booze, and now I feel like a fucking hypocrite." She had finally stopped crying but was still wiping at her tears. "I'm not just sorry, I'm five days sober now."

"One day at a time. Right?"

"Right," Beth agreed.

Sam held out her hand again. "Come on. My place. Let's talk."

SIX

Sam

____

It was a slow drive, the half-mile to Songbird Park.

Sam knew the road like the stains on her linoleum and could have easily driven it better twice as drunk as the crazily cautious way Beth kept tapping at the brake like she was sending Morse code to the engine.

Not that she was in a hurry for another night in her trailer. It was nice enough for what it was, an Airstream she rented from Sycamore, her burnout buddy who owned the grounds, and might have been older than some of the redwoods.

Songbird was just south of town. Upon arriving in Rush, Sam had stayed at the Hillside Hotel. The dump was nowhere near a hillside, or in any way adjacent to being an actual hotel, but the dirt-cheap dive was still slightly more than Sam could afford. So Syc offered her a better deal.

There was a long list of shit to fix in the Airstream, but if she agreed to hack through it, then Syc would give her a better than reasonable rate on her monthly rent. The place was moldy and took a lot of scrubbing, but it was a better setup than Sam had either expected or felt she deserved. Tight and narrow, but orderly. It wasn't like she needed more space. She spent most of her time either outside or in town, and pouting could always be done in a corner. The shower didn't work, but the communal ones in the campground didn't get her any less clean.

"It's coming up." Sam pointed.

"I know where it is."

"Right *there*." Sam jabbed her finger at the turn.

Beth jerked the wheel to her right and turned all that cautious maneuvering into roadkill. The Jeep pounded the ground three times in succession, rising and falling like a wave in the ocean.

But she did make the turn. Barely.

"Sorry," she chirped.

"It's good." Sam felt like laughing.

Beth parked too far away from the Airstream, but that ended up being a boon for Dog, who loped like a deer whenever given the chance. Sam got out and the Siberian Retriever came bounding up to her, nuzzling hard against her leg, whining like he was auditioning for a dog food commercial.

"He's hungry," Sam explained.

"Doesn't Syc ever feed him?"

"Once a week, whether he needs it or not." She shrugged. "I used to take care of it every so often, then feeding Dog sort of became something Syc expects me to do." She shrugged again. "But I don't mind. I like feeding him."

Sam got down on her knees and started stroking the dark gray patches on his bright white fur. "*Shh* ... I'm home. Sorry I made you wait so long."

She started toward the trailer while Dog trotted with a wagging tail by her side. Beth followed a beat behind them, but from the corner of Sam's eye she could see the hint of her smile.

"Where's Syc?" Sam asked Dog. "Is he off getting wasted or laid?" Only upon finishing her query did she realize that it had been delivered in what sounded suspiciously like baby talk.

"Does the dog usually answer you?" Beth asked.

"He would, and probably does. The problem is he only speaks Russian Canine, and there aren't enough cognates."

"*Cognates,*" Beth repeated with a laugh, the mood suddenly lighter. "That's a word you don't hear every day."

Sam set her foot on the single step while unlocking the door, then invited both Dog and Beth into her trailer.

"You want coffee?" she asked as the door slammed behind her.

"Do you have any tea?"

Sam made a face. "I could soak one of my socks for a few minutes. That might taste the same."

"Coffee it is." Beth smiled and took a seat on Sam's micro-sofa.

Sam started the coffee before going to feed Dog, telling him to stop whining the entire time, while finally surrendering to both her slur and the baby talk.

After the coffee, she went to the fridge and pulled out a white sack.

"Do I want to know what's in that?" Beth asked.

"Do you?" Sam shrugged, then explained as she prepared a bowl for Dog. "Customers leave all kinds of meat on their plates. If Syc expects me to feed him, then there's no reason I can't be resourceful. I hate seeing waste at work, anyway. This way Dog gets fed, and I don't have to use my tips to keep his belly full. I doubt Chris would care, even if he knew. Or he would only care because of what everyone else would say."

"You could have just said 'meat.'" Beth shook her head. "Thou doth protest too much."

Beth was right, but Sam didn't need to validate her out loud. She set the bowl full of secondhand meat on the floor for Dog, then went to join Beth on the couch while he buried his face in the bowl.

"You don't talk about her much. Dorothy, I mean," Sam said.

Beth wore her sister like a rotten memory around her neck, though she rarely ever mentioned her name. Sam could relate.

"We were so close before the fire, but talking about her now feels like I'm burning up in it..."

Sam nodded, hoping that Beth would say more about the fire — she always hoped that Beth would eventually say something *real* — but not wanting to push it.

After a yawning moment of awkward silence, Beth bit into it just like Sam had been wanting her to.

"Dorothy was named after our great-aunt. But instead of feeling self-conscious about her old-fashioned name, she wore it like couture. You know the cliché, 'all the guys wanted her and all the girls wanted to be her'? Well, that was Dorothy. She didn't just own her name, she owned everything. None of the girls could ever be mad at her for anything, because she was always so damned nice to every-one. Plus, Dorothy radiated confidence, so she wasn't the kind of girl that ever got messed with ... And oh did she love me..."

At this, Beth gave Sam a lingering smile, soaked in memory. "Thanks to Dorothy, I got to go out with the teenagers, even though I was two years younger than her. We were always going somewhere together … until the fire, of course."

The memory seemed to surprise her, even though it was surely the one that also never left.

Sam figured it was now or never. "What happened with the fire?"

Her nose curled in as though she'd smelled something rancid. "I'll need pills or booze to either start or end that story. Right now, I want to focus on the positive and do everything I can to find my sister."

"Does anyone else know she's alive?" Sam felt stupid for asking but would have felt like more of an idiot letting the question go.

"No." Beth shook her head. "I got scared because I wasn't sure that she was real. So I wouldn't let her in. But then Dorothy started shouting through the door that she was going to get Peter, pull him out of his stupid boat party if she needed to, so she could sort everything out—"

She paled, hiccupping through the end of her sentence and needing a reset before she continued. "But I found a white rose on the porch. That was our symbol for supporting each other. No one else knows about the rose, so it *had* to be Dorothy. The rose was really there!"

Beth dug around in her purse, pulling out a wilting stem with a yellowing rose bud on top.

"Okay…" Sam was thinking. "Did she tell you where she's been all these years? And how she survived the fire when everyone thought she was dead?"

"I'll know when I find her again." Beth shook her head. "Something is wrong with Peter Wilder. I just don't know what, and I haven't seen Dorothy since. But I just *know* he did something to her."

"How do you know?"

"He's a bad man, Sam. *Bad.*"

Another unwanted image of her sweating against him all those months ago. "How is he bad? Specifically?"

"His father owns the town."

The moment was sober, even if Sam wasn't. She stared back at Beth, feeling lost.

"Weren't you an MP?" Beth finally asked. "Military Police?"

Sam nodded, still uncertain. "In another life, long ago."

"What would you suggest I do? Please … you have to help me."

Sam considered her. And again she wondered if aiding Beth Garrick was something Sophie wanted her to do. Even if it was just helping her to see the truth, that her sister was dead and had been since 1993. The woman was dreaming, or hallucinating. "Do you know anyone else who might have been at the boat party? Either crew or caterers or someone that could verify that Dorothy was there?"

Beth nodded vigorously, as if she'd been waiting for Sam to ask that exact question. "I think the Kalamack catered."

"Okay…" With Little Pete involved, that wasn't a surprise.

"Hector from NA works for them sometimes. He might know something. He also works at Mas Amigos. Maybe you could talk to him?"

Maybe you could talk to him? Like that question wasn't already loaded.

"What do you think he knows, and no offense, but why can't you talk to Hector?"

"Because you have experience with this sort of thing."

"I don't have experience with this sort of thing, Beth."

"You have more than I do," she argued, then added an incentive. "I'll pay you."

"I don't need money."

"Of course you need money. Everyone needs money. Even rich people need money. Why don't you ask Big Pete if he has enough?"

Sam shook her head. "I'm not Big Pete."

Beth looked her in the eyes, holding their stare despite the mutual discomfort. "I wasn't trying to insult you by offering you money. But I was hoping for your help and wanted you to know that I value your time. I don't expect anything for free."

"Let me get our coffee and we'll talk."

Beth gave her a grateful nod, then Sam stood from the couch and walked a few feet to the "kitchen."

She was only trying to buy herself a moment to think, but by the time Sam returned to the couch with two steaming mugs, she was feeling more sober than what should have been possible, or maybe just more delusional.

By the time those mugs were empty, Sam was firmly on the other side, wanting to help Beth even though she knew she didn't believe what the woman was saying.

It didn't really matter. *Beth* believed it, and right now Sam needed nothing more than a reason to stay alive. Beth gave her something to focus on that wasn't Sophie.

It was either way too late or far too early when Beth finally stood for the last time with a lingering stretch and her longest yawn so far.

"It's that time," she said.

"Indeed," Sam agreed.

"Can I have a hug?"

Sam should have been better than hating her in that moment for asking, but Beth also should have known better. Not liking to be touched was one of the few things Sam had actually shared with her NA group.

Sam complied, but as they parted from their fleeting embrace, Beth noticed the old scars on her wrists, despite Sam's attempt to cover them.

"Guess how many I've got." Beth gave her a pained smile, then raised both sleeves to prove her solidarity. "You believe me, right?"

Sam wanted to say *yes* but spent a second too long deciding.

Beth pulled out her phone and shoved the screen in her face.

Then Sam was looking at a photo taken right outside of Beth's house, a white rose sitting on her porch that proved absolutely nothing.

"And scroll right."

Sam did. The second picture was more compelling than the first, but still didn't mean much. The back of a woman's head walking down the sidewalk. Reddish-brown hair. But again, this didn't prove much.

"Yes. I believe you. I'll start looking into it tomorrow morning."

Beth gave Sam a second hug that she didn't want before leaving.

She closed the door and went back to the couch, where Dog was waiting for her. She collapsed on the cushion and let him climb onto her lap, nuzzling his snout under her chin.

"So, do you think I should help her? I mean, she might be nuts, but karma's gonna wanna kick me in the ass if I don't help her, right? Everyone thinks she's a fuckup, but doesn't that make her my people? And is it crazy to believe that Sophie wants me to do this?"

Dog whined.

"You already ate."

He whined again, more sympathetic, his tail now wagging.

"Thank you. My thoughts exactly."

But Sam's thoughts soon turned to something else.

And then she was asleep, again dreaming about drowning herself.

SEVEN

Sam

Sam woke up to Dog licking her face.

She pet him for a full five minutes before realizing it was Sunday.

Everything hurt more than it should. Her fault for dancing with the devil last night. She turned with a groan and grabbed her watch. A quarter past noon already. For someone who had spent most of her life rising early, that quality habit seemed to be getting harder to maintain over time.

Her front door swung open without a knock, then Syc barged in like he owned the place, and she wasn't paying rent.

"Afternoon," he said.

"You don't knock?"

"I've been knocking all morning."

"So what, Syc. That doesn't mean you can just come in, anyway. What if I did that to you?"

He shrugged. "Give me a great rate on my rent and you've got yourself a deal."

"What if I had been masturbating?"

Another shrug. "I figured it was more likely you were dead."

"Fuck you, Syc." Though he did have a point. "What do you want?"

"I came to see if Dog was here."

"He sure is," Sam said while stroking him. "And he just told me that he doesn't want to go anywhere with you."

"Did he now?" Syc offered her his crooked little smile.

"What's that, Dog?" He made a sound and Sam made a face. "Oh, okay, I'll tell him." She looked up at Syc. "Dog says you suck."

But he didn't smile, and in truth she was glad to see him. Usually was. She found comfort from the haunting in his eyes. Sycamore might have more than twenty years on her, but his darkness reminded her of a good stare in the mirror, and his torment wasn't a threat. He wasn't like Chris, or anyone in Narcotics Anonymous trying to fix her, or any of the townies constantly judging her. Like Sam, Syc was mostly a loner in Rush, and always would be, no matter how long he called the town home. They were two broken souls sharing their map in a foreign land, generations apart.

"Your canine hates you," Sam informed him.

"Dog loves me more than anything in this world." Syc ran a hand through his greasy long graying hair. "Do you know how much training it's taken for him to pretend that he can tolerate you like he does?"

"Who do you like more?" Sam asked Dog. "Me, or this drifter loser over here who can't stop forgetting to feed you?"

Dog whined and started licking her face.

"*See,*" she said.

"You probably still have some of whatever you ate last night on your face."

"So … Dog likes your mom?"

"I didn't know you swung that way."

"For your mom?" Sam looked at him seriously. "*Anything.*"

"Just so you know … my mom is actually dead."

"Oh. I'm sorry."

"Just kidding. You know I ain't that lucky." Syc laughed. "So, what did you really do last night?"

"Fell off the wagon and onto my face, before I spent the rest of my night commiserating with Beth Garrick."

"Maybe you should have called her *before* you started drinking."

"I didn't call her at all. She scared the shit out of me, looking for her sister in the woods." It sort of felt like Sam was airing the woman's dirty laundry, but it wasn't like Beth's weirdness was a secret, and Syc was the only person in Rush she could really even talk to. Plus, he was the one person that wouldn't pass it on. "Do you know much about Beth or her sister, or any of that old story about the fire and what happened back then?"

"I only know the stories about the stories." Syc shook his head. "I wasn't even here back then."

"Where were you?" Syc wasn't about to answer that particular question now since he never had before, but Sam enjoyed asking him anyway.

"Around," he replied, cagey as ever.

"You make it sound like you were in witness protection. Or a serial killer."

"Do you have preference?" Syc made it sound like a serious question.

Sam shook her head. "You're not a killer."

"How do you know?"

"I know a killer when I see one."

"Oh yeah, and how's that?" Syc seemed genuinely interested.

"You show me yours and I'll show you mine."

"How about you just tell me why you're asking about the Garricks. Are you actually buying what Beth has been selling?"

"Of course not." *Maybe.*

"We watching the bats again tonight?"

"Ask me tonight," Sam said.

"What are you doing today?"

"I'm starting my early afternoon by relinquishing custody of one Siberian Retriever to one brain-fried drifter."

"I've told you a hundred times, drifters can't own property, so by definition I am not a drifter."

"Congratulations, I bet you're the world's only property-owning drifter."

"Besides Clyde McPhatter."

"Who?" Sam asked.

"Never mind."

They said their goodbyes. Dog whined while getting ushered out of the Airstream by Syc, but Sam was glad to be alone with herself, despite cursing her lack of a working shower for the umpteenth time. She would have wanted to scrub the night off of her body regardless, but Sam rarely ever felt like she could go anywhere without at least a one-minute shower. Something about Rush itself made her feel like people always saw her as slightly dirty. But it wasn't like she could wash the Mexican off of her.

It was nearly two o'clock by the time Sam finished showering in the Songbird's public restrooms and was shifting her Jeep into third gear on the way to visit Hector at Mas Amigos, overdue for her day.

She screeched into the parking lot, killed the engine, and entered the restaurant determined for answers.

"Hola!" the server said to her. *"Tienes hambre, o solo viniste a cagar?"*

Hello, then something about her being hungry, but Sam otherwise had no idea what she was saying. "Um … is Nicky here?"

But the server didn't need to answer. Sam saw Nicky just as the bartender looked her way. They had smashed a couple of times, and still liked one another enough. He waved her over.

"Hey," he said when she got there, acknowledging Sam with a lazy gaze. "What's up?"

"Is Hector working?"

"You guys a thing now?"

"You know you're the only one for me," she flirted.

"Then how about a blowjob?"

"No thanks."

"Real quick, out back, no one will know." Nicky was grinning. Probably picturing her naked.

Sam didn't mind. Sex was one of the experiences that made life worth living, and also served as one hell of a distraction. Since most of the other vices were off her table, she took full advantage whenever possible, rarely shy when ordering from that particular menu. Beyond the easy access to all those overheard secrets that kept her curiosity both quelled and inspired, it was Sam's primary reason for working at a bar. And while Nicky wasn't as good as the best of her casual encounters, he was definitely better than most of the prospects in Rush.

"What if I take care of you first?" Just like Nicky to make a valiant final try.

"I already ate. Is Hector here?"

"Hold up." Nicky turned, looking mildly defeated, then disappeared behind the nearest door.

She breathed slowly in and out, wrestling her paranoia. Sam had no idea if she was actually being stared at and wasn't willing to turn around and find out.

Less than a minute of torment later, the door opened again and Nicky emerged with Hector. The man looked almost like a boy. Despite a patch of hair on his chin, his face was cherubic, his cheeks rosy and round. But most noticeably, he was almost a full foot shorter than Nicky, at five-foot-two or so.

He raised his eyebrows at Sam: *Didn't I call you a bitch the last time I saw you?*

"Can we talk outside?" Sam asked.

Nicky was eyeing them both, clearly curious.

She wondered what the hell she was doing, that earlier determination already eroding in the face of her mounting doubt.

"Sure." Hector nodded, then followed Sam outside.

They stopped just in front of the restaurant's widest window.

"I was out of line at NA and I know that. I'm actually helping Beth right now to make up for it."

Hector shook his head. "I don't think you can offer the kind of help she needs."

"Does that mean you won't listen?"

"I'm listening," he said.

"Can I ask you to please not tell Nicky what I'm about to ask you?"

Hector looked uncertain.

"He has a big mouth. If I wanted Nicky to know, I would have asked you right in front of him."

"Nick does have a mouth." Hector nodded. "But I can't make a promise without knowing more."

What else did she have to lose? "You get shifts at the Kalamack Club, right?"

Hector nodded and gestured for Sam to continue.

"Did you work a party the other night on the Fat Chance?"

"Why do you want to know that?"

"Meaning *yes*?"

"Meaning, I just got onto catering at the Kalamack." Hector looked at Sam like she was crazy. "You think I want to lose that gig? Those guys might be assholes, but the *tips*."

"Of course not, and I wouldn't want you to. I know *exactly* how important a spot on the Kalamack catering crew is in this town. Why do you think I didn't want Nicky to know? It's none of his business, but it is mine, and for the next minute, I'm hoping you and I can share it. Tell him we're hooking up if you want, or whatever makes you look good, I don't give a shit. I just have a question, about someone who may or may not have been at the party. Can you please help me with that, Hector?"

Hector nodded.

"Did you happen to see a woman at the party with burns?"

He paused for a beat of thought, then shook his head. He hadn't been around long enough, or really wasn't even old enough to know Dorothy by name. And Sam would be a fool to bring it up unnecessarily.

"No one with burns," Hector said. "Do I get to know why you're asking?"

"She's Beth's sister."

Hector narrowed his eyes. Even his posture seemed more suspicious. "Her dead sister, you mean. Beth thinks she was at the party?"

"Something like that. What if she's not dead?"

"What if she's hallucinating?" Hector looked closer at Sam. Right into her hangover. "You slip yesterday?"

"I don't want to talk about it." She might break if she did.

"You should talk to someone." Her posture seemed to soften him. "And definitely come to the next meeting."

"I will." Then again. "Can you help me?"

"I didn't see her … don't mean she wasn't there." He shrugged. "I mostly worked the kitchen. It's possible I would have missed her entirely. You know how the white don't like the brown outside the kitchen, or serving, unless you look like Francesca."

"Was Francesca working that night?"

"And she's working here tomorrow." Hector nodded. "Lunch shift."

"Now you're answering before I even ask the questions."

Another good-natured shrug. "I've slipped before myself."

"Did you see Peter do anything unusual, or look stressed at any point during the party?"

"I guess he was being his usual self, though he did have a few too many."

"Was he any more obnoxious than usual?"

"He started early and hard. Got sick fast, then ended up spending most of the party locked in his room."

There might be something there. Sam nodded, still absorbing.

"You don't really think her sister's alive, do you?"

"No." Sam shrugged. "But I've been in the position of needing answers before. Just being told to accept the truth doesn't really help."

The death of a loved one was hard enough to accept,

but she remembered begging for answers that her ex couldn't give her and dying more inside with every missing reply.

"Well, I don't think I helped," Hector said.

"You did. Thank you."

"What do you think I should tell Nicky?"

"Tell him I gave you a blowjob."

EIGHT

Sam

SAM TURNED off the radio so she could hear herself think.

It was a short drive to the county courthouse, and she hoped to feel settled prior to her arrival.

The facts were clear. Sam had embarked upon a wild goose chase, and she was almost for sure not only wasting her time, but also making the situation worse by getting involved.

Except that really wasn't a *fact*.

Hector was right that playing into Beth's delusion wasn't helping her. But that didn't mean there wasn't *something* to her story. It wasn't just a drunken thought of Sophie's on the bridge, urging her into action from beyond the ashes scattered nearly two years ago. This was an instinct sharpened by her time in the military.

So following that instinct meant sticking to the facts, and pursuit of the truth led directly to the county courthouse, where Sam hoped to see Dorothy Garrick's death certificate for herself.

She parked her Jeep, then went inside to either conclude the goose chase or find out if there was something more to Beth's story. Sam had never been to the courthouse before, but she wasn't surprised to see that the clerk behind the counter was a bitchy old Fräulein named Grace Holt.

The Holts were a founding family of Rush and might as well have worn that reality like a closet full of sweaters. Grace was the kind of woman who read the news exclusively looking for reasons to prove she was right about the world.

"Hi there," Sam said to Grace, her smile like a genuflection. "I was hoping you could help me."

"Depends what you need." A simple answer, but her scorn was still a grater against it.

"I was hoping that I could see the record of Dorothy Garrick's death."

"Then you can keep hoping," she grunted.

"I'm sorry?" *Even though I have nothing to apologize for.*

"Records are only for residents."

"I live at Songbird Park."

"Please, try not to brag." Grace gave her a vicious smile.

Sam wanted to bash her head against the counter until it got sticky. "I'm a resident of Rush."

"Do you own property?" *Check,* said her expression.

"I don't need to. I am a member of the public, and that is the only requirement for seeing public records. Would you like me to explain how that worked when I was in the Military Police?" *Same way it worked in every other context, really.*

The dried-out smile finally fell from her miserable face. "It's good that you're so familiar with the law…" Grace turned around and started pulling collections of papers from neatly stacked bins, then handing them across the counter to Sam. "You'll understand why we have to follow the rules."

"And the rules in this case are me filling out all of this paperwork."

"I'll also need a copy of your driver's license before I can look anything up."

"Of course." Sam pictured turning her face into batter again as she smiled, then handed the old bat her license and went to fill out her stack of unnecessary forms.

After handing them all in and tolerating a nearly silent yet still semi-abusive exchange, Beth was informed that Grace couldn't show Sam the death certificate, because it wasn't there.

She left the courthouse in fury, not because she was missing the answers she came to get, but because Grace obviously knew that Dorothy Garrick's death record wasn't there from the start. Sam was sure of it.

She drove back to Songbird, wondering if she would ever get a straight answer from anyone in Rush.

NINE

Sam

Syc was sitting in front of the fire pit next to Sam's RV when she pulled up in her Jeep. Dog was laying at his feet, but jumped up and trotted over to greet her, already nuzzling up against her leg by the time her feet hit the grass.

Syc gave her his crooked smile and blew a billow of smoke through his nostrils, holding a freshly lit joint out in offering.

"Care to partake?"

"No, I do not," Sam said, taking her seat beside him and pulling a pack of American Spirits from her pocket and shaking the tip of one into her hand. "But I'm happy to join you."

She leaned back, lit her cigarette, and took a long drag while looking up at the stars, unwilling to break the silence first.

He lasted all of a minute. "If you try to fail but end up succeeding, what did you actually do?"

"Dammit, Syc, have you just been waiting for me to get home so you could ask me that?"

"Sure have." He took another long pull, then blew his smoke like a dragon into the sky.

Sam laughed and considered her reply. Syc liked all the stupid stoner questions, from whether or not Bugs Bunny was attractive when he put on a dress, to *Is there a synonym for synonym?* But every once in a while, he managed to hit her with a question that really made her want to think about the answer.

"I got you, didn't I?" Syc asked a minute into her silence.

"Not even close. That's a word game, not a philosophy problem."

"How so?" He took another puff.

Sam, too, though hers didn't smell nearly as good. "Take the sentence *Syc failed to stay sober for more than a week.* In that usage, we don't give a shit about Sycamore's goals, much like old Syc himself. Maybe he wanted to stay sober and maybe he didn't, we really have no way of knowing. Syc's failure is a matter of note, not intention. In other words, we could just as easily say, *Syc didn't stay sober.*"

"Hard not to feel like you're not judging me here."

Dog whined.

Sam continued. "But if Syc tries to fuck up all his brain cells and accomplishes that goal as he so clearly has, then Syc has succeeded at that goal."

"I'm right here."

"I know. That's why Dog looks so goddamned unhappy," Sam said.

The ensuing quiet was long, deep, and exactly what she needed. Sam lay back in her chair, letting her eyes adjust to the deepening dark. The edges of the redwoods towered above them, making a perfect frame for the bats that were starting to swoop low in the sky. Her favorite time of the day.

She finished her cigarette but didn't light a second one. Syc was already done with his joint and still waiting for her to say something, though he wasn't doing anything to make her Sam like she should in any way hurry.

"I really hate this place sometimes," she finally said, petting Dog as he sighed.

"I hope you mean Rush and not Songbird."

She looked around the trailer park, feigning awe and admiration. "I meant the town, we both know that Songbird is the prize in this cereal box."

"And it's shitty cereal," Syc agreed with a nod.

"Like Special K."

"Ain't nothing special about it." He shook his head, as if the comparison pissed him off.

"It's the people," Sam redirected their conversation back to where it was going. "I love the area more than the town, but that's because it's filled with all these big trees and bright blue sky, instead of the assorted groups and casual racism."

"I didn't know it was casual." Syc was slightly less white than a sack of flour, but he still seemed to take any and all racism as a personal affront.

"It's the lines between the different groups that gets me."

"It takes a while. You're doing great," he said, still looking up at the emerging stars. "I'm not sure anyone could do better than you've done in the … what? A year since you've been here."

"Almost," she replied, before falling deeper into her thoughts.

Understanding the various groups in and around Rush hadn't exactly been easy — it wasn't like they donned matching tees for easy identification. But they did wear uniforms of sorts, with each genus of citizens flashing their telltale markers like the feathers on a peacock.

There were the Good Old Boys. Sprawling families that had called Rush their home for generations. They liked their politics even redder than their meat, always approving of money and guns, boasting a supposed love for their country, but not so much for its government. Good Old Boys bunkered up in Big Pete's Kalamack Club, housed over in the monstrosity that was the Griffith Mansion, where deals were made and nepotism was rife. They dressed like hunters, but with premium apparel that barely got dirty.

Farmers were the group that made Rush both locally and internationally infamous more than any of the others. Unlike those hands working land in America's breadbasket, or south of Rush down in the San Joaquin Valley, these men and women of the Earth grew weed amid the sequoias. The Farmers were territorial, ruthless, and led by local legend Rip Graham. Evolving laws in regard to the legality of cannabis had only heightened the conflict as Farmers fought even harder to control their trade. They were largely based outside of the town but dealt from within its borders. Farmers wore varied clothing, but always looked comfortable, and it was easy to smell both the soil and herb from reasonably far away.

Trippers owned summer cabins in the redwoods outside of town, arriving in waves starting just before then all through summer, though the majority of those cabins stayed empty for most of the year. Middle-class families who couldn't afford trips abroad or all-inclusive holidays, so they used their cabins for annual family vacations.

Tripper and Townie kids got to know each other over the years, but they were always skipping seasons and thus connections stayed tenuous. Trippers wore whatever was both trendy and affordable. Townies hated them for it.

Townies were comprised mostly of families who had lived in the area for years. This group shared some crossover with the Good Old Boys. According to eavesdropped conversations, established patterns of behavior, and many drunken declarations, Sam had observed an obvious and perhaps even indisputable truth: Most of the townie youth couldn't wait to get out of the place, but often returned home to Rush once they were ready to settle down after the low cost of living and strong family values pulled them back in.

Younger townies traveled in packs, got drunk in the woods, and spent an inordinate amount of time in what was one of the shittiest malls that Sam had ever seen. Trippers and townies often hung out together, though the townies saw the trippers as soft and spoiled, which ultimately led to at least a couple of brawls by the end of each season, and sometimes more. A few were legendary.

The town also had an impressively large community of aging hippies. The majority had migrated up to Rush and the surrounding areas after Berkeley became too expensive in the 80s. Like Syc, many of the pilgrims had fried their brains, same as the eggs in those old commercials. But unlike Syc, they had turned too weird for a regular conversation. Thanks to the annual reggae festival, plus the cannabis trade and trimming season, younger hippies were now making the trek as well, landing in late August and sticking around town until winter.

And finally, the group Sam wished she didn't belong to: *Addicts.*

In a community that had been plagued by drugs for over six decades, Rush boasted an unusually large percentage of recovering addicts. But the local NA chapter did take the *anonymous* part of their promise seriously, and most of the town's non-participating citizens weren't even aware that such a group existed, though the Addicts did have members from every other pocket.

Outside of their meetings, they shared a secret kinship, looking out for and supporting one another. Like what Sam was doing for Beth.

Sitting side-by-side with Syc was a sort of salve, helping Sam cling to her sanity. They were both outsiders in this strange town, looking up from their chairs into a diamonds-on-velvet sky, slightly obscured by shadows from the enormous sequoias around them. A symphony of night creatures chittered and chirped in a symphony of wings and legs. Flocks of bats swooped across the sky in peppery clouds across all those stars, like salt across the black.

Syc broke the silence, this time by taking out another joint and lighting it, pulling a fat hit into his mouth, then offering it over to Sam.

"No, thanks." She shook her head, then fished a second cigarette out of her pocket and parked it between her lips as she lit it. "What can you tell me about the Wilders?"

Syc looked over, surprised by the question. "What are you actually asking, Sam?"

His first-naming her made their conversation feel suddenly more dangerous.

"Does anyone have any more money or power than they do?" Sam asked.

"Well, there's Rip, of course." He shrugged. "But it's not like either of them have shared their bank balances with me. As for power, it's safe to assume that both Big Pete and Rip have all the brokers of note in their respective pockets. In short, them boys aren't to be messed with. So again: *What are you actually asking?*"

As leader of the growers, Rip should've been Big

Pete's natural enemy. Yet somehow the two men had maintained a friendship ever since the second grade, when Rip punched Big Pete for calling him a hayseed and Pete found in his new friend something he could respect.

If Sam thought too hard about it, she'd end up saying nothing, so she took a long drag, blew her plume into the starlit sky, then told the truth about Beth either seeing her sister or thinking she did.

"So I guess I'm treating it seriously enough to see what I can find out." Sam gave Sycamore a shrug as she finished.

He didn't respond right away, puffing on his pre-roll and giving her the benefit of his feigned considerations, but it sounded to Sam like Syc had his reply before she even finished her story.

"You still wanting to die? Because I wouldn't go poking my nose in old family business without a death wish."

"I'm not looking to die, but I'm not so sure it'd be the end of the world if I was gone from it."

"It'd be the end of your world. And I'd miss you a little I suppose," Syc said. "Even though Dog would be awful glad about you being gone."

Dog whined his disagreement.

"What can you tell me about the old family business?" Sam persisted. "I know you weren't here for whatever happened with Dorothy Garrick once upon a whenever ago, but you've been in Rush a helluva lot longer than me, and that means you know something."

"You know about the Old Redwood?"

She nodded. "I know about the Old Redwood, and that Abraham Wilder cut it down. I know that Dorothy died in a fire. But more importantly, the Garricks and the Wilders have been at odds ever since that tree got chopped down, and now Beth Garrick thinks Dorothy's back and she's blaming Peter Wilder."

"Do you know what *actually* happened with the tree?"

"No one knows what actually happened, seeing as history is written by the winners and the original participants are all dead, but most folks around here agree that Harrison Garrick was the one to shoot Abraham Wilder."

"The tree was on the property line. And old Garrick went off on a hunting trip and came back to find it gone."

"Sold?"

"Sold at a time when redwood was like gold."

She shook her head. "Imagine killing someone over a tree."

"That little pile of money is rumored to be the start of the Wilder fortune."

"What about the cabin fire?"

"Police said it was some sort of a gas leak. Wrong place, wrong time."

"Who survived?"

"Nobody."

Sam swallowed. "Who died?"

Syc shook his head, death in his eyes and haunting his face. "Dorothy. And the entire Mason family. Mom, dad, and three kids. Beth was lucky she wasn't there, but the trauma is obvious."

"And what about Peter?"

"I'm serious, Sam, you really don't want to do this."

"Do what?"

"Whatever you're doing. The Wilders are beyond dangerous. Even the people I deal with won't fuck with them.

"The mobsters or the serial killers?" Sam asked with the start of a laugh.

"My associates," Syc said, murdering her mirth with

his chilling sobriety. "Even if the Wilders weren't sketchier than a drawing pad, they own the law in this town. You need to be careful."

"I promise, I will be."

Syc looked over at her, like there were another hundred things he wanted to say. But instead, he simply nodded as she stood and stretched before walking away.

Dog bounded up and followed behind her.

"He's only following you because he likes things that smell bad!" Syc yelled.

Sam smiled without letting him see it.

Ten minutes later, she was already in bed, Sophie's face swimming through her mind. The face she could never forget. Was this what it was like for Beth with Dorothy?

Dog whined and she pet him, but really, she wanted some pills.

She kept wanting them, more and more and more with every passing minute.

Until she finally fell asleep.

TEN

Dorothy

1993...

Dorothy giggled to herself again, wondering if she might be in love.

Her wide smile would invite too many questions. She had to wipe it off from her face before anyone saw it.

But Dorothy couldn't stop laughing to herself. She felt like a little girl on a merry-go-round, wanting to spin for eternity, and also like a grownup woman, fully ripened and ready to taste the world.

Peter Wilder was practically a god. He was good at everything, and great at a few things. The kind of guy who knew how to have fun but could also run for class president and win without even trying. Some of it was his effortless good looks, and a lot of the popularity came from his family, but some of what made him special came from pure charisma, and that part was pure Peter.

She took another moment to sober on the porch, then opened her front door to the sound of her sister quietly crying. A strain of whimper that meant their father was raging again.

She heard his verbal brutality next.

"Keep crying and it'll be both of you," he snarled.

Dorothy marched into the living room and saw her sister on the floor, a supplicant to the man who constantly reminded them both where they came from: *I brought you into this world and I can take you out of it whenever I want, so you better pray that if I ever do, it comes when you're sleeping.*

He turned to her, his nose puffy and even redder than his irritated eyes. "Where were you?"

"I was out with a friend," Dorothy said.

"Does that friend look like a fucking toothpaste commercial?"

"I don't know what you mean by that." Even though she did.

"Your sister just told me you're dating Peter Wilder. Is that true?"

Dorothy couldn't help but glance at Beth, though it was the wrong move for sure. She just couldn't believe that her sister would fink on her. They were supposed to look out for each other. *Always and no matter what.* They had promised to do everything in their power to protect each other from him.

So this was a broken promise: instead of protecting her, Beth had handed her over to the biggest monster in either of their lives.

She was still staring up at their father, surely hoping that her ratting Dorothy out was enough to escape the coming punishment. "Yes. Peter and I are seeing each other." No point in lying if he knew.

"What's his last name?"

You know his last name, asshole. "His name is Peter Wilder."

"So why is *my* daughter anywhere near him?"

"Because your business with his family isn't my business, Daddy." Dorothy hated saying Daddy, but the one time she sarcastically called him Master cost her a scar on the back of her thigh.

"Like hell it isn't. You will never see him again."

"We go to the same school, Daddy. Of course I'll see him."

"You're making an even bigger mistake being smart with me, young lady. You know exactly what I mean. You're lucky I let you date at all. You will not be seen in public with a Wilder. Not while I'm alive—"

Just one of the reasons I wish you were gone.

"—And you'll burn in hell for doing it if you so much as try after I'm dead."

"He's taking me to the bonfire at Scorpion Point on Saturday." The aftermath of this would be bad, but then it would be over. If Dorothy was willing to suffer the consequences, then there was nothing her father could do. "And I think I might be in love with him."

"You will *not* be going to the bonfire." He looked down at Beth, then back up at Dorothy. "Neither one of you will be going to the bonfire, or to any event that *that* family is at ever again."

"But I didn't do anything!" Beth started to sob.

Except stab your sister in the back, you fucking coward.

"You would have if given the chance," their father snarled down at her. "But you still look like a freckle-faced little boy most of the time, and even if you didn't, you'll never be half as pretty as your sister, so don't expect the offers to suddenly come rolling in."

Beth curled into a ball on the floor and cried even harder.

Dorothy should have enjoyed the sight since Beth clearly deserved it, but their father's emotional brutality had softened the anger against her kid sister.

She wanted to yell obscenities at the monster standing

like lord of the manor between his daughters, one of them cowering and the other doing everything possible to ignore the years of training that were begging her to. Instead, she said nothing.

"Have you gone to bed with him?"

We've never once used a bed. "Yes, we've had sex. But like I said, I'm in love. And according to Mom, I'm already older than——"

"You better think 'fore you finish that sentence!"

His drooling growl and the memory it inspired got her to drop it.

"Go upstairs," he ordered her.

The command was for Dorothy, but it sent Beth into an even deeper state of hysteria.

But Dorothy knew what to do, and even as furious as she was at Beth, in no way did she want for her little sister to join her. She took the stairs one at a time, careful not to trudge, knowing that the meter of her steps would matter when it came to the monster meting out his punishment.

She tried to ignore the looming sense of him following behind her as she ascended the stairs to their second floor, then went down the hallway and lowered a second set of steps leading to their attic.

She surveyed the chest full of weapons used for punishment, making her choice in the seconds he'd give her: paddle, hairbrush, belt — belt it is.

Dorothy pulled a thick buckled black belt from the box of horrors, then lowered her pants and kneeled over the punishment chair and closed her mind to the pain and the humiliation and the trauma in real time that came whenever she was in this position, suffering through a series of hard slaps, each of them leaving a scar, whether the proof was visible or not.

She wanted her mind to be empty, but instead she kept

thinking of Beth. The thoughts were painful, especially considering Dorothy still felt furious at her.

Still, the rage didn't keep her from picturing Beth, who would no doubt have run to her room and was probably trembling under the bed where she usually hid, even though their father knew her hiding spot, hoping and praying and pleading with the Good Lord out loud in a whisper that she might escape whatever was happening to her sister.

Her thoughts strayed for a moment, and in that blink the pain was blinding. A sharp crack of that buckle biting into her skin. Then she shoved her mind away from the torment and focused again on a pulsing emotion. Compassion for Beth was a compass to follow, even in her darkest hours.

Dorothy couldn't help it. She came into this world first, and Mom would want her to protect her little sister. Yes, Beth could be a little bitch. But they had both suffered under the ugly reign of their father. It hurt to imagine her sister huddled on her floor listening to the grunting and the scraping chair on her ceiling.

But that pain still beat the buckle.

ELEVEN

Sam

SAM WATCHED the Mas Amigos hostess helping the couple in front of her, wondering if the woman was really giving her a dirty look, or if it was only the infection of paranoia that had been living inside her ever since she reluctantly started referring to Rush as her home.

"Can I help you?" The hostess sounded pleasant, and her smile seemed genuine enough.

"Would it be possible to sit in Francesca's section?" Sam asked.

"I don't see why not." She shrugged. "Everyone else wants to, and it's early enough that you won't have to wait." The hostess looked behind Sam like there might be a couple of tiny companions hiding behind her. "Just you?"

"Just me."

"Cool." She nodded in solidarity. "A table for one can be fun. Follow me."

The hostess grabbed a menu, then led Sam to a small table in the corner of what was apparently Francesca's section.

"Thanks." But then Sam kept it going. "What's good here?"

"Don't order the queso. Everyone goes on and on about how great it is, but it's the only thing on the menu that comes from a can."

"What should I order?"

She looked thoughtful. Even put a long finger to her pointy chin. "The *chilé relleños* are killer, and the steak enchiladas are as good as the menu says they are, assuming you like eating meat." Another shrug. "If not then you should probably order the quesadilla."

"What if I'm vegan?"

"Then you should eat somewhere else." The hostess left with an implied wink that helped to dull her ever-present paranoia.

Reading the menu, Sam couldn't help but feeling like everyone in town probably thought this was the kind of place she ate all the time. Or how she ate at home. But she barely ever ate Mexican food and was still far from deciding what she wanted to order when her server arrived at the table.

Sam would have known it was Francesca even without the name tag. She understood in an instant why everyone wanted to sit in her section. Francesca was a beautiful brunette in her twenties, with tan skin, twinkling blue eyes, and a smile that rested neatly between devilish and angelic.

"What can I get you?" Francesca sounded neither kind nor cruel, but was clearly not used to working hard for her tips.

"I heard the queso is good."

"It's great," Francesca agreed, and Sam could see the lie behind her smile.

"What do you think I should order?"

"The steaks are all great."

Of course they are. "I think I'll order the enchiladas."

"What kind?"

"Chicken. But I'll also order a steak if you'll tell me whether you were working a party out on the Fat Chance—"

"Oh. It's you. Hector told me someone was asking about the party."

"That's me." Sam smiled. "I'm trying to help a friend find her sister."

The smile had frozen on Francesca's face, but Sam plowed ahead anyway. "Can you tell me if you saw a woman with a burned face on the boat?"

"Sorry. Never seen anyone like that before."

"And the queso here is great, right?"

"I'm sorry?"

"I think you saw her, which means I know you can help me."

"I don't want no part of whatever's going on." Francesca shook her head. "That's between her and them."

"The fact that you know there's anything between her and them proves that there must be something you can tell me."

"I like my job ... I like my life." Francesca visibly flinched as she looked around the restaurant. "I'll be right back with your order."

She didn't wait for a reply, just disappeared into the kitchen and never came back.

Ten minutes later a different server arrived: Juana Aguayo herself, the owner of Mas Amigos. She brought an order of chicken enchiladas, with rice and beans, plus both corn and flour tortillas — Francesca hadn't asked — then set it all on the table next to a plate of taquitos with a side of guacamole.

"*En la casa,*" Juana said, pointing to the taquitos. "*Ellos son muy delicioso. ¿Hay algo más en lo que pueda ayudarte?*" Then, when Sam stared back at her blankly, she added, "Is there anything else I can help you with, Señora Salazar?"

It sounded like she threw an extra syllable into Salazar, Señora sounded like an insult, and the proprietor's Español now sounded like a setup, but Sam ignored what was still probably only her paranoia. "Only Francesca. She promised to give me the lowdown on dessert."

"Francesca is gone."

"Gone?"

"Her shift ended."

"Really?" Sam asked, knowing she was pushing it but incredulous nonetheless.

"I'll have an order of sopapillas brought to your table for dessert. I hope you enjoy the meal, but then I expect you to leave, and only come back if it is to work on your palate."

At least the sopapillas were scrumptious.

TWELVE

Sam
____

"You doing okay?" Chris asked.

"I'm fine," Sam replied, looking at her boss from across the bar. She was only a few minutes into her shift and he was already being weird. "How are you?"

"The last time you left here … you weren't your best self. I just wanted to see how—"

"I'm fine. Nothing to worry you. I just had a lot on my mind."

"Anything you want to talk about?"

"Not even a little." She shook her head, then met his eyes, hoping that might make it easier for her to earn a *yes* to this next question. "Can I work the Back tonight?"

"Bill's on tap for the Back Bar."

"I know what the schedule says, that's why I'm asking."

"I need you out front."

"Nope." She shook her head again. "You need *someone* out front. But I need to work somewhere quieter tonight to do my best job. So, whaddaya say, boss?"

"How about I repeat that Bill is on the schedule, then

give you this one anyway because that's better than you browbeating me."

"You're the boss."

"It might be nice if you started treating me like one," Chris replied with a wink before walking away.

But then he was gone, and Sam began to relax, looking forward to a calmer night away from another potential skirmish between the trippers and townies, but also eager to be in a place where she could keep her ears primed and her eyes open for answers.

Big Pete was holding court at his usual table, with Rip by his side and Reginald Jonas rounding out the threesome. Jonas was round, fat, and odious. Strong rumor declared that in his psychiatrist days the doc was more likely than not to prescribe electroshock therapy. Now retired, Jonas spent most of his time too drunk to string a full sentence together.

At first it seemed like the universe was working to make it an easy mission for Sam when Ralph Colton sauntered in and the chief of police took his spot at the table. But despite the ripe opportunity, there was nothing easy about it. Nina's dad liked to bluster and boast, and he could easily brag for an hour about anything. But he was also Big Pete's crony, and even if Sam could get the officer talking, the Czar of Rush could shut him up with a blink.

She used the table's first, second, and third rounds to observe the mood, prove her competence while staying invisible — same as always — and work a lot harder than usual to charm them. There would almost for sure be a fifth round, but it was far from guaranteed, and subsequent rounds grew increasingly less likely after that.

So Sam set their drinks on the table and figured it was do or die. "Hey Chief, I was wondering if you could answer a question for me."

Big Pete kept ignoring her, same as he had nearly every second she'd ever spent in his presence, still talking across the table at Rip like she didn't exist.

"Just don't ask me about any of that gender or pronoun stuff, because none of it makes sense to me." Colton grinned, like he was being clever instead of cliché.

Sam smiled back. "I was down at the county courthouse earlier today, because I wanted to get a look at an old death certificate, but the record wasn't available."

Colton was instantly suspicious. "Whose death certificate were you looking to see?"

"Dorothy Garrick's," she replied.

Colton's suspicions spread to the table. Big Pete stopped talking and Rip looked like he knew why. Only Jonas kept guffawing, clearly having missed the moment in his drunken state. The other three men were now staring at Sam, waiting for her to leave. Which only made her feel like she needed to stay.

"Grace Holt said it wasn't there."

"Grace Holt was right," Colton confirmed with a decisive nod.

Again they all waited for her to go.

But she pushed it. "Why wasn't her death certificate at the county courthouse if she died in Rush?"

"Because she was airlifted out of here and died in some other hospital," Colton replied.

"Which hospital?"

He shrugged. "How should I know?"

Because it's your job. "But wouldn't there be a record?"

Big Pete, Jonas, and Rip watched him laugh at Sam like she was the village idiot before he replied, "Not if she died in a different county." He snorted. "Maybe you should find out which county it is so you can start harassing the public servants up there."

"That's a good idea. You said 'up' … does that mean it wasn't San Francisco?"

The chief leaned forward, his jaw set and face stern. "I assume Beth Garrick is responsible for encouraging your frivolous little questions. She keeps calling the station, asking us hard-working cops to help her find Dorothy. I highly suggest you stop encouraging those delusions."

"I'm sure you're right." Sam shrugged, like it was all no big deal, but she still had to lob a final ball before going. "It's just that Dorothy was last seen getting on Peter's boat—"

Big Pete rose slowly to his feet, halting Sam's words and commanding the table's attention, looming over Sam and sending flecks of spittle onto her face as he growled, "You need to mind your own business, señorita. You've no right coming in here and sticking your nose into things that don't concern you."

"I work here."

"Then why don't you bring my table another round and work a little harder to remember your place. Faster this time. Neither one of us needs to pretend like I couldn't get you fired with one nod."

"I'm sure you could," she agreed, giving the bully what he wanted, but only in a way that let Sam keep living with herself.

"Are you being smart with me?"

"No, sir." She absolutely was.

"I'm sorry." Chris suddenly appeared on-scene to rescue her. "Sometimes Sam's tone is hard to read. I've been working with her long enough to get it, but—"

"I don't need you to defend me."

"Maybe you do, señorita." Big Pete turned his attention to Chris and nodded toward the Redwood. "Maybe the other place is a better for outsiders."

"I hear you." Chris gave him a nod, then pulled Sam away from the table and sent her into the Rings, fuming.

It was a long hour before she looked out the window and saw Big Pete leaving with his buddy and his pet police officer in tow.

"So, you're just going to stop letting me work the bar because that asshole snaps his fingers?" Sam said, now that Chris was finally willing to discuss what happened.

"He didn't snap. And of course you can still work in the Back."

"Unless he's in."

"Big Pete has a short memory. He'll forget about it."

"I'd argue the opposite."

"I promise you can still work the Back when it makes sense. But remember, I had you over there tonight, anyway. I do own this place and I've been keeping it relatively peaceful for over ten years now. Maybe I know what I'm doing."

"Maybe." But she was smiling, and a bit more willing to concede. "Sorry if I made it harder on you."

"It's fine. Can you please just remember that if there ever comes a day when Big Pete decides I'm his enemy, I'm done in this town."

"I promise to remember, but wow, is that shitty. It's like you're a sharecropper."

"It's nothing like that," he protested.

"It's a little like that." Sam left it there, and they parted with a smile.

She returned to the front bar and finished her shift, then started her drive home only to notice someone following her almost immediately.

But Sam wasn't sure the person in pursuit was truly that incompetent. Maybe they wanted her to know there was a gray sedan behind her, staying just far enough back to remain a mystery for most of the way.

She lost the car for a while, but the momentary relief was slapped right out of her when she saw the gray sedan again, this time coming from the opposite direction and nearly clipping her Jeep right off of the twisting road and into one of the many looming trunks on either side of it.

Sam slammed on her brakes, then sat in her seat panting as the sedan raced away, wondering what she'd gotten herself into. There was definitely something rotten in Rush.

THIRTEEN

Beth

Beth woke with a start.

She was suddenly upright in bed, certain that she heard the sound of something breaking downstairs. She swallowed hard, trembling for several long moments until she finally gathered enough courage to toss the covers off of her body and plant both feet on the floor.

She lifted her mattress and grabbed the small pistol she kept hidden there for precisely this kind of emergency.

Her old Victorian had a long history and sometimes what seemed like a mind of its own, the elderly structure always wheezing and creaking like a senior who shouldn't be walking but doing it anyway. Right now those little noises sounded dangerous in the otherwise painfully quiet pre-dawn.

Beth looked out the window and stared into the forest but saw nothing. Her home backed right up to the woods, and she'd spent most of her life terrified that an army of ghosts might one day drift out from among the trees to end her.

Something wasn't right … she wanted to hold her

breath as she crept down the stairs, unreasonably certain that every step would be her last…

Because something evil and ugly was going to end her.

But by the time Beth was inspecting her living room, mindlessly turning cushions on the couch and looking through the foyer closet, feeling dumber and dumber with every moment wasted on her fruitless investigation, she realized that it was just another nightmare, and as much as Beth hated the hauntings in her sleep, she couldn't exactly keep her eyes open for the rest of her life.

So she went to the kitchen for a glass of water, and stopped mid-stride, her foot hovering above a cluster of shards littering the floor.

A glass must have fallen from the counter.

And that meant someone probably was in the house, since glasses rarely if ever fell on their own.

She found herself whimpering *no, no, no* as she went to the look out the window again.

This isn't real, she tried to insist, first in her mind and then out loud.

You just need to take your meds.

Yes, that was exactly what she needed. A couple of her antipsychotics and everything would be better than new. They were right upstairs on her nightstand. She just needed to turn around and—

But Beth couldn't move.

She could barely even breathe.

A trio of shadows emerged from the woods, sentries from that army of ghosts, burning as they bled out from the trees and drifted toward her, three pillars of fire, bright flames making the black sky glow orange behind them.

This isn't real … this isn't real … this isn't real…

But it was. It had to be.

The flames died and Beth could see only their wretched black burns.

And still they kept coming.

She was rooted in paralysis, unable to so much as scream.

But then Beth opened her mouth and—

—woke up screaming to find a gun in her hand.

In a way, finding herself suddenly armed was even more horrifying than anything she had lived through in her nightmare.

She probably shouldn't keep the gun in her bedroom, or anywhere near her bed. She might shoot herself while sleeping.

She walked to the closet, stowed her weapon on the top shelf, then went downstairs to the kitchen for a glass of water, for real this time.

She filled it to the top and gulped every drop, glad to see that there were no shards on the floor. She set her glass in the sink then left the kitchen and took a look around her living room.

Her heart stopped.

There was broken glass in an untidy pile in front of her door. And the centerpiece of all those shattered fragments: a large rock with a paper tied to it.

This wasn't a dream, and there was no way to convince herself that it was.

So she slowly approached the rock, trembling as she bent to retrieve the note, then read it as her forehead beaded with sweat. The warning was scrawled in red marker that might as well have been blood.

STOP LYING.

She checked the door to make sure it was locked, then called the cops.

Of course this had something to do with Peter, or

someone close to him … someone who knew that Beth was looking into him and whatever it was she knew he had done.

She just couldn't remember what.

But Beth couldn't report such a thing to the police, at least not over the phone. Instead, she said that there had been a break-in and that she needed an officer to come out and take a report.

Lenny Harrison showed up forty minutes later — with no excuse for his response taking so long, seeing as Rush was a tiny town and it was the middle of the night with nothing going on. Beth knew she shouldn't have bothered.

"My sister is missing, and Peter knows where he is," she insisted for the third time in a row.

Lenny shook his head again. "You're talking about your sister, Dorothy."

"That's the only sister I have!" she snapped.

"Dorothy Garrick is dead."

"Not anymore," Beth insisted, trying to shove the rock and its note into his hand. "Can't you dust this for prints?"

Lenny laughed in her face. "You think we're CSI up here in the sticks?"

"I don't know, Lenny, I thought you might do your job!"

"It's probably some fool kids thinking you were someone else."

"No." Beth shook her head. "My sister is missing. I tried to report it yesterday, but no one will listen to a word I say, or do anything about—"

"We looked into it…" Lenny's face softened with his first note of sympathy. "But nobody's seen your sister, Beth. And you need to leave folks alone or…"

"Or what, Lenny?" She might be breathing fire

through her nose. "What's going to happen to me if I keep looking for my sister?"

Lenny looked at her, likely deciding on the best way to answer.

"Are you threatening me, Lenny?"

"No, I am not." He gave her a decisive shake of his head. "But I am wondering if you're off your meds again, or if maybe you're overdue for another stint at—"

"So you are threatening me!"

"I'm simply saying that when people aren't right up here"—Lenny tapped at his temple—"they tend to send those folks to a mental hospital."

"I'm not the problem here! Peter Wilder is the problem here!"

"I would strongly advise you to leave Little Pete alone. You're lucky the Wilder family isn't pressing charges as is."

Then Lenny left Beth to her impotent fury.

She went back to the kitchen, poured herself another glass of water, gulped it down without even breathing, wanting to hurl the glass onto the floor when she finished, then finally claimed the three calming breaths she required to steady herself.

Beth bellowed rage into her empty house, screaming until her throat began to burn. Then she went upstairs, no longer screaming, now shaking and feeling nearer and nearer to hyperventilation.

She went to her nightstand and grabbed one of a half-dozen little orange bottles. She shook two anti-anxiety pills into her palm, swallowed them dry, then repeated the sequence with another to dull the sharpest edges of her undying agony.

She stared down at the hardwood floor while waiting for the drugs to kick in, thinking she might need another anti-psychotic … or two.

Because surely all that blood on the floor had to be a hallucination.

She looked closer and realized that the bottom of her foot was throbbing.

She lifted it up onto her knee and found a small piece of glass from the living room floor lodged into her heel.

She pulled it out, watching as the blood swelled from her ruptured skin, doing exactly nothing to stop the flow as a rivulet of dark red blood dripped from her freshly opened foot and onto the floor.

FOURTEEN

Jenny

1993 ...

JENNY WAS over the moon as she sat on the bus for the twenty-minute ride to Scorpion Point.

Tonight would be one of the biggest nights of her life so far, and she couldn't wait to get started. She had been looking forward to the big bonfire all summer. Not just this one, but every summer for as long as she could remember. In all the years that the Masons had been coming to vacation in Rush, there had never been a time when Jenny wasn't intrigued by the locals, fascinated by their ways of having fun, and willing to do just about anything to join them.

This wasn't just her first chance to experience the legendary party always held at the end of summer. She was getting to visit Scorpion Point with all the tourists and locals *all by herself.*

The Garrick girls were in BIG trouble. While Jenny did feel sorry for them, she also couldn't believe her luck.

Without Dorothy distracting all the boys like she always did — especially Peter Wilder — and no Beth holding her back with all of her worrying (seriously, it seemed like she'd be happy to stay home playing with her old My Little Pony and Strawberry Shortcake dolls most of the time), Jenny's time had finally come.

She had never been to Scorpion Point without her parents before, but Jenny loved the feeling of light danger as she left Rush behind her, getting closer and closer to the small town's even smaller neighbor. The air felt different in Scorpion Point. Jenny had learned what marijuana smelled like a few summers ago when some teenagers were smoking and Beth and Dorothy told her what it was. Jenny had smelled it a lot since then, not only every summer in Rush, but once at a park back home in San Francisco. But in Scorpion Point, the smell of weed lingered in the air and mingled with the aroma of patchouli and what her parents referred to as "human funk."

She loved every dirty inhale of that air into her body. Sometimes when Jenny was all alone, she would imagine what it would be like to live up here instead of just visiting, and wondered if she could ever be one of the wild souls who ended up in Rush, wearing brightly colored clothes and weird hair, often with flowers woven into it, even for the guys.

Jenny was almost there, but her eagerness to reach the bonfire meant she was almost an hour early. Only the dorks would be there. Or little kids like her who were in too much of a hurry to play it cool.

So she stopped into a gift shop called Paper Moon, located on an even shorter Main Street than the one in Rush. She wandered the aisles like she belonged there. The shop was full of crystals and toys.

Jenny paused in front of a large display and read the sign: *Crystals For Healing, Self-Love, and Energy Clearing.*

She didn't need to heal from anything, or clear her energy, but Jenny did like the idea of self-love and had a small box of assorted crystals in her hand before she even realized that she'd reached out for it. She read the box:

This assortment of crystals will emit uplifting, energizing, and calming vibrations to help you feel more positive one hundred percent of the time. Achieve a more peaceful mind and a revitalized state of being.

The box was filled with three different kinds of quartz — clear, rose, and smoky — plus a bunch of other crystals that were hard to pronounce: black tourmaline, selenite, kunzite, lepidolite, and malachite. Jenny wanted to buy the box but was shocked to discover a sticker price of nearly fifty dollars. She only had a ten, though that had felt like plenty upon leaving the cabin.

Jenny finally settled on a small red box of "river rock" chocolates, shaped like the pebbles that lined the Copperhead River shoreline, the assortment drenched in a glaze of various colors — just like the pebbles on the river she loved so much. The chocolate rocks only cost ten percent of the real ones, and even though five bucks still seemed like a lot for a box of candy, considering she could get a jumbo bag of Hershey's Kisses at the Mom & Pop by her house with twice the chocolate for half of the price, this was a vacation purchase. And the box of chocolates weren't only for her.

She paid for the chocolates, imagining herself handing them to Peter while wondering if she could have possibly gotten away with putting the box of crystals in her pocket and leaving Paper Moon without getting caught.

That was the kind of thing Jenny might suggest to Beth if they were together, only to have the fraidy cat start listing all the reasons they would probably get caught. But even without Beth there with her, Jenny knew that shoplifting the crystals wasn't even close to worth the risk. Not only would she be in more trouble than she'd ever known in her life if she got caught, Jenny would also miss the big bonfire on Copperhead River.

And no way could she ever allow that to happen.

After killing enough time and making her purchase, Jenny finally made her way to the beach. But it wasn't as easy all by herself — or without her parents and their car — than she had imagined. A steep slope of silt stood between her and the rocky riverbed below. Her flip-flops were cheap, but even if her mom had bought her that pair from Esprit like Jenny had begged her to, the flimsy footwear would have still had her slipping and sliding down the hill.

Jenny managed to stay upright most of the way, but eventually lost her balance and rolled down the hair, covering her hair in a dressing of silt. There was no way to disguise what had happened, and of course the guys weren't about to let her forget it.

"THE CIRCUS IS THAT WAY!" Gary bellowed at the top of his lungs as Jenny approached the group. Her eyes went right past him, to Peter standing slightly off to the side in his bright red Airwalks, sending a careless grin her way.

The gentle ridicule kept coming, getting louder and louder as Jenny got closer to the fire. But once she was finally standing in front of the group, Peter said, "Are you okay?"

Her insides melted into a puddle.

She nodded. "It didn't really hurt."

"That's good to hear." Peter grinned again, then

pointed at her slightly smashed box of chocolates. "What's that?"

"Oh…" Jenny laughed, almost absurdly self-conscious but doing her best to keep it together. "I got these for you."

She handed him the chocolates and he took them with an appreciative laugh, looking down at the box, then back up at Jenny with an even wider smile. He stuffed the gift into his back pocket like he was stowing a wallet, then put a casual hand over her shoulder.

Jenny's heart was a drum line.

"You want something to drink?" Peter asked.

"Yes, please."

He started her off with a beer, but soon Jenny was drinking something fruity with vodka, she wasn't sure what. An inner warmth began to fill her, a relaxing wave that she'd never felt before.

By her third drink, the bonfire was roaring, and everyone was either sitting or dancing around it. The hippies gyrated with wild abandon. Jenny felt like she was watching MTV.

She rested her head on Peter's shoulder, thinking, *It's just like I imagined.*

Jenny had gone after what she wanted, and now she finally had it.

That was exactly what this summer was supposed to be about.

FIFTEEN

Beth

Beth opened her eyes to another morning, wanting to die.

She wondered how deep this could go. She hated herself for being so morose, but she already hated herself for hating herself, and all that self-loathing was chewing through her like Ruthie through a tray of holiday fudge.

She considered taking pills, mentally flagellated herself for the longing, then determined that she needed to get the hell out of her Victorian before the siren song of that little orange bottle finally grew too loud for her to ignore.

Ruthie didn't need groceries so much as Beth needed to bring them over. She should really take a shower first. She didn't really want to, but she had soaked her pajamas with sweat through the night.

She drew a bath instead, doing her best to ignore the darkness of her accompanying thoughts, then put a pot of tea on the stove while hot water filled her century-old clawfoot. She drank the first cup in the bath because she needed it, and the second after she was all dressed for a better day simply because it was there.

In between her steaming mugs, she soaked in lavender

saturated water and wispy bubbles. The calm of her bath and the caffeine in her Earl Grey battled it out as she drove to Provisions, then as she loaded her handbasket with groceries, less so as she paid for her items due to a complicated transaction involving eye contact and money, but then her anxiety was back with a vengeance all the way to Ruthie's.

Beth didn't even need to knock. The door swung open on her second step away from the Honda. "You look glad to see me," she said, surprised by the delight on her aunt's typically cantankerous face.

"I'm just hoping you have ice cream."

Beth sighed and stepped past Ruthie into the house.

She walked over to the table and started unpacking the groceries, setting them in a neat display across the top. Ruthie loved to see her items arranged, but it was a frivolous preference started by accident thanks to Beth herself appreciating a bit of show and tell. She did it one time, then the next, and one more after that. Ruthie threw a fit the fourth time when she didn't.

But Ruthie wasn't looking at the paltry array of items. She was studying Beth's profile with narrowed eyes.

"You're here early."

"I'm here most days."

"But never before nine."

"I didn't have a lot to do this morning."

"So what is it?" Ruthie's voice was sharp. "You're bored, or depressed, or wanting to beat around the bush until you finally get to whatever you came here for."

"I was wondering what you remember about Jenny."

"Who's Jenny?"

"Jenny Mason."

"That's a—"

"*That summer.*" Then, just to double clarify: "What do

you remember about Jenny Mason the summer of the fire, Ruthie?"

She made a face. This was obviously the last thing Ruthie wanted to discuss, but it was her fault for making Beth get to the point without massaging her way in.

"I never did like the Masons. It wasn't anything specific, so much as everything about them." Ruthie made that face again, but this time she wrinkled it even harder. "They were just another group of trippers looking down on the folks that actually lived here." She shook her head in sorrow. "But that doesn't mean they deserved to die. It was a crying shame what happened to them."

"Did I ever tell you anything about Jenny or Dorothy or Peter back then?"

A different face, this one wary. Ruthie took a moment for what seemed to be serious consideration, then drew in some air with a shake of her head. "Nothing out of the regular. Why?"

Beth sighed, wanting more but not enough to raise an issue Ruthie didn't already know about. "I just really miss her. Dorothy, I mean. It's like I have this giant hole in my heart that won't ever close up, no matter what I do."

"I know what you mean." Ruthie was suddenly there, an affectionate hand patting her gently on the back.

Ruthie used the silence to study her groceries. Once she was done scanning them, Beth expected her to go on and on about the items.

"You turned out to be a good girl," Ruthie said instead.

The simple sentence lifted her spirits tremendously. "Thank you."

Beth went to hug her aunt, but Ruthie batted her away before picking up a box of pasta with glee. "Is this really made with brown rice?"

It was, and the news seemed to delight Ruthie instead

of turning her suspicious like usual. Ruthie had recently declared herself as a "gluten-free kind of gal," but that didn't mean she wanted to experiment with alternatives to the stuff she liked.

In sharp contrast to her warm embrace of the brown rice pasta, Ruthie referred to the cashew milk chocolate ice cream as "frozen dirt."

Beth said, "I bet it's delicious."

"*You bet?* You haven't tried it?"

"I've tried the vanilla. But I don't like chocolate and—" She stopped, ready to get out of there, knowing it would take at least ten minutes to ease her way out the door after the launch sequence had been initiated.

"You know what, you're right. I wouldn't want to poison you." Beth grabbed the cashew milk ice cream. "If it's delicious, I'll get you more next time. If it's not, then I'll never buy you frozen dirt again."

Ruthie shrugged. "Do you want to watch TV?"

Not really, but Beth did end up watching two hours' worth. The couch was comfortable and that bottled blue glow was a good friend that never stopped trying to soothe her, even if she only had Ruthie instead of a family like Peter.

TWENTY MINUTES after leaving Ruthie's, Beth was walking her neighborhood and plastering the hundred fliers she had printed with Dorothy's last high school photo all around town, while asking anyone willing to answer her — sarcastic or not — whether they might have possibly seen her sister.

She ignored all the sideways glances, all the strange looks that seemed to blend pity with fear. Most people avoided her entirely, turning the other way or pretending that they couldn't see her coming. But the kids weren't shy about laughing at the crazy lady, both behind her back and straight to her face. She had spent most of her life so far wishing she could fade into the background.

Beth ended her search party of one at the library, first by stapling one of her fliers to the top of the return box outside, then taking the remainder of her stack inside to ask Mrs. Davidson for permission to post them around the library.

The librarian gave her a halfhearted nod, gesturing to an empty spot on the checkout counter. "You can leave them there," she said, with an air suggesting that the stack of posters might find its way to the garbage five minutes after Beth was back outside.

"Thank you." She offered Mrs. Davidson a smile, but the librarian didn't return it, or let her know she was welcome. "I'm just going to use the restroom before I go."

The smile fell like a dead leaf from Beth's face as she walked away from the counter, feeling like she might as well be invisible.

She opened the bathroom door, then stepped inside, the hair on the back of her neck rising.

"Hello?" Beth called out to no one's reply.

She kneeled down and looked under the stalls, cursing her paranoia and muttering a mild prayer that no one came in before she was back on her feet.

She slipped into a stall and closed the door, then sat on the toilet while trying not to cry.

A few moments later she heard the bathroom door swinging open, then footsteps shuffling across the tile floor before a banging on her stall.

She jumped and the exclamation left her like a belch. "It's occupied!"

But whatever was on the other side of her stall door

refused to leave, getting louder instead, multiplying into an army of whispering voices.

She saw shadows, a few and then a multitude, crowding the area below the stall door. The sight made her want to whimper, filled her with a need to scream as she saw a cluster of feet.

Beth fell back with a squeal, slamming her spine down onto the toilet and reactivating an old injury that screamed bloody murder through her nerves.

She reached into her purse, fishing for the pills. Anything would do. Anti-anxiety, anti-psychotic, or anti-whatever the hell was on the other side of her stall door still banging to get in.

She pulled out a bottle and twisted the cap off before it flew from her hand.

Pills spilled onto the tile and scattered across the floor.

Beth fell to her knees, scooping them up off of the filthy ground and popping them into her mouth, then leaping to her feet and grabbing the plunger, ready to end anyone who made the fool mistake of trying to attack her.

She kicked the door open and came out swinging, yelling as she spun around in circles, around and around in an otherwise empty bathroom.

She fled the library in tears, flying out of the bathroom as the sobbing started, dashing past Mrs. Davidson at the checkout counter, then screaming down the street, this time truly oblivious to observers on both sides.

Beth kept running toward the hidey hole under her bed.

SIXTEEN

Sam

Sam was late. After a night staring up at the moldering ceiling of the Airstream, she'd finally done the only thing she could think to do and went for a walk through the redwoods surrounding Songbird.

Unlike the crunch of the woods in Ohio, the floor beneath the giant trees was muted. The thick layer of red dust soaked up the sound of her feet until it seemed she wasn't even really there. Sam kept shrinking until she was surely no taller than Sophie had been — and would be forever.

Despite her dark thoughts, it had been a balm to let her daughter into her mind. To imagine the curve of Sophie's face and the weight of her hand tucked tightly into Sam's.

The woods had felt like the safest place in the world. And upon returning to her Airstream, she slept like the dead.

Only to be woken by Dog begging for his dinner, just twenty minutes after she should have been dressed and ready for work.

She roared through two yellows and ran one red

despite her intention to stop, screeching into the Redwood Rings lot with a minute to spare. Fortunately, Sam didn't have to pass through that asshole speed trap that would have surely landed her a ticket.

But by the time she entered the Back Bar, Sam was a minute late and Bill was ready for her.

"Arriving late tells people that you think your time is more important than theirs, you know."

"Seriously, Bill." Sam stowed her bag under the counter, then reeled around on him. "I ran one minute behind, and the place is practically empty."

"Practically empty isn't empty. What if those two customers needed something at the same time? You would be making them wait, just because you were—"

"*One minute late.*"

"If you are chronically late, then you are chronically rude."

"Did you spend the morning looking at quotes on Pinterest again?" Sam asked. It wasn't an unreasonable question. Bill liked Pinterest more than most brides.

"I was here fifteen minutes ago."

"Congratulations, Bill. That's admirable of you. But I'd still rather show up a minute late than a quarter hour early acting like an asshole."

"I'm not being an asshole," he defended himself without evidence.

"You know I hate being late, and yet you can't help reaming me on it every time I am."

"You're super good at it for something you hate."

"You think the good ol' boys don't like you because you're gay, but maybe it really is your personality they have a problem with."

He shrugged. "I'm okay not being liked."

Sam shook her head. "I don't think you are. Where's Nina?"

"She's off tonight."

"Okay, then where's Chris?"

"Sorry..." He dramatically reached into his pocket, produced a handful of air, then mimed a few swiping gestures before looking up at Sam seriously. "My Chris tracker says he's..." He looked down at his invisible screen again, then back up. "It says *None of your business.*"

"As in 'actually none of my business,' or more like 'you don't really know'?"

"You should sweep before more customers get here."

She looked around the bar. The place looked spotless. "Looks like it was swept before we opened, and like nothing's happened since. Oh, and you're also not the boss of me."

Bill went to pout in his favorite spot behind the bar while Sam got to work. She didn't need or want his direction. Not because she wanted to shirk her duties, but because Bill loved bossing others around. But Sam always knew what to do without waiting for orders and would prefer to stay busy than standing idle like most of her coworkers, including Bill.

With roughly an hour before the place would start filling up, she went through her usual opening routine, starting with a quick walk around the exterior to clear any debris from the entryways and windows. She wiped down the countertops and tables, which last night's shift (including her) had done a shit job of cleaning, then replaced and refilled the condiments and tabletop items. Sam's last stop on the checklist was the woman's bathroom. The mirror was smeared with bright pink letters written with lipstick: *Fuk this place.*

Her sentiments exactly. Sam wondered who wrote it as

she wiped the slur off of the mirror with Windex and a washcloth, not because she was upset at having to clean the graffiti, but because she wanted to give the author a high-five.

The Back Bar filled up faster than usual. By the time she was done with the mirror, the place was close to packed. A good thing. She wanted to stay busy.

But Big Pete's table was occupied instead by Peter Wilder — Little Pete if she wanted to piss the asshole off — sitting alone.

Sam saw him before he saw her, but only by less than a second, and he was already giving her a lecherous grin that filled her with the wrong kind of chills before she could turn away.

He raised a hand to nab her attention: *A little help over here, please?*

Sam walked over, nodding at Peter as she stood adjacent to his table. "Hey."

"Hey, yourself." His grin split wider and turned even flirtier. "What've you been up to?"

Sam took a second to think, trying to see through to the other side of that question. Did Peter know that she'd been talking to Beth? Or that she'd been snooping around on her behalf? Was he really wanting to know what Beth might or might not have told her?

"The usual," she answered, "serving alcohol, then figuring out who's drunk and who's stupid."

"How can you tell?"

"It's not that hard." Sam really wanted this conversation to end.

But Peter wanted it to keep going. "So, tell me: what's the difference between *tipsy* and *drunk*?"

"A tipsy customer still has control over what they say and do, while remembering everything that happened the next day. Drunk customers run the gamut from low control to no control, have to battle their bodies reacting to remove the toxins through vomiting, and often forget what assholes they were the night before."

"Why do I get the feeling that you're talking about me?"

Sam shrugged. "Probably because you think everything is about you."

"Not everything." He grinned again. "Just all the good stuff."

"What can I get you?"

"Maybe I should be asking you the same thing."

"Great. I'd like a Shirley Temple."

"What time do you get off?"

"Late," she said. "You'll already be home with your wife."

"So, does that mean you don't want to get off after you get off?"

"Wow. And right after I bring up your wife. Is that really any way for a mayoral candidate to behave?"

He shrugged, managing to look impressively indifferent. "Nobody needs to know."

"Sorry, Peter." She gave him a smile to stay on his good side. "I just don't get off on married men."

Or narcissistic assholes like you.

He grinned. "You did before."

"You didn't tell me you were married."

"Fair enough." He nodded. "For now."

"So, what can I get you?"

"A bourbon sour."

"I'll be right—"

"And a mojito!" Peter's companion arrived at the table, ordering as he sat.

"Got it." Sam offered them both a nod, then went to make their drinks behind the bar.

Fucking mojitos. That might be the only drink she hated to make more than a lemon drop. At least it was early. She usually got that particular order when the place was packed — either the Back Bar or the Redwood Rings — and she was four or five drinkers deep, when the last thing she wanted to do was spend five of her valuable minutes muddling mint leaves.

She made the mojito, then the bourbon sour, glancing over at the table as she did, unsure of whether the unsettling vibe rolling off Big Pete's boy like a stink was a legitimate scraping against her instinct, or whether Beth's paranoia had managed to poison her.

She delivered their drinks just as Peter's companion was complaining about the current mayor, Adam Westhoff, a little too loudly. An everyday conversation. The election was in November, and according to a lot of Back Bar patrons (most of whom also bitched a bit too loudly), the soon-to-be former mayor had been preventing the council from doing the "right thing," which in this case apparently meant approving the companion's development.

Peter looked up, saw Sam standing there, and practically winked while making no effort to edit his response.

"You're going on and on about a temporary problem. We're not even talking a quarter year from now. Once I'm the mayor, it will be a snap"—the asshole actually snapped his fingers—"to articulate the wisdom of our offer to the council."

His tablemate glanced at Sam, clearly uncertain.

Peter shrugged — *she's nobody* — and continued. "This isn't confusing, Charlie. Westhoff is popular with enough of the folks around here to stand in our way, and those are the sort of folks we're not about to start seeing eye to eye on when it comes to most things. Now, if you want to make sure these little hurdles all get gathered up and stacked in a warehouse somewhere, then you need to make sure you and your associates are all showing up both now and on voting day."

"Maybe we should talk about this later," Charlie suggested.

The hurdles were metaphorical, and while Peter hadn't said anything illegal, there was clearly something untoward about their exchange. Sam would have probably sensed it anyway, but Charlie's bristling reaction to her presence felt an awful lot like a teenager trying to avoid getting caught.

For what, Sam didn't know. Peter's daddy was powerful enough to force the council's approval on most things. But he wanted the votes instead. The farmers weren't going to vote for him, not this election or ever, and Rip had all the pull with that particular crowd.

Peter was looking for power. "She knows how to keep her mouth shut," he said, still eye-fucking her.

"I didn't hear anything worth shutting up about." Sam gave him a hard smile. "Enjoy your drinks. I'll be back later to check on you."

"Or you could just come back in fifteen minutes with another bourbon sour and a mojito," Peter said.

Charlie raised a hand. "I'm good."

"One bourbon sour in fifteen minutes it is."

She returned to the bar, weighing the benefits of staying closer to Peter's conversation with the many obvious costs of going anywhere near the fucker. A knowing sort of menace wafted off of him, and instinct warned her to stay away.

"You can have my tips tonight if I can swap with you and work the Redwood," she offered Bill.

"Deal." He didn't even hesitate. Everyone preferred the Back Bar.

Her shift continued with the type of bullshit Sam considered to be the norm in the Redwood Rings. Tonight that included customers requesting that she choose their drinks, because they didn't know what they wanted and enjoyed wasting her time; three separate customers all getting pissy at her for not remembering their orders from the last time they came in, even though she only remembered one of the customers at all; two women launching into a loud argument that was just inches away from a slapping match before Sam ushered them outside; one guy who thought he was approximately three hundred times more charming than he was asked Sam if she could "help him remember that drink he had one time" and then gave her ridiculous clues, eventually leading to an X marking the spot on his crotch; another insistent asshole who kept reaching across the bar — it's called a *bar* for a reason, asshole; and too many people waving money in her face, snapping to get her attention, or slapping the bar like they were killing a fly.

But at least Chris had stepped in to work alongside her to keep everything moving and make sure she stayed sane. They worked in a duet, with Sam making drinks and Chris taking them out to the customers, the two of them constantly trading jokes and laughter, taking turns with their predictions, both of them more accurate than not.

Sam knew she was making a mistake playing with Chris like she was, especially with the way their bodies kept constantly brushing against each other. Of course he was going to ask her to stay in his apartment upstairs after closing.

But Sam was a big girl and could take comfort where she wanted it without committing to anything else. And tonight she planned to head back to the comfort of her Airstream.

Chris challenged her resolve slightly ahead of schedule, a couple hours before closing when a lull in customer needs left them both cleaning up behind the bar. "So, you wanna hang tonight?"

"I can't," she said.

"Oh. I don't mean we have to do anything or anything … I just wanted to maybe talk … or whatever."

"I wish you'd asked me earlier. I just made plans a little while ago and it would be shitty of me to change them."

Judging by his expression, Chris wished that he'd asked too, on any one of his hundred-plus opportunities. Little did he know that Sam would have only manufactured another excuse.

It was his fault for not letting their thing be what it was. She didn't want to talk. She didn't have time to talk. Not with him. Not when she was helping Beth with a serious problem.

"Maybe tomorrow?" He looked so hopeful.

"I can't."

Why? She could see the question in his eyes, but instead he said, "Oh. Okay. Maybe some other time. If you—"

He stopped. Then they both turned and ran toward the commotion exploding in the Back Bar.

SEVENTEEN

Beth

BETH STOOD outside the Back Bar fuming, clenching and unclenching her fists while wishing that her best breathing techniques were enough to calm the constantly raging storms.

But everything about the Wilders made her angry. She had come to the bar to see Sam. To see if she could unravel the truth from the wild thoughts that were like a tangle of forgotten Christmas lights in her mind. But seeing Peter's Mercedes in the lot, and his mayoral smile through the window where he was holding court to the people of Rush, made her want to scream with rage.

He was so ... so *pompous.*

The Wilder family had made its fortune through lumber, back when it was still okay to slaughter redwoods indiscriminately. If her great grandfather was to be believed, their fortune had all started by stealing the ancient old growth on their property line, and triggering the family feud. The Wilders had gone on to earn their surname, hacking through wild forests at a furious speed, determined to outrun the coming legislation, and doing their damndest to slow it down with payoffs for as long as they could.

But even all those new laws couldn't do much to stop an empire. The Wilders had owned most of Rush forever, and that was a truth that would likely never change. There was a good chance that if a local business wasn't owned by the family outright, the Wilders were probably still the landlords no more than two payments removed.

Of course they were treated like royalty. Even in the places they didn't own, like Redwood Rings and its Back Bar neighbor, the Wilders acted like they had done everything from laying the original foundation to covering the restaurant's property taxes for the prior quarter. The Wilders thought that all of Rush belonged to them.

Beth's family was virtually gone. While the Wilders' power had only grown, the once mighty Garricks had dwindled to nothing. Only Beth and Aunt Ruthie remained ... unless Beth could figure out what Peter had done to Dorothy and get her sister back.

She was breathing steadily in and out, her fists no longer clenching and unclenching, her mind no longer dashing between fight and flight, her soul no longer willing to settle for the suffering of inaction.

She drew another long breath, exhaled as she crossed the short span of parking lot to the Back Bar's entrance, then swung the door wide and entered without giving herself another second to think.

She marched to Peter's table, not stopping to think as he raised his eyebrows in surprise.

"I need to talk to you."

"Take a seat." He pointed to the empty chair beside Charlie, who was grinning at her. "I notice you didn't bring your yearbook, so I'm guessing this isn't about old times."

She sat, but not because he ordered it, and did her best

to ignore what was clearly a sneer on his silver spoon face. "Where is she?"

"Are we talking Amelia Earhart or Carmen San Diego?"

She held in her snarl. "We're talking Dorothy Garrick. She was on the Fat Chance during your party."

He looked at her with pity, which only stirred her furor.

"I'm not crazy," she said.

"I didn't say you were."

"But you're looking at me like I'm crazy, when we both know you're a liar."

"I'm worried about you."

"People would never vote for you if they knew what kind of man you really are."

"I'll be the mayor of Rush *precisely* because of who I *really am.*" Peter smiled, and even looked pretty doing it, despite his ugliness. "The people in this town know that I care. Especially about you, Beth. We go back, and I'm worried about you."

"You're lying."

"I don't mean to be insulting in any way—"

"Then you should probably swallow whatever you're about to say."

"—but have you been taking your meds?"

"And there we go." Though Beth couldn't really say for sure. One of the many downsides of being off her meds was the not knowing whether or not she was on her meds.

But that wasn't what this was.

"*Here.*" She showed him her phone, and the picture of a white rose. "*See.* You know what that rose means. She's not dead, she came back, and she was going to talk to you."

His face was unreadable. And considering Little Pete Wilder was a man who had been wearing a mask the entire time she'd known him, even the things he didn't say couldn't be trusted.

"What is it you think your dead sister would like to talk to me about?" Peter finally asked, his tone as unreadable as his expression.

"I don't know. Something important. Something about … that night."

"What night?"

"You know what night." It was so hard to say, but Beth forced the words past her lips. "The night of the fire."

"Why would she want to talk about that night?"

"You know why."

Peter raised an eyebrow. "I mean, why would she want to talk to *me*?"

"What do you mean?" Beth was too unsettled to say anything else.

"Don't worry about it." He shrugged and leaned back in his chair. "You should probably get home."

"I want to know what you meant by that, Peter."

"I'm not sure what you want me to say." He shrugged again. "I wasn't even *there* the night of the fire. You can't even tell me whether or not you've been taking your meds. I'm happy to help however I can, but I'm seriously wondering if I'm really the person you should be talking to."

His voice fell to a whisper, as if he didn't want the world in on their secret. "I'm thinking this conversation, and the kinds of questions you're asking, are best exchanged between you and your shrink."

"Just tell me what you did to Dorothy and I'll go."

"I'm requesting that you leave immediately."

"You can't throw me out of someone else's bar."

"That was me asking you nicely, Beth. I only do that once. I'll have to get Ralph on the line next, and believe me when I say that he'll come, whether I own the bar or not."

Her fists were back to clenching, but Beth had been hiding them in her lap. She forced her fingers to stay straight as she stood, glared at him, and did the only thing she could think of.

She leapt on Peter, swiping her nails across his face.

EIGHTEEN

Sam

"I KNOW YOU KNOW WHAT YOU'RE DOING!" Beth screamed at Peter as she clawed him.

Sam and Chris rushed forward, managing to pull a sobbing and snarling Beth off of Peter before she ripped the skin from his face.

The asshole stood straight, looking around at the bar while accepting the reality that he now had an audience. And though he might not have asked for the onlookers, the mayoral candidate and career narcissist would use it to his advantage.

"I'm so sorry about whatever it is that happened to her," Peter said to Chris while speaking to the room. "I'm not sure what's going on with Beth, but I think we should all be worried about—"

"YOU KNOW EXACTLY WHAT'S GOING ON WITH ME!" Beth shrieked.

"Shh..." Sam tried to soothe her.

"You should get her some help," said Peter to Sam. "I'm pretty sure she's off her meds."

"We're good. Thank you." She took Beth by the arm and began to lead her away.

Peter kept going, still speaking to her while addressing his audience. "If she needs anything, of course you know that I'm happy to help with whatever—"

"I said we're good." Sam's smile was a strain on her face.

"Well, just let me know…" Then a photoshoot ready smile as he made eye contact with the room. "And my apologies for the commotion."

The bar returned to their drinks. Except for another small scuffle brewing in the corner. JJ, laughing at the looney losing her shit with his cadre of cackling syco-phants, and Chris quietly telling him to shut the fuck up or get the hell out of here.

Peter excused himself and made for the exit, leaving Sam and Chris to deal with Beth. He was a leaky wound of a man, which made Sam want to dismiss every word from his mouth, but even if his bluster about Beth's health was a performance designed to make it appear to the room that he wasn't antagonizing a mentally ill woman, he did have a point.

"Let's find you somewhere to sit for a few minutes, okay?" Sam said.

Beth nodded, then let Sam lead her into the back room.

Sam assured her that she would be back in just a few minutes, then went outside to call Meredith while chastising her own poor judgment. She hated that Peter was right, but this had gone too far. And like it or not, Sam had dragged it at least half of the way here. It was in her best interest to stop encouraging Beth and finally see if she could get her some help instead.

"I was just about to call you," Meredith said, instead of *Hello*.

"Why were you going to — don't tell me you've already heard?"

"How big do you think this town is? I'm already on my way."

Then Meredith hung up. Sam knew from experience, she didn't like to talk while driving.

Sam stayed in the back room with Beth while Chris manned the customers until Meredith arrived around ten minutes later. She requested a moment alone with Beth, so Sam excused herself from their company, then went back into the bar to help.

She offered Chris a quarter hour of assistance, which seemed like a reasonable length of time for Meredith to get what she needed from Beth without Sam around, and just long enough to catch up on all of the customer orders.

Sam returned to the back room, but Meredith didn't seem pleased to see her.

"What's up, doc?" Sam said after Meredith pulled her to the side.

"Why didn't you call me sooner?"

Guilt flooded her immediately, because of course Meredith was right.

"I'm sorry," Sam said, sheepish in her embarrassment. "I was wrong not to."

But Meredith didn't acknowledge Sam's acknowledgement. "This is a problem for a psychotherapist, not an ex-MP with her own issues to deal with."

"I know." Sam nodded. "Of course, you're right. I'm sorry."

Meredith softened. "You should really come to a meeting again."

"I promise to think about it."

And she did. But first Sam started thinking about drinking, right around the time Meredith walked Beth to her car. First a little, and then a lot.

Then she thought about taking some pills all through closing time, finally turning her mind to a meeting while driving down the winding road through the trees to her trailer park. Sam managed to keep her thoughts on the things she might say in NA, until they turned sour and she started thinking about the gray sedan, wondering if she had really just seen it.

Her paranoia was a cancer, but Sam hoped that reaching Songbird might be a cure. But even once home her sense of unease only deepened. She parked in between the trailers, then went to knock on Syc's door.

Five times, and still no gruff responses or barking.

So, what, Syc was out and he'd taken Dog with him? Sam didn't need them, because she didn't need anyone. Except that by the time she reached her own front door, Sam knew that was a lie.

The disappointment felt like a sunburn inside her. The sudden truth was disgusting, but she couldn't argue with it: at some point Sam had apparently started to rely on others again, and that defied the inarguable law that she was better off alone.

She stopped with her hand inches from the doorknob, not exactly afraid to enter so much as aware that something was off. More specific than a bad feeling, her MP senses were insisting that someone had been in her space. She couldn't have articulated what was different and might not have been able to spot the *why* in a lineup, but paranoia or not, Sam wasn't about to go inside without protection.

She never needed a lot of home protection, and never really cared about protecting much of anything she had, including herself. But she did keep a taser in her Jeep for emergencies, so she walked back and dug it out of the glove box, then slowly approached the front door, pausing in front of the knob again, now armed and ready.

She threw the door open, registering that it was already unlocked, but not slowing as she rushed inside. Whirled around but saw no one waiting.

Her heart was pounding and she couldn't slow it down, refusing to believe that she wasn't in danger. Maybe someone was in the bathroom?

But no. That same MP's instinct was now insisting that she was alone.

So why—

Her heart stopped, the pounding no longer a problem as she spied something that was not as it should be: a little orange bottle of pills had appeared on her counter.

The yearning was thunder, and the anger like lightning.

Sam staggered back, physically stricken by the sight, and the reality that someone would stoop so low. To hit her hard on such a brittle bone.

She fell back another step, then stood paralyzed between the pills and her door.

After several frozen seconds, she ran.

Out of the trailer and into her Jeep.

Racing down the winding roads with nowhere to go but away, so preoccupied with the pills on her counter that she forgot about—

The gray sedan driving the opposite way as Sam was heading back into town. The sight of it would have been enough to startle her, but the flashing blinders sent her swinging too hard around a dangerous bend, nearly flying off the road before she managed to right the Jeep again.

Her heart pounded all the way to the bar.

NINETEEN

Jenny

1993 ...

JENNY WANTED TO REMEMBER.

But first she wanted to stop hurting.

Or at least understand why she was hurting in the first place.

She sat up on the tiny ripped old piece of towel she'd been sleeping on and looked around again. But same as the last two times before she had laid back down again, Jenny was still alone.

The beach wasn't exactly empty, but the scattered survivors of the party were mostly hippies, and she didn't see a single person she knew.

She tried to stand and had to sit back down. Most of the pain was concentrated between her legs. It was so obvious once she knew it that Jenny wondered why it had taken her so long.

She checked herself and gasped when she saw that she wasn't wearing underwear.

Jenny looked around again, sweaty as she saw the entire world as a threat. The hippies were suddenly menacing. What seemed so friendly yesterday had been pushed through a funhouse mirror and was now a horror show. She didn't want to approach those weird people for help. They might have even done something to her.

The hippies were still awake. Had they been watching her sleep?

Or doing something to her while she did?

It was a terrifying thought that throbbed in her mind like the pain between her legs.

Nothing happened to you, Jenny told herself. *You fell asleep in a weird way, probably on a rock or something. Nobody hurt you or anything. You drank too much. Peter probably kept trying to wake you, but like Dorothy says, "You could snore through a storm!"*

Jenny felt a flush of embarrassment, thinking of Peter bearing witness to her snoring. But that was so much better than the other thing that kept filling her with dread and poisoning her mind.

She scoured the beach for her panties, looking all along the sand and in between the rocks, hunting not only for the panties, but for the memory of what happened that might accompany the discovery.

She returned to the small towel she'd woken up on, hoping that she'd simply overlooked the scrap of material.

Her mother was going to kill her. It was impossible to believe that she wouldn't want to know what happened to Jenny's missing pair of Fruit of the Looms. She didn't know how to answer a single one of her inevitable questions, so she practiced the many things she might say in response to Mother's queries while looking for her—

Jenny didn't see her panties. But she did see something that stopped her cold.

Peeking out from under the old, worn towel was the red corner of something familiar. Lifting the towel, Jenny found her box of chocolates, a lot more mashed than when she'd given it to Peter. She desperately wanted to believe that this was a different box, but the heel print from his Airwalks made the truth too obvious.

Jenny abandoned the bonfire for good, then made her way up the steep silt hill, not even caring how much harder it was to ascend than it had been coming down, but needing to get the hell away from the riverbed as tears rinsed both sides of her face.

Jenny kept trying so hard to remember.

But by the time she reached the top of the hill, she wondered if she wanted to.

TWENTY

Sam

SAM PULLED into the Redwood Rings just as Chris was locking the front door.

She tapped her horn lightly, twice to snag his attention.

He spun around, primed to be bothered, but then he smiled at the sight of her Jeep and gave her a little wave. It was too dark to see his expression, but Sam could practically smell his happy surprise.

And again, she felt like an asshole.

"Did you forget something?" he asked as she approached, his hope that she hadn't getting clearer on his face as she neared.

"Just a drink." She smiled.

"You're drinking?"

"It just has to be wet. It doesn't need alcohol."

"Well okay, then." He turned back around and opened the door, still seeming uncertain but willing.

Sam sat at the bar while Chris made her a drink.

She looked around the bar in surprise. "What the hell happened here?"

He sighed. "It turned into a long-ass night, right after you left."

"What happened?"

"It was sort of happening for a while, then things just exploded at the end."

"Why didn't you say anything?"

"The Beth thing was just the beginning. And you weren't exactly in the mood."

"Sorry." She took her drink, then sipped through her straw. "I could have helped, you know."

"I had it handled."

"Had *what* handled? I still don't know what happened."

"Double Rainbow came in."

"Oh…" Double Rainbow was an old hippie who sounded enough like that poor bastard from the *Double Rainbow* video on YouTube that it had become his new name shortly after the video first went viral, and now there was nothing he could do about it. Double Rainbow was fucked in the head, and legend said that he'd been that way since late last century. He started flipping out about Y2K and never went back. He could never quite cotton onto the truth that though he was well known around Rush, his celebrity identity was *village idiot.*

Double Rainbow was a problem every time he entered either bar.

"What did he do?" Sam asked.

"He came in looking to score, even though he knows that the Redwood is neutral ground and there can't be any buying or selling here, and he's reminded every time, both before and after he's told to leave." Chris drew a long breath. "Tonight he was so obvious about it and kept refusing to go, insisting that his friends were coming to have a drink with him. That they'd be there any minute."

"Then they did, and his friends were all dealers?" Sam finished.

"Exactly. That led to this whole thing between the trippers and the townies, with both sides making fun of Double Rainbow, though also weirdly defending him in a way, but each group doing it differently so they could still stay at odds. And guess who the dealers were?"

Sam stopped sipping her Shirley Temple to gasp. "*No...*"

"Oh yeah. Eddie, Levi, and Christian."

"They know they're not supposed to pull that shit in the Rings."

"I called the cops, but five minutes after the brawl had already started."

"This was all after I left? In the last hour?"

"Yup."

"Damn. But also, that's nothing compared to the shit I used to see." Sam laughed, because it was true.

"You're going to leave it there?" Chris raised his eyebrows. "No story?"

She should have kept her mouth shut.

"You don't have to tell me..." he said into her silence.

"Maybe I tell you upstairs?"

He smiled. "I'd like that."

Sam followed Chris to his apartment, admiring the view from behind.

He was another of Rush's blow-ins. It didn't matter that he was 42 and had lived in the vicinity ever since leaving San Diego at the age of 18 to attend college near Rush. Investing more than half of his life and all of his money in the town had turned him into a staple of the community, though even if he doubled his years, he'd still be something of an outsider.

He wasn't truly a townie, nor member to any of the founding families. It had been more than two decades since he had been a tourist. Chris was tolerant of the drug trade, but in no way involved. He had two sleeves of tattoos, the body of an MMA fighter, and a generally gruff demeanor that gave him the physical authority to handle most altercations that might erupt inside the bar.

Add his ability to stay perfectly calm, and he was an excellent arbiter of the disputes that regularly occurred both in and around the bar. By not being a participant of any group, Chris was respected by all of them.

"So, do you want to tell me old stories, or do you want to tell me why you've been a bitch lately. Well, more than usual." He was tentative, clearly not wanting to poke the bear but no longer willing to say nothing as he plunged his French press, then poured her a fresh cup of coffee.

Sam felt in equal parts the pressure to tell him *why* she'd been so difficult to be around, and a desperate wish to run back downstairs.

But Chris would eventually find out about her daughter. It might as well come from her.

"Has anyone ever told you about Sophie?" Sam accepted the coffee, then held it close to her.

Chris shook his head. "No."

Not a surprise, and something of a relief. The only people she'd told about Sophie in Rush belonged to her NA group.

She gulped her coffee. It was too much, and the swallow burned her throat. But it was no worse than the scorching story that was about to leave it. She took another sip before starting.

"I had a daughter. Her name was Sophie, and Sophie was an accident. But still the best thing that ever happened to me, planned or otherwise. I had a three-night stand with a younger soldier named Ian. We met at a bar while I was investigating one of his superiors. We had a great time together for a couple of days. But it was what it was. Until I found out I was pregnant."

Another sip. "I had no intention of telling Ian. He was a kid, not a father. It wasn't fair to him and — it doesn't matter, he wasn't part of the picture and that was all there was to it. My mom argued with me from the start. But I stuck to my guns, even after Sophie was born, insisting that having a daughter was the last thing Ian would ever want to hear about. But she refused to drop it, and when she finally argued that I might be willing to listen better if my baby shared her blood, I finally broke. Not because I believed that, but because it hurt so much when she said it."

This time when Sam took a sip, it was to obscure the truth that she wanted to cry. "My mom was right about Ian. At least when it came to how happy he was to hear the news. He looked like a five-year old holding a fistful of balloons when I told him. This was right before her first birthday, and of course Ian was there at the party. After he first met her, they had regular play dates. I was usually there with them. My mom lived with Sophie whenever I was on assignment. But—"

Sam held the mug to her lip as she sipped, slightly longer than she needed to. "My mom fell down the stairs and broke her arm when I was five days away but still in Afghanistan. I agreed to let Sophie stay with Ian while she was in the hospital. Because I didn't really feel like I had any other choice ... and it was just five days away."

Then she repeated it out loud to Chris, just like she repeated it to herself all the time when alone. *Just five days.*

Another long sip. "But it doesn't matter, because even

if I came home the next day, it would have been too late. Ian lost our daughter the first chance he got."

The coffee couldn't help her this time. Sam's first tear had already fallen. "On the first morning she was staying with him, Sophie wandered out the back door. She wasn't seen again for a week."

Chris looked at her patiently as she gathered her strength and thoughts.

"The next time anyone saw Sophie was when her body washed up on the shoreline of the lake next to Ian's place." She took a breath, her first true exhale since before starting the story. "The other night. When I left early. That was the two-year anniversary."

Chris looked into her eyes. "So you came to Rush to lose yourself."

She blinked, teasing him to smother her emotion. "Don't play psychiatrist with me."

"Anything to get you onto my couch," he teased her back, seeming to know exactly what she needed.

Sam surprised herself. "Psychiatrists aren't supposed to fuck their patients."

He surprised her too. "Technically, bosses aren't supposed to fuck their employees, but I still can't stop wanting to see you naked at some point in between the time you finish that coffee and when you're on the way back home."

"You're not seeing me naked." She couldn't surrender all the way.

He didn't respond. Or need to. Sam was wrong. She did get naked, and he did see her, and she honestly liked both parts of that.

But then she lingered, and that was a mistake.

She never meant to fall asleep in his arms. Doing so

made her itch. Sam woke up on three separate occasions, in and out of her slumber with the most pressing of thoughts: *I really need to go.*

Instead, she stayed the night.

TWENTY-ONE

Beth

Beth was alone.

She assumed it was her preference when telling Meredith to go home. She hadn't wanted the sharp-eyed psychiatrist to know that Beth felt certain the cupid statue on the mantel didn't normally face toward the street, or that the picture of her mother sitting atop the piano had *always* been on the credenza in the hall. Meredith would have her committed.

She pulled the throw up to her chin and looked over at her boarded window. An ugly reminder of last night, same as that shard of glass that had opened her foot. She felt the pain but did her best to ignore it.

She looked at her gun, sitting a few feet away on the coffee table, and wondered if it would be better if she was holding the weapon instead. Sure, that seemed dangerous, but so was lying on the couch unarmed and prone. She might as well beg the universe to let Peter send one of his minions to murder her.

But soon the silence was screaming, and Beth needed it

to shut the hell up even more than she needed the gun. So she grabbed the remote from the coffee table, then aimed it at the TV and ended the oppressive quiet.

Her empty living room was suddenly flooded with a scripted exchange as a pair of anchors started swapping unfortunate news onscreen.

The noise helped her to think.

She pondered harder, wondering what Peter wasn't telling her.

What had he *done?*

Beth wished that she knew.

Why wasn't anyone willing to tell her anything? She was sick of Rush treating her like a ghost.

She turned off the TV, then tossed the remote on her coffee table with a sigh. Again she considered grabbing the gun, but knowing that would only stir her anxiety further, she finally stood from the couch and went to the dining room instead.

She opened her purse, took out her phone, and made a call. Two rings, then she hung up.

She couldn't keep calling Sam. Not after her little display in the Back Bar.

That was when the noises started. Gentle at first. The whispering she was almost used to, but then a THUD from upstairs.

No … the attic.

Beth could barely breath.

It was *that* noise. The one that always came before Dorothy came to bed covered in bruises and crying.

She ran upstairs to her room, slammed the door, and practically dived under the bed.

And she hadn't even stopped to pick up the gun.

•　•　•

FIVE MINUTES … ten … twenty … and then an hour later, Beth was still lying in the tight space, listening with all of her might. It had been ages since she'd heard so much as a whisper.

The silence grew intolerable. There was no way she could sleep, and she definitely couldn't spend her entire night cowering under a bed. She was in her *forties*.

She crawled out from under her bed but felt something sharp under her foot as she stepped toward the door. A single white rose lay on the floor of her room, next to a drop of blood from the new cut in her foot. Terror engulfed her. All the positive self-talk in the world wouldn't make the real-life evidence of her sister disappear.

She threw on some clothes, then got into her Honda and started driving without any destination in mind beyond escaping.

Except, Beth knew exactly where she was going. Even if the top of her mind wasn't aware of her journey's end when grabbing the car keys, her port of call became clear before she made it halfway there.

She parked across the street from Peter's house and stared, first through her window and then through his, into the living room where the asshole was playing Family Man in front of the TV.

It wasn't their fault. Peter performed the mayoral savior role well. His wife likely had little if any clue how big of a scumbag he actually was, and his children, probably tucked in bed upstairs, were surely even more in the dark.

His wife was a victim. Same as Dorothy, and Beth in her way.

She remembered Peter pledging his eternal love to her sister, and how badly she'd wished he had been saying those things to her.

He probably made the same vow to his wife before kissing her goodnight, probably not meaning it now every bit as much now as he never meant it back then.

Little Pete Wilder probably wasn't capable of loving anyone other than himself — and maybe the daddy who always bought his son out of trouble.

He turned from the glowing TV and cast his gaze out the window upon her. Beth felt sure of it.

She held his stare, neither of them blinking.

Until his face started to change. First it shifted into an inhuman smile, before distorting all the way into a visage that could only belong to a demon.

Beth blinked, but even with her eyes back open, she saw that he now had long horns and sharp fangs, dripping with blood.

But then she blinked again, and Peter was no longer staring. He wasn't even looking at her, still watching TV with his wife as if he'd never turned her way.

She threw the car into drive and pulled away, faster than she intended and with a tease of squealing tires. She was scared that Peter had seen her, frightened that he would call the cops and she'd find them on her porch, terrified that something might happen while she was sleeping, and that after closing her eyes tonight, she might never wake again.

She made it home safely but was far from feeling safe.

Beth took the meds Meredith had carefully laid out for her, and then opened the bottle on the nightstand and took a few more — it was hard to count when her thoughts and feelings and worries were scattered all over the place.

She collected the gun from the coffee table and tucked it back under her mattress, then climbed into bed, begging the universe to grant her some sleep, growing ever more desperate for the kind of shuteye that came without nightmares of burning innocents drifting out from the woods.

Sleep eventually found her.

But the nightmares refused to stay away.

TWENTY-TWO

Sam

SAM OPENED her eyes to the smell of bacon and a sickening realization.

She reassembled a montage of damning events, starting with her blowing Chris off, followed by her horrifying discovery of some asshole's sick joke — the bottle of pills on her countertop — that capped her long night into a full retreat, first into Chris's arms, then into his bed, and now into the same bullshit domestic fantasy he'd repeated a few too many times already.

She sat up in bed, then blanched in surprise. She knew his loft window looked out onto the lake — Sam stared at that water every time she was here. But it was different waking up to the sight, and even in the brilliant sunlight streaming through the glass and promising Sam a beautiful day, in the moment she could only think about how much she wanted that lake to drown her.

She kept staring at the calm surface, picturing herself thrashing and sinking beneath it, when a clatter came from the kitchen. Sam looked over to see Chris standing over the stove.

"You're making breakfast, I see." She shouldn't have opened up so much last night. More, she should have left after getting what she needed. "I'll be out of here before it's done."

"Good morning. And don't be silly. I'm almost finished. Look."

"I'm not hungry."

"I bet you are."

"I'm really not." In truth, she could eat a double cheeseburger with triple the fries.

"Five minutes. Then ten to eat."

Sam shook her head. "One minute to piss, and another half or so to get out of here."

His face fell. "I know that you're only leaving right now because doing this with me makes you feel vulnerable."

"Doing what?" she snapped.

"This." He gestured at the couch, the empty plates, him, then her. "All of it."

"You know that, huh?"

"I think I do." He nodded. "It's okay to be vulnerable. I'm not going to hurt you."

Sam laughed in his face. "You think you could hurt me?"

"I think anyone could hurt anyone."

"Eggs sound good."

They did, and they were.

"Sorry I was being an asshole," Sam said.

"You don't have to call yourself that." Then, as if that wasn't enough, "You're not an asshole."

She shrugged. "These eggs are honestly some of the best I've ever tasted."

"It's the Cholula sauce."

"The what?"

"Cholula sauce." Chris returned to the small kitchen

and waved an orange and red bottle at her. "Juana Aguayo gave me a bottle. It's changed my life."

"No shit?" Sam reached for the bottle and liberally sprinkled more onto her already picante eggs.

"Go easy." He laughed. "You're a spicy enough woman already. That's going to send you over the edge."

Sam set the bottle on the table and looked at her plate.

"You eating those or taking a mental picture?"

She smiled at him. "Thanks for a good time, but now—"

"You've got shit to do."

"—I've got shit to do." Sam sighed as she finished, shaking her head with a reluctant laugh. "Asshole."

"Better me than you. I'm glad we had breakfast together. Now go get your shit done. You only have a couple of hours before your shift."

By then, she almost didn't want to go.

But of course she had to, so she did, cursing herself for being so needy and indecisive all the way back to Songbird Park, several hours later than she should have been pulling up to her trailer.

Then she remembered the bottle of pills on her counter, and the reason she'd gone back to the bar.

Instead of parking, she drove the grounds looking for Syc, finding him less than five minutes later, sweeping red dust and old pine needles from one of the campsites, Dog laying in the sun several yards away.

She stopped her Jeep a few feet from Syc and rolled down the window. "Fresh booking?"

"You think of any other reason I'd be sweeping all of this dead skin up?"

"Dead skin?" Sam looked down at his pile.

"The forest sheds too. Now what's up? I know you didn't drive over here to ask me about my commerce."

"I was wondering where you were last night."

Syc started laughing and swatted her with a hand. "You know I can't tell you that, not unless——"

"Someone was in my trailer."

Syc sobered immediately.

"I found a bottle of pills on the counter, and they sure as hell weren't put there by me. Plus, my door was unlocked, and you've gone in there enough times without my permission to know I always lock it."

"That you do." He nodded, his face still serious. "I went fishing up at Scorpion Point with a buddy of mine. Alamo figured it was a good idea to get out there while we could, before the tourists really started pouring into the park. I figured Alamo was right."

"That can't be his real name."

"Only a few of my friends have real names, but Alamo swears his is real."

"His name isn't 'Alamo'," Sam insisted, despite never having met the man.

Syc shrugged. "Okay. I'll let him know that Sam the All-Knowing says that his parents have been lying to him."

"How is the security in Songbird?"

"You mean Dog?"

Dog barked and came running over.

Sam said, "It's sad how much he hates you. Laying all the way over there, just waiting for me to maybe pull up, hoping that I will, and trying to sleep so that he could dream about a life away from you."

"Now I'm glad that I can't offer you free security."

"What about paid security?" Sam asked.

"You work in a bar."

"How about one of those guys without a real name?"

"Guys without real names cost more," said Syc.

"Shouldn't it be the other way around?"

"How many guys without names do you know?" Then when she didn't reply, "There's no security in the park, but you know I'll keep an eye out for you, kid. I always do."

"I know. Thanks." Sam paused and Dog filled the silence with another bark.

"What is it?"

"It's just … Dog can smell hooker on you, and he thinks it's kinda gross."

"What is it really?" Syc asked, still serious.

"What can you tell me about Rip and the farmers?"

"Same as everyone else." His face was unreadable.

"I know you've done some kind of business with them…"

He looked back without blinking, neither confirming nor denying her accusations, and leaving the space for Sam to continue.

So she did. "I don't really care how much you're breaking bad, man. I just want to know if you have access to a lab."

"Well," he chuckled, "of course I have access to a lab."

"Would you be able to analyze a sample for me?"

Syc nodded. "Indubitably."

"Thanks," Sam said. Dog barked and she added, "He just said you suck."

TWENTY-THREE

Sam

SAM COULDN'T BE late for work again, but she felt compelled to check on Beth ahead of her shift.

After knocking on her front door for more than a minute with no response, Sam began to wonder if she'd made a mistake. She imagined checking in on Beth with a quick in and out. Part of her needed to know she was okay after everything that happened at the Back Bar last night. She wasn't exactly worried, but the unanswered question sat like a splinter in her head.

Now Sam was annoyed. She saw movement behind the curtains, but still no answer. She was risking being late for work again and suffering yet another round of Bill being petty with his bitching, while Beth was playing hide and go seek inside her house.

Sam took out her phone and gave her a call.

Still no answer.

She spent another two minutes peering through three different windows, one on the porch and each of the others on opposite sides of the house. But that time Sam didn't see anything inside and wondered if she'd imagined the moving curtains.

She went back to her car, but before getting inside, she saw the gray sedan parked across the street from Beth's house. First time she might have been able to see the driver, if not for the glare on the windshield.

But they could see her. So she gave them a friendly wave, followed by the finger, then she got into her Jeep and drove to the Redwood.

Despite the stop, Sam was on time for once, but Bill wasn't there to express his shock. Nina's cheerful face awaited her instead. Even though she was annoying, and usually got "the good room," Sam couldn't help but like her.

She wished that Chris was working, and also that she didn't keep wishing for stupid things that made her ashamed of herself.

Chris was probably giving her space after last night. If so, then awesome. It was definitely easier with him upstairs, or wherever he was, and her working the front bar.

Sam crushed one-half of a cigarette under her heel, then went inside, approaching the bar warily, unsure if she was about to be sucked into a sob story about Nina's deadbeat boyfriend Wayne or a barrage of questions about what had happened with Beth Garrick last night.

But Nina's opening line was about neither. "Some guy is looking for you."

"Some guy." She nodded for Nina to continue.

"He wanted a drink."

"Okay…"

"He started a tab."

Sam gestured with a rolling of her wrist: *Get the fuck on with it!*

"He drank the first one fast and then he ordered another."

And that was it. "Thanks, Nina."

Sam looked and saw the stoner looking at her again. Staring.

She walked over, her littlest hairs all bristling, stopping with a glance at his empty glass. "Need a refill? Is that why you keep looking at me?"

"The service is pretty slow here."

"It's not her fault. Her Daddy is Chief Colton."

"You Sam?" Shaggy asked after a second of it seeming like he wanted to say something else.

"I am." Sam nodded — not like she could keep that a secret. "Do we have someone in common, or are you playing a game of Solitaire Guesser?"

He leaned in and mumbled, "I have information from Francesca."

This was now a different conversation. "What is it?"

Sam was rattled by how much she needed to know.

But Shaggy shook his head. "It's gonna cost you."

Of course. "How much? Is it somewhere around the market price of an ounce?"

"It's not that much," said the stoner defensively. "And besides, there isn't a 'market price.' It all depends on the strain and—"

"Hey. Toker nerd. I don't give a shit about aromas or terpenes. Can you please get back to shaking me down?"

"I'm not shaking you down. This is a simple transaction, man."

"Cool, man. So how much are you not shaking me down for?"

He looked down at his glass. "Why don't we start with another one of these?"

"We don't have anything with cannabinoids in it."

"It's a vodka on the rocks. Make this one a double."

She held her tongue, then made the drink and set in front of him. "Vodka on the rocks. Now—"

He raised a hand, palm out to silence her, and used the other to lift his drink and sip it down to half-empty. He set it back on the counter and gave her a nod: *Continue.*

"So, our simple transaction, man…?"

Shaggy looked at her.

"How much?"

"Oh. A hundred bucks. Like I said, not that much."

"Are you and Francesca splitting that, or—"

"Do you want it or not?" He was done being played with.

"Sure. A hundred bucks." She went to her purse, got the money, then came back and handed it over to him while Nina watched the whole thing, with Sam strongly wishing that Nina was anywhere else.

Shaggy took the money and looked down at his empty glass.

"No," she said.

Shaggy went on anyway. "That woman you told Francesca about. The one with the burns. She was there. At the boat party. But you can't tell anyone you heard it from her, and she really strongly like totally all the way advices you to not say anything to anyone at all, because people were being really weird about it."

"*Advises,*" Sam said.

"I'm sorry?"

"No, I'm sorry, Shaggy. Keep telling your story."

He looked at her, slightly uncertain before he continued. "Someone ran into the lady when she was hiding somewhere on the boat. Security was called and they brought her to Peter. He took the woman to his room, and then never came out. I'm here because you can't go back to Francesca, not after I leave here and never again. She doesn't want this coming back on her, so don't make her regret telling you."

"For a hundred dollars."

He offered her a nod in lieu of a legitimate answer, then slid off of his stool and — no shit — straight up Shaggy walked (really, it was almost a shuffle) to the door.

It hit her with a wallop as he left: *Beth wasn't hallucinating about her sister coming back.* Sam felt terrible for doubting her.

Beth said that Dorothy intended to confront Peter about something. But what? Did she blame him for the cabin fire that ruined her life?

Whatever the truth, Peter was definitely hiding something. And Beth had been telling the truth.

Sam finally had some fresh information, but not a clue what to do with it.

She picked up the phone, but her call to Beth hit a wall of voicemail. Just as well. Affirming that Beth had seen Dorothy would likely send her new friend into even more of a tailspin.

And right now Sam had more questions than answers.

Like Peter's secret. And Dorothy's whereabouts.

Unless Peter had actually killed her.

There were a lot of places to hide a body near Rush.

The forest itself was a balm to her. Red dust on everything, chattering insects, trees that stretched halfway to the twinkling sky. But it could as easily hide one burned and damaged body. Chopped up and left for the wild animals. Stuffed in one of the many yawning cavities inside the trees themselves.

Burned in the fire pit of an empty cabin, finishing what was started back in 1993.

And then the worst thought of all. The Pacific shelf. A

body going into the ocean could be sucked under and never seen again.

Sophie's face, bloated, mangled and mostly missing floated in her brain. The image came hard and fast, like a punch to the solar plexus.

She couldn't breathe. Her hand almost instinctive reached toward the vodka bottle, but instead of picking it up, she smashed the glass and sent an arc of shards to the floor.

"What the hell?" But Nina's voice fell on empty air as the back door swung shut behind Sam.

TWENTY-FOUR

Beth

WAS THERE A PHONE RINGING SOMEWHERE?

BETH WASN'T SURE, but something shrill kept screaming at her. And that something was distracting her from the still drifting nightmare, coming closer and closer.

Maybe that was a good thing. She didn't want to see Jenny on fire, begging and pleading as she came.

"Please, Beth … you have to help me!" Then she made it worse. *"You're the only one who can."*

Beth was desperate to turn around and run, but her heels might as well have rooted in the soil. She was paralyzed by terror, unable to move a muscle, forced to stare at Jenny as the flames went from a light campfire licking her body to a burning inferno that could (and would) reduce a cabin to ashes.

The closer Jenny came, the louder she screamed, no longer able to beg for Beth's help now that she was being burned alive.

Then that ringing again. More insistent.

She needed to answer it, even if the other line came with heavy breathing from the Grim Reaper himself.

Anything was better than seeing Jenny on fire.

But a moment later, Beth discovered that she was wrong about that. Because now she was staring into Peter's angry eyes as he jabbed a finger in her face.

"Look what you've done! You ruin *everything!*"

"No!" she yelped. "I didn't mean anything … you have to tell me what happened!"

Then, spoken like the Devil himself: *"You know what happened."*

"I can't remember." She shook her head, tears like a spilled glass of water slopped down her cheeks. "You have to help me remember."

His smile radiated evil. There might have been tiny horns growing from the back of his head. He laughed, the sound like lava boiling over the lip of a raging volcano. "What happened, Beth?"

"I don't know!" she sobbed.

"YOU DO." His declaration crashed upon her like a fallen redwood. She tried to squirm away from the truth, but the overwhelming weight held her to it. "YOU DIDN'T HELP HER. IT'S ALL YOUR FAULT."

She knew it was true.

That's why she lived in this nightmare.

Because it was her fault and—

THIS TIME the ringing mercifully ended her nightmare.

Beth woke up whimpering to find that she had soaked through her pajamas and sheets again. At least some of those tears had been real.

Her phone was still ringing.

She fumbled on the nightstand until her fingers closed around it, then she answered the call without looking.

But too late. Whoever it had been was already gone.

She looked at her screen, saw that it had been Sam

making her fourth such attempt. The phone lit with a new voicemail, her only one from all those calls.

Beth pressed *Play*.

"Hey, Beth. I really need you to call me when you get this."

Two sentences, and she felt chills through every part of her body. It wasn't the nightmare, nor her usual paranoia. Something in Sam's voice had affected her very marrow. Not what she'd said, but all that she wanted to say but couldn't.

She had to call Sam back and—

CRASH.

The sound downstairs wasn't a nightmare or paranoia. Someone was inside her house, Beth was sure of it.

And after all that had been happening, and the haunted sound of Sam's voice, she had to believe that the only reason for anyone to be in her house right now would be to kill her.

Probably by lighting her on fire.

She got out of bed, quietly as she could, then got slammed on two sides by nausea and a fog of lingering haze.

Could she have taken more pills than she realized last night?

The thought filled her with doubt.

Maybe that's all it was. Maybe it really was the nightmares and the paranoia. Maybe there wasn't anyone in her house at all and she was going out of her goddamned—

BANG.

Someone was absolutely inside. But Beth was also high as fuck.

Both could be true. Both *were* true.

Beth was trembling on the floor because of the nightmare and because of her paranoia, but there was also someone in her home — because they had broken in — and she was swimming in a murky fog of pharmaceutical muck.

None of that changed the fact that the cops or Peter were probably on a mission to kill her.

She gathered the courage and put her hand under the mattress.

Only she pulled out a pair of scissors instead of a gun.

She stared at them with an open-mouthed whimper.

They had most definitely been a gun before. She really was losing her mind.

But a weapon was what she needed now, so the scissors would have to do.

She crept to her bedroom door, slipped out into the hallway, and inched toward the stairs.

Made it all the way into the living room, still gripping her scissors like the edge of a cliff.

Beth's eyes blurred as tears filled them. The terror rising to almost stop her heart. *The noises were coming from her kitchen.*

She jumped into the doorframe with a wild yell as a figure fell on her from the other side. Its arms outstretched.

Beth screamed as she stabbed.

And stabbed.

And stabbed.

And stabbed.

TWENTY-FIVE

Beth

1993 ...

WHITNEY HOUSTON'S "I Will Always Love You" came on the radio.

"Again," Jenny complained.

"I like this song." Her defense of the tune was sincere, but Beth was still glad that Jenny had finally said something. She'd been unusually quiet all afternoon.

"I liked it too. The first four thousand times. Now it makes me hate the radio. It's either that or 'Whoomp' half the time I turn it on."

"Have you noticed how often they play them back-to-back?"

"No." Jenny shook her head, the most she had moved in a while. "As soon as one of those songs comes on, I always turn it off."

"It's better than 'O.P.P.'. Remember how much they used to play that?"

Jenny made a face.

Beth said, "We can turn it off now if you want."

"That's okay…" The end of Jenny's thought never came. For another quarter hour or so, the still-active radio was the only thing keeping them company. Sir-Mix-A-Lot bragging about how his baby had an impressive amount of back, followed by too many commercials, then a hit from last summer that was still one of Beth's favorite songs. And best of all, Jenny loved it too.

So she cranked up the opening notes to "Under the Bridge," the first verse echoing throughout the otherwise empty cabin.

"Anthony Kiedis is so super-hot."

Jenny rolled her eyes. "The radio has even managed to ruin this song. Ugh."

Then she turned away from Beth and toward the wall.

Beth killed the radio. "Just tell me what's wrong."

"Nothing is wrong," Jenny insisted.

"*Something* is wrong."

Jenny turned back around — too fast for Beth to believe in her innocence. "I said that nothing is wrong! Are you going to be obnoxious about it all day?"

"I'm not trying to be obnoxious, Jenny. But what am I supposed to think? You're usually a Tootie, but today you're acting like Jo."

"I'm not acting like Jo." Jenny crossed her arms, an awfully lot like Jo would. "And stop comparing everyone to characters from *The Facts of Life*. It's like something your Aunt Ruthie would do, and it's super annoying."

"Is there anything I'm doing that's *not* annoying to you right now?"

"Right now?" Jenny repeated. "No."

"Well, I'm sorry that I'm so annoying," Beth said, more hurt than she wanted to admit.

"No, I'm sorry." Jenny sighed. "I just … well, maybe—"

The cabin door swung open, and Jenny's parents entered the cabin.

"Hey girls!" they called out together.

The Masons did *everything* together. Jenny's parents only walked without holding hands half of the time, and she didn't seem to find *that* annoying at all.

"Hey, Mom and Dad!" Jenny called, her mood immediately more buoyant. "Me and Beth were just about to head out for a walk."

"Don't do drugs," Dad said.

"Or elope with any strange boys," added Mom with a laugh.

"We'll be too busy selling our bodies for change," Jenny kept the joke going.

"Too much," her parents replied in unison.

Outside the cabin while walking the shoreline toward Miller Bridge, Beth waited for Jenny to start talking. The cabin was out of sight before she finally spoke.

"I've been thinking…"

"Yeah?" Beth said.

"I don't think Peter and Dorothy are good for each other."

But of course Jenny would say that. Everyone liked Peter. Not just Dorothy. Jenny and Beth did too, even if neither of them were ever dumb enough to admit the truth out loud.

Beth shrugged. "I think they make a good couple."

"Why?"

"They like each other. They're both popular and good looking." Then, because Beth's argument sounded like the brittle reasoning of a fourteen-year-old that it was, she added, "And everyone knows it."

"Those aren't really reasons…" It seemed like Jenny couldn't have made another word if she wanted to. Her body seemed suddenly heavier, as if an invisible wind was dragging her back in the sand. She took a long breath, then finished her thought. "Peter Wilder thinks he can do whatever he wants."

It broke her. The second that last word left her mouth, Jenny started to cry.

Beth stopped walking and put a hand on her arm. "Are you okay?"

Jenny plopped on the ground while shaking her head and blubbered, *"No…"*

Beth sat, hugging her until the sobbing began to subside. "What is it, Jenny? You can tell me anything."

Jenny nodded as she recovered her breath, then blew a long gust from between her lips. "Something happened on the weekend. I went to the bonfire. At Scorpion Point. Peter and the other boys were there. But of course you and Dorothy couldn't go." What she didn't say: *Because your father was being an asshole. Again.* "And we drank beer."

"Who drank beer?" Beth felt several emotions at once, like judgment, and anger, and envy.

"All of us."

"Who is *all of us*?" Beth was trying extra hard not to be mad.

"Peter, Gary, Levi, Christian, and Eddie."

"You were the only girl there?" Beth couldn't believe what she was hearing.

"See." Jenny shook her head. "This is why I didn't want to tell you."

"I'm sorry," Beth said, only half meaning it. "But you know what we promised each other about drinking." Then, because Jenny had obviously forgotten: "We weren't going to drink until we turned sixteen, *at least*. And in the tiny chance that we broke our promise and did it before then, we would have to do it *together*."

"I'm sorry." Jenny shook her head, her tears now falling. "But this isn't even about the drinking."

"Then what is it about?"

Because what could be worse than—

"You had sex!"

"I think Peter raped me."

A stunned moment of silence, then: "You *think*?"

Jenny took a long breath. "I passed out … and woke up without my underwear."

"That doesn't mean—"

"I just knew, Beth. *I know*."

"Okay," she said, trying to restart the conversation. This was spiraling fast. "Let's say you were really … taken advantage of. How do you know it was Peter that did it?"

She shook her head without answering. "I should never have told you."

"Just answer me, *Why Peter?*"

"WHY NOT?"

"Calm down, Jenny. It's okay, I'm your best friend, I'm not saying that I don't believe you … I'm just asking questions." But Beth *couldn't* believe it. "Peter could have any girl he wants, so…"

"Not me. Not like that."

"He has Dorothy … and she … you know … she has sex with him."

"*Peter Wilder raped me.*"

"But you don't remember what happened. Couldn't it have been one of the other guys? Like Gary or Levi?"

"It. Was. Him."

Beth had never been in a standoff with Jenny before, and she had no idea what to do. "Okay."

"Okay, what? It doesn't sound like you believe me."

"Okay, let's stop talking about it," Beth said.

Jenny leaped to her feet and started stomping down the shoreline back toward the cabin.

"Wait!" Beth scrambled to catch up. "I promise I'm not saying that I don't believe you, Jenny — I just don't understand why you don't think it could have been Gary. He calls his penis a DNA rifle!"

Jenny kept walking. Beth caught up to her and put a hand on her arm. Jenny flung it away and reeled to face her. "Don't touch me."

"I'm—"

"No, Beth. You're not. Peter is your sister's boyfriend and you've secretly liked him since forever, so it's fine that you can't hear what I'm saying right now."

"I can!"

"*But you can't.*" Her words sounded so final that Beth couldn't bear to follow.

They wandered off in two different directions, and Beth wondered which of them felt more alone.

TWENTY-SIX

Beth

BETH WOKE up on the kitchen floor.

She was sticky again, but the coppery smell hitting her nostrils wasn't sweat.

Beth looked down and saw that her hands were covered in blood, the horror and clenching panic inspired by the sight was raw and immediate.

Human nature itself was scraping against both her nerves and her psyche. She frantically surveyed her body but noted no wounds.

What have I done?

She thought it over and over while trying to make sense of what she was seeing. She kept flashing on a series of strobing images, but she had no way of knowing whether they were frames from a memory, or from one of her innumerable nightmares.

The figure that had invaded her kitchen wore the same face as that monster drifting out of the woods. Neither could be real.

No. No. No. Beth stood from the floor, wildly shaking her

head, wondering where the scissor blades and the blood could have possibly come from.

Blood on her hands and all over the floor.

There had to be a logical explanation, and she needed to know what it was. She also needed to clean up all of this mess, starting with herself.

Maybe she was being framed for murder.

That was just the first of a hundred awful possibilities to assault her as she showered, dressed in fresh clothes while stuffing her sweat-soaked and bloody pajamas into a 32-gallon plastic bag that she would dispose of later — after filling it with the evidence she was about to make downstairs.

She scrubbed down her kitchen, freaking out but not totally losing her shit, stuffing all of the towels and cleaning supplies into that same bag when she finished, just in case.

The bag was a hot potato, and she had no idea what to do with it. The attic might have been a good place, but then Beth would have had to look at her father's treasure trove of horrors. So she put the bag under her bed, in the only place that felt safe.

She picked up her phone from the nightstand. It was dead, but that didn't even matter. Beth realized as she looked down at the blank screen that she had no idea what she would even say.

Hey there, Sam. Can you please call me back? I woke up with blood everywhere — don't worry, that's not the problem. I'm just not sure where to bury the evidence.

Maybe she *should* bury it.

Except the cops could probably tell if the dirt in her backyard had been recently unearthed.

She plugged in the phone to charge while considering all the infinite areas in and around Rush where one could easily bury a large plastic bag and leave the site with every confidence that the bag would stay buried there.

She surprised herself with an inappropriate laugh while thinking that Rip surely had at least a hundred such places.

Maybe—

A sharp single knock on the front door, followed by three insistent raps.

She started toward the stairs, grateful that her kitchen was clean and her body freshly scrubbed.

Unless that made her *too* obvious.

She looked through the peephole and saw two men in suits. "Who is it?"

"I'm Detective Bacon," said the man on her left, pointing to his partner. "And this is Detective Young. Are you Beth Garrick?"

She felt sweat break out over her scalp and swallowed hard, glad that they couldn't see her. "Yes."

"You've called in about your missing sister?" asked Detective Young.

"And your department wouldn't file a report because you said she was dead."

Detective Bacon looked down, sheepish.

Beth opened the door. "Do you have any news?"

Bacon nodded. "We'd like you to come with us, ma'am."

"To where?"

"A body was found—"

"Are you okay?" Bacon cut his partner off and reached out a hand to steady Beth. Bright spots appeared in her vision as the detectives walked her to the couch and sat her down.

"Are you here to arrest me?"

The men exchanged an unreadable look before Young

started overusing the voice she was used to. The one saved for small children and crazy people. "The body was found next door. On the Wilder's front porch." Bacon interrupted him with a cough. "Point is, a body was found that could be your sister, and we'd like you to come with us to the coroner's office. For identification."

She nodded, no other choice, numbed by the icy realization that the same knock just fifteen minutes ago and she would have still been scrubbing blood from her kitchen floor.

NEITHER OF THE detectives said much of anything, though both eyed Beth with compassion as they led her into the morgue.

She was prepared to feel just about anything as the coroner pulled back the sheet, just enough to see the dead woman's face.

Her first gasp came from the stab wounds, clearly made from the scissors she couldn't explain. The site of all those furious incisions pocked across her body raised the bile in Beth's throat. She swallowed it hard, but that same bile gurgled back up like a burp when the burns and the red hair and Dorothy's birthmark all hit her at once.

"Thatsmyglurgster." The words were rancid meat in her mouth. She parted her lips to try again and made everything worse. She clapped a hand over them and urgently whimpered, *"Whrsthebthrom?"*

The detectives both looked at Beth in confusion.

But the coroner had apparently seen this before. "It's right outside, second door on your left."

She fled to the restroom, crashing into a stall at the final moment, falling to her knees and vomiting convulsively into the toilet bowl, sobbing hard as she emptied her tear ducts and stomach.

Then she pressed her back to the stall and palmed her knees, breathing in and out, wondering how long she had by herself before one of the men came to check on her.

This was worse than she had imagined. Worse than anything that had ever happened to her.

Beth knew she had done something terrible after waking up covered in blood. But this was … *unthinkable.* Her sister had come to her for help, and in her drug-addled nightmare haze, she turned on her.

No, it was worse than that, and Beth forced herself to acknowledge the truth in her mind: *She had murdered Dorothy.*

Instead of sitting on the bathroom floor, she should go back into the room with all the bodies. Confess to the detectives. No reason to prolong the inevitable.

She made her way back to where her murdered sister was still lying on a slab, with every intention of spilling her guts and accepting the damnation she so clearly deserved.

But the detectives weren't in the room. She peeked in next door, saw them talking to the morgue attendant one office over, then went back to look in on Dorothy—

Beth stopped cold in the doorway. Eyes bulged and hand clapped over her mouth. She had to trap the scream inside her or everyone would know she was crazy.

Because that couldn't possibly have been Dorothy, sitting up and staring vacant eyed at her sister, bloody, phlegmy, drool dripping down from her slackened jaw.

"Why did you do this to me?" Dorothy couldn't have possibly asked her, in a childlike voice that didn't really exist.

Beth pressed her hands harder against her mouth, forcing the bile back down her throat. She closed her eyes, then opened them again. Her sister was still there.

"Why did you do this to me?" Dorothy repeated.

But this time Beth knew for sure that she was seeing the sights and hearing the sounds of hating herself.

She blinked to prove it, and her slaughtered sister was back to lying on the slab like the murder victim she was.

"Are you okay?" asked one of the detectives as he strolled back into the room.

Like it mattered which.

I'm fine, was the last thing Beth remembered saying.

Then she was in her car, driving home, confronting the truth that she was a murderer, and thus deserved to die. Just like she would have wanted for Peter, if this was really all his fault like she so desperately wanted it to be.

For years now Beth had been holding on … waiting for the missing pieces to fill in. *The fire … that night.* She still didn't know what had happened.

And now with Dorothy dead, she likely never would.

The solution was obvious. Beth needed to get home and swallow enough pills to douse what was already lighting her insides on fire, then make sure that she could never open her eyes again.

Beth would be dead before she could learn anything more, because escaping the truth was her only means of besting it.

TWENTY-SEVEN

Sam

WHILE WINDING her way toward Rush, Sam reminded herself to slow down. She had been calling Beth steadily, and then urgently, since last night without any answer. At first it had been to tell her new friend that Dorothy *had* been on the Fat Chance during the boat party, but now it was to reassure herself that Beth was still alive.

The pit in her stomach was rotting.

And now Sam was approaching a speed trap with almost no chance of making it through without getting pulled over. Locals were supposedly immune to the trap, yet for some reason the radar gun had captured Sam's speed several times. She had yet to get a ticket, but every officer in the rotation seemed to enjoy fucking with her.

So Sam kept it a mile under forty through the infuriating five-mile stretch. But on the other side she floored it harder than ever until she pulled up in front of Beth's Victorian fifteen minutes later. No way to tell if she was home (dead) or not looking from where she was.

She got out of the Jeep, then went to the front door

and knocked, feeling unreasonably nervous on her way, then through every second of waiting.

Her anxiety worsened as she knocked and knocked and knocked, that last round considering a little breaking and entering.

But no. She was being ludicrous. Yes, the danger was real, but that didn't mean there weren't eyes on her. Sam looked over from Beth's pink and white home to the dark blue monstrosity where Big Pete hung his hat next door.

Beth could be anywhere. Grocery shopping, visiting Ruthie, or any of the other things she did with her day that Sam had no idea about.

Even if her car was right there in the driveway. And that board covering a broken picture window didn't make her feel any better.

And still, she really should be answering her phone.

Unless she's taking a nap, seeing a movie, or breaking bread with a friend.

Does Beth Garrick even have any friends?

Of course she did. Beth was probably helping out with a bake sale somewhere. And she'd taken an Uber.

Sam got back in the Jeep and started toward work, calling Beth yet again on her way.

"Hey, Beth. I really need you to call me when you get this."

"ARE you going to bite my head off if I ask why you seem so distracted?" Chris asked.

Sam looked over at him. "Did you know it's a scientific fact that when a person is asked if they're going to bite someone's head off, the odds of said head being bitten off dramatically increase?"

"It's a fair question coming from your boss," Chris replied.

Of course it was, but that didn't make Sam appreciate the query, or encourage her best work. She knew she was distracted, and all the reminders in the world weren't about to change that. It was actually shocking, how consumed she suddenly felt with this mystery that had nothing to do with her.

"I just have a shit ton on my mind," Sam said.

"Anything you want to talk about?"

She looked at him again, trying not to show her irritation. "The bar is mostly empty and you keep wanting to chat. Don't you think I would have initiated an exchange if I wanted to talk?"

"Nope." Chris laughed, but Sam only found the sound mildly insulting. "Not even a little. Don't you think I would have let you start the conversation if I thought there was a chance in hell of that actually happening?"

She looked over at Chris yet again, this time with dueling emotions. Half of her wanted him to shut the hell up and never ask her anything ever again, but the other half — which seemed to be growing despite her surface desires — felt like confessing everything than basking in some back and forth.

"I'll tell you tonight. After we close. But only if you stop bugging me until then."

"Deal." He nodded assent, then stayed true to his word and left her alone.

Curiosity was practically carved on his face, but even if Chris was constantly questioning her with his eyes, not a single query left his lips — not even when Peter Wilder came in like he owned the place an hour later and her mood and behavior must have both withered into something even more mysterious.

Peter wasn't alone, taking a seat at his daddy's table with a local asshole named Gary Travers that Sam could barely stand. The kind of beefy redneck who dragged his dick into at least one out of every two conversations. His incessant mentioning made her think he was probably hung like a field mouse.

She walked over to their table, her gait broadcasting the usual message that she was only doing her job and couldn't give a shit about Peter Wilder, though in truth her insides had sparked to life. With confirmation that Dorothy had been on his boat, she *needed* to know what he might be hiding.

"What can I get you?" she asked them both at once, not bothering to wait for a break in their conversation, hoping to inspire Peter's agitation and maybe engage the asshat in a bit of back and forth where he'd let vent more than he meant to.

Gary stopped talking and looked up at Sam with a salacious grin. "You asking about now, or later?"

"What do you want to drink, Gary." Sam stared at him, making her eyes appear as dead as his chances.

"Two fingers of Artemis Tull, then." He gave her a grin and a nod; she knew what was coming. "Two fingers sounds about right, am I right?"

She turned to Peter. "How about you?"

He seemed to be assessing her, and there was something in his gaze that tickled her suspicions further. She wanted a better read on him, but he was more guarded than she was used to seeing. Peter always acted like he was above the rules and had nothing to hide since punishment for breaking even the worst of them probably wouldn't lead to much more than a grownup's version of timeout. Tonight he seemed nervous, and maybe off his game.

Unless that was more of her paranoia and suspicions playing tricks on her.

"I guess I'll take the usual," Peter finally said.

"You don't have a usual. You order something different all the time."

"Well then, why don't you surprise me?" Peter gave her an uncomfortable smile.

"Why don't you surprise us all and grab a seat?" said Gary. "Or I could head next door and see if there are any fine ladies who might be interested in a little quality time at the shooting range with the old DNA rifle."

Peter shook his head. "Jesus, Gary."

"A surprise it is." Sam nodded, then turned around and headed back toward the bar, feeling their collective gaze the entire way there.

"We almost never work together!" Nina chirped while Sam made their drinks.

"That's because there's only four tits on staff right now, and it isn't smart to have all of them in one shift working only one side of the bar."

Nina laughed. "One of us might get pulled into the Redwood later. Chris said they're extra busy over there." She laughed again, pointing at the drinks. "That's a lot of tequila. Is Gary wanting to get drunk fast? That's a lot more than a couple of fingers." Then she made a face. "He didn't joke about a whole fist or anything, did he?"

"The tequila's for Peter. Gary ordered the whiskey."

"Peter wanted a Big Gulp of Tequila?"

"It's slightly more than a triple. I guess he had a shit day." Sam left it at that, nodded at Nina, then went to deliver the drinks.

"Because of *the body*?" Nina practically squealing at the opportunity to gossip.

Sam froze, an image of Beth bloated and floating in the lake out back rose into her mind.

"What body?"

"*Dorothy.*"

"Dorothy Garrick?" Sam's eyes pinned Nina and the other girl squirmed.

"Just about the only Dorothy around here." Nina shrugged. "We all thought she was dead. But then she turned up dead … again."

"And what does that have to do with Peter?" Sam had a furious itch to see the full picture, then share it with Beth the second she could.

Nina grinned. "That's the best part. Dorothy was dead *on Peter's Wilders front porch.*" She shrugged again. "Well, it's his daddy's porch, I suppose. But still. Sucks to be him."

"Give them these." Sam shoved the tray into Nina's hands and nearly toppled Chris in her rush to the back door.

"What's wrong?"

She didn't have time to tell him.

Because now she knew that Beth was *not* okay.

SAM WAS IN HER JEEP, trying not to speed to Beth's Victorian for the second time today.

The knots inside her writhed harder by the mile. Her instincts were screaming but she didn't know why, wanting or perhaps needing to retch as she passed the grisly spot in the road where she'd seen the fallen deer.

The animal's corpse had been cleaned up, but the red patch left behind made the memory like an open sore on the road.

She pulled up in front of Beth's with a forehead full of

sweat, controlling her breath on the way to the door, knocking as the hair on her arms came to life.

No answer.

And the light upstairs made Sam's bad feeling worsen.

Another knock, but still no answer.

Finally, she was pounding on a door that stayed relentlessly shut.

Sam reeled back, then slammed her foot against the board above the window. It snapped into pieces and clattered on the ground.

She ran inside, screaming Beth's name as she ran through the house, every room downstairs, then up the stairs two at a time, and finally into the bedroom.

"You'll be okay," Sam promised after finding Beth curled in a ball under her bed in a pool of her own vomit. "I'll call 911."

Beth couldn't answer.

Sam made the call, then waited for emergency services, petting her and repeating a promise that it would all be okay. She managed not to sob until the ambulance had pulled away, its sirens screaming into the night. And again she was alone.

There was nothing more she could do for Beth. But she still felt that she had to do *something.* If she had trusted her instincts and shown up earlier, Beth might not be on her way to the hospital to have her stomach pumped.

So she took the time to dress the broken window. She tried to reassemble the pieces of broken board she'd kicked back together over the gaping hole, but it looked unsettling.

Sam went to the kitchen in search of a cereal box or something she could use to cover it. But the kitchen was practically bare. Everything Beth needed to bake cookies was there: flour, sugar and chocolate pieces. But nothing to keep herself fed. Even the pad on the fridge had a list of *Groceries for A. Ruthie,* but no sustenance or sundries for the woman that actually lived here.

And now Beth might die, without seeming to ever really have lived.

Sam looked around again but decided that the broken boards would have to do. All that was left to do was clean up the puke under Beth's bed.

That's where she found a bag full of bloody clothes and towels.

The discovery was not only chilling due to its unsettling nature. Sam had to admit that she didn't really know Beth Garrick at all.

And she knew even less about her sister.

Solving a mystery was impossible without the information required to put all of the puzzle pieces together. Scrubbing vomit off of the floor while wondering about a bag full of bloody clothes, Sam knew where she might get some answers to her many looming questions.

And that was exactly where she needed to go.

TWENTY-EIGHT

Sam

Sam stood on Ruthie Garrick's front porch, not exactly regretting that she had taken it upon herself to check in on the old woman, but deeply wishing for any other road forward.

She knocked for the third time while telling herself that if Ruthie didn't answer now, it would be perfectly reasonable for her to turn around and get back in the Jeep. Go home and … what? … ask Syc *again* if he knew anything more about the Garrick sisters? Then what was the point of being here now?

She knocked again, harder, more irritated, six times in a row, two sets of three knocks with a neat beat in between until someone finally answered.

"No solicitors!" Ruthie barked from the other side of the door.

"I'm not selling anything. Beth asked me to come and check on you." *Sort of, not really.* "It's me, Samantha Salazar."

The door parted a crack and Ruthie shoved her

eyeballs in the slit. "How do I know you're telling the truth, and that you're not really here to rob me?"

"Why would I want to rob you, Ms. Garrick?"

"Why does anyone get robbed? Probably for drugs."

"I'm sober. Beth is my friend. Like I said, I just came to check on you, and I don't mind saying that if I was inclined to rob an old lady for drug money, I'd pick a nicer house, or one with something German in the driveway instead of that old Nissan."

"You don't have to be insulting!" Ruthie snapped as she unchained the door, then opened it. "So, what do you want?"

"To see if you need anything. Like Beth wanted me to." *And like I keep telling you.*

"Beth will be here on Sunday."

"It's Thursday now," Sam said.

"You think I don't know what day of the week it is?"

"Is it possible that you'll need something in between now and Sunday? If so, I would be happy to get it for you." Only half of that second sentence was true.

Ruthie looked at her suspiciously. "I don't need anything."

"Okay then, great." Sam started to turn around. The chances of getting anything out of this cantankerous old lady were almost certainly nil.

"Wait!" Ruthie called out. "I need a refill of my diabetes medication." She finally offered Sam a freshly baked smile. "Could you be a dear?"

"That's why I'm here … to be a *dear*."

The door closed all the way, then a few moments later it opened again and Ruthie shoved a ten-dollar bill through the part. "I expect change."

Sam looked at the money and said, "I'm hoping for the

same thing. But social media has really polarized us. Makes it easy to stay stuck in our antiquated thoughts."

She took the ten-dollar bill from Ruthie, while the old woman stared back at Sam in confusion.

"Or insulting," Sam added before waving the money like a flag. "So, diabetes medicine. I assume it's at MedSavvy on Main? Under Ruthie Garrick."

"How do you know that?"

"Logic. Geography. Math. Basic reasoning."

"Are you being smart with me?"

"Nope, like I said, just the basics." Sam smiled to keep things friendly. "I'll be right back with your meds and your monetary change."

Sam got back into her Jeep, figuring the conversation had gone as well as it was going to. She had to butter Ruthie up and would be happy to deliver her diabetes medicine if Ruthie delivered some answers. She turned on the radio instead of the usual silence and started toward MedSavvy on Main.

But the song — "Off With Your Head" by the Yeah Yeah Yeahs — died during the second chorus when Sam suddenly required the silence. She saw the gray sedan one street over as she pulled into the MedSavvy parking lot. She offered the car a friendly wave while swinging into her spot.

Inside she bantered about Old Ruthie with Arnold, the pharmacist, paid the $11.47 to get her pills, then hurried back to the Jeep, driving with her eyes half on the rearview the entire way back.

Ruthie had the door open before Sam could knock.

"Beth called. She said I could trust you." Ruthie opened the door all the way and gestured for Sam to enter.

"She called you, did she?" Beth was likely still comatose in a hospital bed.

"Why does that matter?" Ruthie snapped as Sam stepped inside.

Ruthie was rather round, but even if Sam ignored all of those pictures on the mantel, she could tell that the old woman had started her life on the smaller side, probably adding a pound or so a year in her 20s, drawing on a balance she didn't have without ever adding funds or settling the account. Now she waddled around with a begrudging smile, her aging apple face resting under a shock of bright white hair like the puff of a Q-Tip atop her head.

The living room was drenched in the scents of cigarette smoke and must. Something told Sam that the rest of the house probably reeked even worse. Of many things. If Ruthie wasn't a hoarder, then she was doing her damndest to join the sorority. There were knickknacks everywhere. Magazines stacked like monuments to Country Living, Victoria, and (ironically) Good Housekeeping. Piles of detritus in varying forms: fading papers, a box of broken toys, waterlogged books that could never be read again. To Sam's eye it was all garbage, but garbage (like beauty) was in the eye of the beholder.

"Your meds." Sam handed Ruthie the bag.

"You really are a dear." Another almost warm smile. "And guess what?"

"You're hiring a maid?"

"Oh, this?" Ruthie laughed and gestured around at her mountains of trash. "Believe it or not, I know where everything goes!"

"I believe it." Sam rattled the bag to remind her.

Ruthie took it and delivered her news. "I made cookies."

"Congratulations."

"They're oatmeal. Do you want to know what I call them?"

"Oatmeal cookies?"

"Oatrageous."

"Clever." Sam was surprised by how delighted she felt seeing Ruthie so pleased with herself. "Are they just oatmeal?"

"Oatmeal, peanut butter, and chocolate chip. Do you want one?" Sam almost said no, but then Ruthie added, "I made them for Beth, but I'm sure she'd want you to share."

"I'd love one." Sam smiled, her easiest so far.

"Why don't you take a seat on the sofa and I'll go get our cookies." Ruthie turned around and shuffled off to the kitchen before Sam could answer.

So she went over to the sofa, trying not to breathe. It said everything that she could be in a house with freshly baked cookies but smell only cat piss, even though Ruthie, to Sam's knowledge, didn't have a cat.

To Ruthie's credit, the couch was one of the few clear areas. Sam sat all the way to the left, leaving plenty of room for her host.

Ruthie returned with a plate full of cookies. She set them on the coffee table and nestled herself next to Sam. "You can have as many as you want."

"Just one, thank you." But Sam knew one bite into the cookie that she was going to have more. "*Wow.* This is *really good.* You're a great baker, Ms. Garrick."

"*Ruthie.* And thank you. Do they make cookies in Mexico?"

"I'm sure they do, but I've never been there."

"Oh. What kinda Spanish are you? Puerto Rican? Cuban? Are Dominicans Spanish? Are there other kinds? I don't mean to be an ignoramus." Ruthie smiled. "Beth is always on me about this stuff."

"She can be persistent." Sam smiled back. Now that she was here — and eating a cookie that tasted better than it had any right to, especially considering the layer of dust that was surely coating her tongue — it was time to dig a little. "But Beth's persistence is one of her best qualities."

"She's a good girl." Ruthie sounded almost begrudging.

"Who is that with her?" Sam pointed to a picture on the mantel, knowing exactly who it was.

Ruthie followed her finger. "Oh. That's Dorothy."

"So ... Beth's sister?"

Ruthie's lips pressed together. "I'd really rather not talk about her."

"Seeing as she just came back from the dead?"

No answer.

"And then died again?"

Ruthie dropped her eyes and started picking at crumbs on the cookie plate. Clearly, she wasn't going to give Sam anything. She surveyed the pictures again.

"And who's that in the picture with you?"

Ruthie looked up, a smile at the change of subject, "Oh that's Shelby. *My* sister."

Then she clapped both hands over her mouth like she'd said something wrong. Interesting.

"Shelby, huh?" Sam pressed. "What's she like?"

"Well. She's a little..." Ruthie's tongue dangled out of her mouth, and she made it look like her head was too heavy for her neck, the way it was suddenly wobbling around. "You know."

"You mean her mental health is deteriorating?"

"Apparently."

"Where is she? Do you see her much?"

"Oh, never." Ruthie sounded almost cheerful again. "She's down in Ukiah. It's a real shit hole."

She fanned her face like the heat of Ukiah had suddenly shown up in Rush. "She's also a bit of a miser." Ruthie whispered like it was a secret. "I'm not exactly rich, but I know how to spend my money."

"So you weren't close."

Ruthie shrugged.

"But Beth and Dorothy were?"

"Sure," Ruthie scoffed. "Sometimes they were."

"What do you mean?"

Ruthie made a face, but Sam didn't know what the expression meant. "They were two different sisters."

That didn't clear things up. "And Beth was always looking up to Dorothy?"

"More like Beth has a screw loose, same as my sister."

"She and I have talked about her childhood a little. It sounds like she had things kind of rough growing up."

"That's true." Ruthie nodded. "Her dad, Jack, was hard. But more on Dorothy than Beth."

"Because she was the oldest?"

Ruthie shook her head. "Probably because Dorothy reminded Jack of her mom."

"Beth never told me what happened … to her mom."

"Jack never got over Brooke killing herself. The girls were both so small, and he didn't know what to do. He was younger than you are now, I imagine. The darker the skin, the harder it is to tell how many years a person is hiding. What are you? Thirty-five? Forty-seven?"

"I'm forty-one."

"Well, how about that?" Ruthie beamed, pleased with herself. "You're right in the middle!"

"I suppose I am." Sam smiled. "So, Jack never got over things?"

"He sure didn't. He was always a drinker, but a happy drunk when he was young. All of that anger made things different. He drank to forget, and as an excuse to get mean. I honestly don't know if Beth would have been like she was if not for Jack setting an example, or if it's in her blood, same as Shelby's. I'm sure they have that saying about the apple and the tree wherever you're from."

"Yep. I heard that all the time in *Ohio* growing up. Sometimes I'd hear someone saying it one table over while my family was eating at Bob Evans."

Ruthie didn't know what to do with that.

"What do you mean about Beth 'being like that'?" Sam asked.

Ruthie shook her head. "Beth can be sweet as pie, but too much sugar can give a person diabetes."

"And Beth is the sugar-slash-diabetes in this scenario?"

Ruthie nodded toward the cookies. "Do you want another one?"

She did. And as Sam chewed through the oatrageous crumbles of chocolate and peanut butter, she began to wonder what kind of aunt Ruthie was to be saying these things about her niece to a relative stranger. She was also curious about Ruthie's siblings, Shelby and Jack ... and what might be in Ukiah.

"You might want to slow down," Ruthie warned her. "My friend, Ginny, choked on her pecan pie because she was eating too fast, and that filling slides into your throat like it's greased."

"It was probably the pecan that got her," Sam said, finishing her cookie as she stood. "Thank you so much, Ruthie. Those were delicious."

"Would you like a couple to go?" she asked, hopeful.

"Sounds oatrageous."

Sam called Chris from her Jeep before starting the engine to tell him that she wouldn't be back in.

"Is everything okay?" Concern in his voice both a comfort and lashing.

"Good as it's gonna get in a place where everyone thinks I look like the lady on a box of taco shells, I guess."

"Why aren't you coming back in?"

"I need to go somewhere," she said.

"And that's as specific as you're going to get?"

"How about: *To see a crazy lady.*"

TWENTY-NINE

Beth

BETH'S HOSPITAL bed felt like a prison. But no matter how much she begged and begged, they refused to discharge her. She might as well have been shackled.

"When can I go home?" she kept asking.

Nobody was willing to give her a straight answer, but when she finally looked up and saw Meredith Graham standing in the threshold with an understanding smile, it felt like someone throwing her a lifeline, like there might be a way out of this place. Sooner rather than later.

"You came to check on me." Beth knew there was more to it than that. "Are you going to tell them that I can go home?"

"I'd really like to do that." Another smile as Meredith walked over to her bed, then dragged over a chair and sat like a lady. "Do you mind if we talk?"

"Isn't that what we always do?"

"You had a lot of drugs in your system when Sam found you."

Beth nodded but didn't otherwise respond. What the

hell was she supposed to say? They both knew what had happened.

"Were you *trying* to overdose?"

"No. Of course not."

Meredith looked at her, narrowing her eyes without saying anything.

"I don't remember," Beth finally said. "Really, I don't."

Meredith slowly nodded, but still didn't speak.

"Am I in trouble?" Beth asked.

"Your pills were all legal … though I am surprised to find that you were taking painkillers. And we need to be really careful considering your history of abusing."

"My back has been acting up. I swear, it's not like I was taking them to get high."

"Someone needs to be monitoring your medicine." Meredith followed her declaration with another long look at Beth.

"I don't remember what happened," Beth explained.

"What do you remember?"

Beth closed her eyes, thinking hard, trying to draw her last and most relevant memory from the pile, same as she'd been trying to do since opening her eyes in this antiseptic room in this stupid sterile bed. "I remember how much pain I was in."

"What kind of pain?"

"I fell over in the library bathroom and slammed my back into the toilet."

"Why were you in the library bathroom?" Then, the real question: "What's going on?" Meredith didn't wait for her answer. Instead she stood, walked back over to the door and closed it, then returned to the bed. "Tell me everything. I promise, this is just between us."

Beth could trust Meredith a whole lot more than she could trust herself. She grew up hanging out with the townies, same as Beth and Dorothy and all the other kids around their age in Rush. But Rip Graham was Meredith's daddy, and that impeded her friendships. Everyone knew Rip was a killer, including his daughter. So Meredith made a furious effort to live a life in contrast to her upbringing.

Most of the blue bloods in Rush carried themselves with a haughty, superior posture, while Meredith's bearing was a well-maintained balance between self-assurance and grace. She ditched Rush to attend Brown, studied psychology, and went on to become a well-respected psychotherapist — all the way across the continental map in Providence, Rhode Island.

But when Rip had a heart attack ten years ago, Meredith gave up everything like the good and perhaps even over-accommodating soul she had always been, returning to Rush and setting up shop as the only family her daddy had left.

Starting an honest conversation with Meredith wasn't the problem, so much as knowing where to find *Go*.

She repeated her questions, this time reversing their order. "What's really going on with you, Beth? Why were you in the library bathroom?"

"I was posting pictures of Dorothy."

Meredith nodded, her expression intentionally blank, same as it always stayed in psychiatrist mode. "And why were you posting pictures of Dorothy?"

"Because she was missing."

Another nod. "Missing, not dead?"

"She came back to Rush. She was missing. Now she's dead."

"Is it possible that you're hallucinating?" Not so much as a hint of judgment in Meredith's question. "You've been seeing things that aren't really there for years."

"This was *real*," Beth insisted.

"Maybe it's time we reassess your meds."

Beth reached over and grabbed her purse, then produced her guest pass from the morgue. "She. Was. Here."

Meredith stared at the pass for a long while. Something changed on her face — not all the way there, but Beth knew she saw something.

"And you were there to identify Dorothy," Meredith acknowledged. "But it's been a while, and nobody's seen her since she was a teenager. Plus all the burns."

"It was my sister," Beth said, almost defiant. "There was a birthmark, and besides, I talked to her."

"In *the morgue?*"

"Of course not." *Yes.*

"Before she died?"

"Yes."

"What did she say?"

"She was trying to figure out the truth. About what happened in 1993. She wanted to sort things out. With Peter Wilder."

"*Why?*" Meredith asked.

"I don't know. She disappeared. But she went to a party on the Fat Chance before that."

"What *do* you remember?"

Beth thought back. She remembered a fight. She remembered feeling hurt and angry, whipped in with an enormous helping of guilt.

"Would you like to do EDMR right now?" Then when Beth didn't answer, "Maybe we can figure out what Dorothy was talking about."

Eye Movement Desensitization and Reprocessing was a mouthful for what amounted to psychotherapy that enabled people to heal from their trauma.

Beth had always been told that severe emotional pain

required a long time to heal. But Meredith promised that EMDR therapy would heal her mind from the psychological trauma, much like physical therapy helped to recover the body.

Meredith would target a memory, then ask questions about that memory while moving her hand back and forth in front of Beth's eyes in a way that mimicked the biological mechanics inherent in REM, the deepest kind of sleep. This supposedly encouraged the processing of the surfaced memories to transform her on an emotionally permanent level.

In talk therapy, clients gained insights from their therapist's interpretation of what they are saying. In the EMDR therapy they had done so far, Beth had been able to draw her own conclusions.

But still, Meredith was there to guide her. And at this point Beth would do anything to either get some answers or stop feeling crazy. Meredith's treatment might give her both.

She agreed and it started to work ... even though the avalanche of images and emotions was almost an assault.

Beth remembered her fight with Jenny ... not just the words but the gut punch. She remembered blowing Jenny off when she tried telling her about the rape ... then a flash forward to the memory of fire ... and...

Dorothy coming out in flames with—

"IT'S OKAY..." came Meredith's soothing voice. "You're in the hospital having an EMDR session. Can you hear me, Beth?"

"Yes." She sat up in bed to gather her bearings.

"How are you feeling?"

She shook her head and started to cry. "It's awful ...

how Dorothy looked." Her tears began to spill. "I can see the flames all over her, lighting up the night … and it's too much."

Meredith was patient, waiting for Beth to stop crying. Fourteen tissues later, she had enough breath to make a sentence without hitching.

But it wasn't the image of Dorothy that brought on the tears. It was Jenny. She still wanted to sob with every thought of her friend. The shame of not believing her or helping her was so heavy, Beth might die beneath the weight of it.

She couldn't tell Meredith.

When the silence had lingered too long and it was clear that Beth had nothing to add, Meredith said, "I should go. But I'd like to come back in two days."

"Won't I be home by then?"

"Do you think you should be?" Meredith asked.

She nodded.

Meredith looked hesitant. "I need to know if you're in any danger to yourself."

"No, Meredith, I don't want to die. Like I keep telling everyone, I didn't mean to end up here, and don't even remember what happened."

"That's exactly what concerns me. The doctors will keep you here for observation for another day or two, just so we can be sure."

"There's no *we* about it. I'm in this smelly bed and you're about to leave me."

"Does your bed really smell, Beth?"

"Yes." She hated herself for pouting. "It smells like abandonment."

"I'm sorry." Meredith put a hand over hers.

"No, you're not."

Meredith looked at her.

"How long do I have to stay? Is it a day? Or two?"

"Yes. And you need to stay on your meds—"

"I hate my meds."

"I know you do. I also understand why you would want to quit them, and I'd be happy to help you do that. But we need to wean you off and find a substitute. You can't just decide to stop taking your meds without telling anyone. Or worse, try to self-medicate."

"Thank you." She swallowed, feeling the incremental improvement. "I'm already better than I was."

"You don't have to stop thinking about Dorothy. But do your best to focus your mind on the questions you *can* answer instead of fixating on the ones you cannot."

"Okay," she said, defeated yet hopeful.

Her heart started to pump again once Meredith left, and Beth could feel cold sweat trickling down her forehead, now that she finally remembered.

Not just Jenny and her terrible news, or the argument that followed. The icicles of guilt that had been sharp enough to lodge themselves into her skull for decades.

What if Jenny wasn't lying?

What if Peter raped her, then blew up the cabin to keep her from telling?

She looked out the hospital window at the ever-present forest line and realized that despite the clarity of her recall, she had to be sleeping. Because Beth felt certain that at any second now, fiery figures would emerge from the forest.

But after a quarter hour of wide-eyed staring, those fiery figures never came.

Her neck and arms and palms were drenched in sweat, and Beth wasn't sure what was worse — the fiery figures that kept her waiting, or the unending line of darkness, hiding its bounty of secrets at the forest's edge.

THIRTY

Sam

It was a relatively long but beautiful drive to Ukiah, and one Sam would have preferred to make with Dog or Syc, or even with Chris. Being alone probably only felt this lonely because a long day preceded by a night of craptastic sleep had her running on fumes, and that turned a three-hour drive into something that felt more like six.

Sam might as well have had a broken radio. She turned it on for fewer than five minutes, starting with the end of an absurd mattress commercial promising the "best night of sleep you've ever had in your life on the night you bring your new mattress home!" and finishing four minutes later with the start of "Girls Like You" by Maroon 5, featuring Cardi B and aptly embarrassing them both.

The grating track was enough to give Sam faith in the isolation of her thoughts. Soon she got lost in them and found herself sinking deeper and deeper into the belief that something was wrong about this whole situation.

Beth, Dorothy, and whatever the hell had happened back in 1993 was now playing out in what should be Sam's life of solitude and penance among the sequoias. But the entire town was less than peaceful.

There was something bubbling under the surface in Rush. The groups, the power plays, the brawls in a neutral bar. Beth might be nuts, but she also might be onto something. Maybe that same something she'd never managed to identify, despite it being like a permanent breeze blowing through Rush.

She remembered her night with Peter six months ago and a barb of regret wormed through her. Only once, before she knew he was married. But she deeply wished she could take it back. It wasn't that one-night stands bothered her. Or even guilt over a marriage she didn't know about. It was that Peter Wilder grew ever more odious the longer she knew him. Sam couldn't help but feel disgusted by the thought of that night on his boat.

She shook her head and turned her mind from the Wilders to the Garricks, wondering if all Rush's founding families were steeped in secrets.

By the time she was parking in front of Aunt Shelby's — down to a warning light's worth of gas but unwilling to fill up ahead of her arrival unless she absolutely had to — Sam was burning with curiosity, with no idea what answers might be awaiting her behind the faded red door.

Three knocks and no response.

Another five got her knocking harder.

After seven, Sam was seriously wondering what to do next.

Because the woman was home. Sam went to the window and saw Aunt Shelby — or someone else who could easily be an Aunt Shelby, with waist length silver hair spilling into her lap — leaning back in a beat-to-shit armchair and staring at the TV.

Sam tapped on the glass, then a half-minute later

began banging, hard and then harder until Aunt Shelby or whoever finally turned from the TV to note the commotion.

Her eyes about fell out of her face. From alarm or surprise, Sam had no idea. If she had to pin it down, she'd say it looked something like *unbridled delight.*

Shelby rushed up from her seat.

The front door flew open before Sam could get there.

"Katy Jane!" she exclaimed.

"No…" Sam felt like she had deeply disappointed Shelby and couldn't finish her sentence. Shelby's face fell. Her shoulders lost their bones, and all four limbs seemed to linger in place. "I'm sorry."

"Who are you?" Shelby didn't sound mad, but she did sound suspicious.

"I'm a friend of Beth … Garrick."

Shelby nodded slowly but didn't otherwise respond.

"I was wondering when you last saw Dorothy."

Shelby brightened. "I just talked to her a week ago. But she's not home right now. She went away." A cloud of suspicion turned her overcast. "Why do you want to know?"

But this was excellent news. Sam had just figured out where Dorothy had been hiding all these years.

"I'm helping Beth to figure out what happened to Dorothy."

Shelby stared back at Sam in confusion.

"Dorothy came to Rush and visited Beth, but then she disappeared and— " She stopped, not wanting to tell the confused old woman that her niece and probable caretaker was dead.

"Beth?" Bewilderment still knotted her face.

"Dorothy's sister."

"Dorothy doesn't have a sister." For a moment, as she

said this, Shelby sounded unnervingly sober, but then the muscles in her face all seemed to surrender at once and her very presence went as slack as her body.

"Shelby?" Her eyes went from vacant to lost, so Sam tried again. "*Shelby?*"

Shelby stayed perfectly still, cognizance fighting for life in her eyes. Then like the flicking of a switch: "Hello."

"We were talking about Beth. Dorothy went to—"

"Nice to meet you, Beth." It was like the woman had entirely reset.

Fine. She smiled. Started over. "My name is Sam. I'm—"

"Nice to meet you, Sam." Shelby smiled.

Sam smiled back, harder this time. "I'm a friend of Beth Garrick, looking into the disappearance of her sister, Dorothy. You said that you saw Dorothy last week, so—"

"When did I say that?"

"About two minutes ago, ma'am. Did you see Dorothy last week?"

"NO I DID NOT!" Shelby stood boot camp straight, glaring at Sam.

"I'm sorry?"

They stared at each other. Probably around thirty seconds.

Then Shelby's face finally settled again. "Hello."

Sam took a deep breath, then smiled as wide as her cheeks would allow. "Do you happen to know Dorothy Garrick?"

"Of course I know, Dorothy! But I don't care to know you."

The door slammed in Sam's face.

Returning to Rush with nothing to show for her three-hour drive was disappointing, but there wasn't anything else she could do. Sam was heading back to the Jeep and trying to remember where she had passed a gas station when Shelby's next-door neighbor opened the front door and a woman walked out onto the porch in a robe and slippers, clearly more with it than Shelby.

"Did I hear you say you're looking for Dorothy?"

"Yes" Sam replied, instantly on the alert.

"Can you please tell her she needs to come home when you find her? Shelby's been shouting at the kids again … and I just really don't think she should be left alone like this."

"When did you last see Dorothy?"

"Oh…" The woman rubbed her forehead like that might nudge the memory. "I think it would have been a week or two ago now." She snapped her fingers. "Yes! It was ten days ago when her sister was here."

"Beth was here?" So, this is going to keep getting weirder.

"She was." A shout and scream from inside, and the woman went scurrying back into the house, calling over her shoulder, "They are lovely girls, those Garricks."

The door closed and Sam got into her Jeep.

She drove back to Rush, now almost looking forward to the long drive. She needed time to think.

Why wouldn't Beth have told her that she visited Dorothy first?

Sam thought back to her many NA meetings with Beth, at first only searching for another piece to the puzzle. But digging into that group meant discovering something obvious. Something she should already have noticed, and likely would have if not for all the moping and obsessing she'd been doing.

A truly awful thought: Only the NA group knew about Sam's addiction, so one of them must have told the

Wilders, and that's why they left that bottle of pills in her Airstream.

Anger bubbled up like bile in her throat. The one place where Sam thought she was safe. The one place she had believed impenetrable to the bullshit in Rush turned out to be just as broken as the rest of it.

She fumed on the way back to town, feeling suddenly trapped in a web.

With Big Pete the spider dead in its center.

THIRTY-ONE

Jenny

1993 ...

JENNY STOPPED across the street from the Wilder homestead, staring at the dark blue Victorian.

She had planned on marching right up to the front porch, then pounding on the door and demanding entry. But the place was intimidating up close. Looming enough to make her feel like an intruder.

The Wilders could even make people who lived in Rush feel like outsiders. Jenny didn't stand a chance of feeling like she was worth anything around them.

But none of that mattered right now. She had to gather her courage, cross the street, then pound on the door and demand entry exactly like she had imagined.

Jenny couldn't let Peter Wilder get away with this.

She marched across the street, though it might have been more of a light stride seeing as at least two of her steps were so tentative. At least she'd put on the purple Docs and could pretend it was a march. She pounded on the door, or semi-aggressively knocked — surely she was loud enough to be heard even if there was some noise in the kitchen.

A professionally dressed maid answered the door. Her black and white outfit looked more like a costume to Jenny than a uniform.

The maid obviously had a few opinions of her own. She looked Jenny over, judging her from denim cutoffs to the baby doll tee she had completely forgotten about. "May I help you?"

"I'm here to see Peter. Please."

"Might I ask what this is regarding?"

"I just want to talk with him. It's private. Please…" Why was she being so polite? To hell with this judgmental maid! "If it's not too much trouble…"

"Your name?" She made her request for Jenny's moniker sound like a gold-plated favor.

"I'm Jenny. Mason." Then she made herself look like even more of an idiot. "He'll know what it's about."

But her unnecessary finish turned out to be true. Peter came swaggering to the door like her panties were stuffed in his pocket, smiling like a serpent as he scraped her soul with his eyes.

The maid disappeared down the hall without even a nod goodbye.

"Good to see you." His smile widened and he nodded vaguely at the second story, presumably toward his bedroom. "Interested in some seconds?"

Jenny had no idea how to answer that, aghast as she was. The fucking asshole had zero remorse. She'd imagined him denying that he had done anything wrong, not standing in the doorway like a conquering hero.

"You can be on top this time." He reached out to touch her and she slapped his hand away.

"I never wanted to have sex with you!" Then twice as loud, but not yet a scream. "You took advantage of me!"

Surprise flooded his face. "What?"

"You took advantage of me." She said it again, slower this time.

He looked her in the eyes for a moment before he shifted, raising his hand and stepping back from the threshold. "It wasn't me. You were—"

"Are you kidding me? You literally just admitted it!"

Peter shook his head. "I didn't admit anything."

"I'll tell."

"You have nothing to tell." He infuriated her further with a shrug.

She leaned into the doorway and gave him one more chance with a whispered growl, "*You raped me, Peter.*"

"That wasn't rape. Someone needs to buy you a dictionary."

"I never said yes."

"You're kidding me, right?" Peter leered at her. "What do you call slobbering all over me all summer, and following me wherever I go, and *spying on me* when I'm going at it with Dorothy? That all sounds like *saying yes* to me. You can't act like you want it all summer and then act all innocent when you finally get it."

"I never—"

"Make sure you look up 'slut' when you get that dictionary."

"I'M GOING TO TELL EVERYONE IN RUSH THAT YOU RAPED ME — STARTING WITH DOROTHY!" Jenny bellowed at the top of her lungs.

Peter paled with terror before quickly regaining his composure with a snarl. "You better watch yourself."

"Or what, Peter? What are *you* going to do when *I* start telling people that you got me drunk"—Jenny leaned even farther into the house—"and RAPED ME!"

"Keep your voice down!" he snapped.

"Why? You don't want your maids to know what you

did? Are your parents in there? How will mommy and daddy feel knowing that their little boy—"

"You better stop it."

"Or what? You still can't answer me. Is your daddy really so powerful that he doesn't even need to follow the LAW? I don't think so." Jenny took a step forward, feeling her confidence swelling, not yet inside his house but only a hiccup away. "You can't even look me in the eye and say you're sorry for what you've done?" She shook her head. "You're going down for this."

"Have fun destroying yourself."

But Jenny could see the fear behind his armored words. "You have until tomorrow to do the right thing and turn yourself in. Maybe it will go better for you that way."

For a moment she thought he might back down right then, but her moment of triumph was barely a blink. Jenny would never let him get away with what he'd done to her, but she wanted Peter to save her the humiliation of having to tell the police herself.

He smiled and unsettled her instead, his confidence fully back. He had gone from being an unarmed man pretending to have a gun in his pocket to one with a bazooka behind him.

Peter opened his door all the way, and there stood Big Pete himself.

For a moment, she made the mistake of believing that the father would hold his son accountable. Instead he laid into Jenny with a slow and measured menace that was far scarier than shouting would have been.

"So, I was hearing that right? You think you can go after my boy? The son of a Wilder? You think some tripper bitch is going to get *anyone* in this town to believe her?" Missiles of spit hit her face as his got nearer and nearer. "You'll be lucky if you can get your momma to believe it, and I can promise that testing my theory'll be the sorriest thing you'll ever do — I'm talking lifetime regret, not just for you, but everyone you drag into it by being a whore who can't keep her legs or mouth shut. Do you understand what I'm saying?"

He didn't wait for an answer. "Just try opening your slut muzzle again and see what happens." He dared her with an empty second that she was smart enough to refuse. "You'll never be welcome back in Rush. And your daddy sure as hell won't be landing that contract for the new library they're building. So I guess no migration for the Masons like you guys have been talking about."

Big Pete gave her an ugly leer, just like his boy, still looming at Jenny, expecting her retreat.

Jenny was taken aback. Her parents hadn't breathed a word about a move to Rush, although they'd known full well it was her dream since she was six years old. It would almost be worth swallowing the terrible truth to finally get what she'd wanted forever.

But Peter looked so damn smug, and she knew she couldn't stand to see his face *every day* if she moved here.

So she rolled her shoulders back, unwilling to surrender another inch of ground. Not after losing several feet to Big Pete's verbal assault.

Jenny stared at them both, frozen but not paralyzed. "This isn't right." She shook her head in defiance. "And I *am* going to tell."

"ARE YOU NOW?" Big Pete's quiet menace gave way to a roar as he stomped out onto the porch in a blink and forced her into further retreat.

But he wasn't coming at her — he went to the side of the house and grabbed the hose.

Then he turned on the water and aimed the nozzle at Jenny.

Even seeing it coming, the blast of cold was still a shock.

"THAT'S WHAT YOU GET!" Big Pete yelled as he drenched her. "NOW STAY OFF MY LAND!"

Jenny ran to the fence, just outside of the reach of Big Pete's stream of water, and shouted her final thought at Peter. "THIS ISN'T OVER!"

He was on the porch, watching the scene like he was missing his popcorn.

Until Big Pete grabbed his boy by the collar and threw him inside the house, then he turned toward Jenny, sending another blast of water her way, forcing her to jump back and lose yet another foot as he boomed:

"DAMN RIGHT IT'S NOT!"

THIRTY-TWO

Beth

BETH WOKE FROM A RESTLESS SLEEP, sitting up instantly and looking around the room, trying to identify either the sound or its source, ideally both.

She was dismayed to find herself still in the hospital. She hadn't forgotten exactly, but Beth had allowed herself to think about other things than how much she wanted to get out of there while trying to sleep.

It was hard enough anyway without being so certain that the nurses were all looking at her funny and whispering about her.

Beth laid back down in bed, but she couldn't shed the overwhelming sense that she wasn't alone. So she sat back up and looked around the room again.

Still she saw nothing, and still that nothing unsettled her.

Closing her eyes made it even worse, because then it was easy to imagine the sound of someone breathing. She sat up again, this time looking one bed over to where Beth thought those inhales and exhales might be coming from.

No more sounds, but something almost for sure moved under the bed.

Or probably not since now everything seemed so perfectly still, and practically silent. Beth was obviously still attending a sold-out performance of crazy town.

Something moved under the bed again. She was even more sure this time. A single white rose slid out onto the hospital floor.

And then to prove it wasn't a hallucination, the hand that must have been moving came out from under the bed, crimson where it wasn't charred, skin crisped in shades of red, purple, and black … unless that was the lighting.

The hand preceded a body, covered in a white robe, the monster's smile rotten and garish.

Except it wasn't a monster … at least not exactly.

It was Dorothy … though this version was nothing like the happy big sister that Beth used to know. Her features had been warped by time and the sins committed against her, hair wild and sticking out from every angle like satellites on her head.

This Dorothy was angry, and rage fluttered about her more than the robe.

Beth closed her eyes, positive that the Dorothy would disappear, same as it or something like it had vanished so many times before.

She opened her eyes, saw her twice dead sister staring at her, then closed them tightly to try again. Of course the apparition would go the hell away.

But it didn't. And this time it had drifted closer.

Beth was sure she could smell it, though ghosts were odor free, and she really-truly-deeply needed for the Dorothy not to be real.

She reached out, compelled to touch Dorothy's angry face.

And despite her rage, Dorothy let her.

Beth ran her fingers across her sister's skin, feeling the bumps and planes of her burn scars as she whispered, "Are you real?"

Angry Dorothy whispered back, "You killed me."

"No!" Beth whimpered, both hands retreating back into her lap.

"You're a murderer, and you should pay. You don't deserve to be here getting help."

"*No … no … no…*"

"You should be back where it all began."

Beth shook her head, squealing *No* over and over, desperate to end this exchange with herself.

The nurse would come back in at any moment. Then all of this would—

Dorothy ran from the room.

So Beth had no choice.

She stripped herself of every wire attaching her to the monitors, then ran out of the room and after Dorothy, gown trailing behind her, feet pattering down one hallway, around the corner, then out a side exit.

She had to find a way to make everything right.

Sam

SAM WOKE up to the sound of a torpedo exploding in her living room.

In reality, it started with a soft knock on the Airstream's front door. Sam planned to ignore the knocking, but the beats were metronomic. A Bolero of rapping, coming harder and harder (louder and louder) until the demand for her attention reached a crescendo she could no longer ignore.

Sam opened the door to Beth looking up at her with worried eyes, holding a paperboard drink carrier with two large cups.

"I know it's early, but I brought us enough of the wake-up juice that there's no way we'll run out."

Sam turned around but leaving the door wide open, because what else in the hell could she do?

"Why aren't you in the hospital?"

"They let me go." Beth's eyes were a little too wide. She was trying to look innocent.

"After less than 24 hours? After an OD?"

Beth's shoulders sagged, and her explanation fell out in

a rush. "Okay, I snuck out. But for good reason. There were some memories … plus Dorothy was angry and those nurses are total bitches."

"Dorothy was there?" Beth must be hallucinating again.

"Angry Dorothy." Now she held up a rose. Again her proof that she was telling the truth.

"What's up, Beth?" Sam sat beside her on the tiny bench seat.

"I wanted to talk."

Sam took one of the coffees, but it was too hot to gulp. "So talk." She took a tiny, disgusting sip. "Gross, what's wrong with the coffee?"

"What? Oh, that's mine." Beth swapped the cup in Sam's hand for another. "Macha. Tea."

"Isn't that the one that looks like liquid boogers?"

"Well, it's green."

"Turns out it tastes like them too." Sam was relieved to see Beth laugh and maybe relax.

"I just couldn't stay there. And wanted to see how things were going. You're my partner in all of this … and there's something I have to tell you."

"I was planning on coming to the hospital to give you an update sometime around after I woke up."

"I'm sorry."

"The coffee is delicious." Sam nodded in satisfaction, taking a sip of the cup actually intended for her.

"It's fair trade."

"The trade can be a total rip-off if the coffee tastes like this." She took another sip, lightly scalding her tongue. "How is this still so hot?"

"So … you were planning on giving me an update?"

After taking a long moment to drag her burned tongue

back and forth against the roof of her mouth a few times, Sam said, "I went to see Shelby."

"My *Aunt* Shelby?"

"I'd prefer to give a smart-ass answer right now, but I can't think of a single famous Shelby. Yes, your Aunt Shelby. The bad news is that she isn't all with it. The good news is that it looks like that's where Dorothy has been hiding all of these years. Did you know that?"

Beth shook her head.

"You had no idea?" Sam pressed.

She shook her head again. "No idea."

But still Sam didn't couldn't tell if she was lying. "The neighbor said you were there last month."

Beth burst into tears, still shaking her head, even wilder. "I'm so confused.

"We'll get it figured out," Sam assured her, feeling sorrier for Beth than she had been just a few minutes ago. "Maybe something in your update will help?"

"I did remember something…"

Sam took her first actual gulp. Damn that was good, and not just because it wasn't tea. "I would really love to know more about that memory, and by more, I mean *anything*."

Beth spit her next sentence out like a mouthful of rotten food. "I remember Jenny telling me that she thought Peter raped her."

"*Thought?*" Sam repeated, the cup of coffee hovering in front of her lips.

"She didn't have proof, but she said she knew, and I didn't believe her." Beth shook her head, clearly angry with herself. "We got in a big fight about it. Maybe that has something to do with this?"

"Maybe." Sam set her cup on the floor and leaned back on the couch, no longer needing or wanting the caffeine. "Is it possible that Dorothy knew? And that's why she went to confront Peter?"

Beth nodded like a scared little rabbit. "That's what I'm thinking."

"She did, you know."

"What?"

"Go to Peter." Sam spoke softly, unsure of how this update might land. "On the boat. I got confirmation."

Beth's eyes widened.

"Does Peter know that Jenny told you what he did?" Sam asked.

"I'm not—"

Beth stopped talking at the sound of a car — or cars — pulling up in front of the trailer. Sam was already over at the window looking out at a pair of vehicles she didn't want to see. One plus the other equaled something nefarious: a police cruiser, and that same damn gray sedan.

No surprise when a cop got out of the cruiser, and only slightly more so to see a second officer in plain clothes climbing out of the sedan. They traded a nod and an underhanded grin while converging upon her front door.

She recognized both men, but not by name. No one Sam had ever seen hanging around with the chief, but that was almost worse — underlings looking to curry favor were dangerous.

"We've got assholes to deal with," she said on her way to the door.

Beth looked frightened. "Do you think Peter sent them?"

"Are Trix for kids?" She opened the door. "Yeah?"

Uniform spoke first. "I'm Officer Rue"—he nodded to the asshat right next to him—"and this is Officer Reedus."

"Does he always do the talking for you?" Sam asked Reedus.

"You always wake up acting like a bitch?" Rue replied.

"Whoa." Sam acted more shocked than she was. "Do you protect and serve with that mouth?"

Rue again. "I bet I can name a few things you do with yours."

"Like file a complaint?"

"You need to stay away from Peter Wilder," Reedus said.

"*See.*" Sam looked at Rue. "Your buddy Reedus knows how to get to the point. But either one of you can tell Peter Wilder to fuck himself. Or both of you, if that sounds like more fun."

"I see Miss Garrick is with you." Reedus nodded at Beth, standing behind her. "Mr. Wilder has complained that you *both* have been harassing him. We're here as a courtesy, to avoid a formal complaint."

"That's very generous of Mr. Wilder. And it's also total bullshit."

"You better—"

"Peter Wilder did something to my sister!" Beth shouted. "*And* he raped my best friend in 1993!" She barreled forward before Rue got started, ducking under Sam's arm to bark in his face.

Reedus looked slapped.

"You off your meds again, fruitcake?" Rue laughed. "Maybe they should have let you OD."

"Say something like that again and see what happens," Sam dared him.

Reedus gave his buddy an uncertain look.

Rue laughed again. "Maybe I should remind you who has the badge here."

"Maybe I should remind, or I guess probably inform you, that one of us has military training while the two of you are both washed up, and one of you has rage issues on account of his being hung like a loquat."

Rue wasn't laughing.

Reedus raised his voice. "Stay away from Mr. Wilder."

"Stop trying to run me off the road," Sam shouted back.

"PETER WILDER IS A RAPIST!" Beth roared.

Rue grabbed her hard by the arm, wrenched her out of the trailer, then dragged her down the three stairs and dropped her in a grassy patch of dirt.

Sam leapt to the ground, claimed Rue's free arm, and shoved it behind his back — one wrong beat from breaking before Reedus could do dick about it.

Rue whimpered and relented as Beth scurried back inside.

"You're making a mistake," Reedus said to Sam.

"Damn right she is," Rue added through obvious pain.

Sam finally let him go with a hard shove to the dirt before marching back up the stairs.

"We could arrest you right now!" Rue shouted.

"Then do it," Sam dared him again. "But you won't. Because something tells me that you're not here on official police business and you'd rather — or Peter would rather — there not be a record of this little encounter. So you go ahead and tell him that his message has been received."

But Rue clearly wasn't done. Without moving his eyes away from Sam, he slowly walked over to her Jeep, holding the stare as he opened the passenger side door then started digging through her glove compartment.

He pulled out her taser.

Sam took a step closer. "What are you—"

Reedus threw out his arm, clearly prepared for another brawl.

Rue carefully pocketed the taser. "I'm confiscating this illegal weapon."

Sam rolled her eyes, "Tasers aren't illegal."

"They are if you're addicted to narcotics."

The worst punch was knowing they were right. Sam was an addict, she went to the meetings and introduced herself as an addict at the start of every one. But the realization that she had never categorized herself as such when it came to her right to carry protection was a shock.

The staredown lasted nearly another minute, until the conflict fizzled into grumbles and mutters, then the officers finally turned away from Sam's RV and got back into their cars.

Once their backs were turned, she slammed her front door without giving either Rue or Reedus the satisfaction of seeing her staring out the window.

"What did you do?" Sam said.

Beth was shaking as she sank down onto the tiny bench seat. Sam lowered herself in front of Beth and gently took her hands.

"I threw a rock through his window." It was barely more than a whisper. "After I left the hospital."

"And?"

"I attached a note telling him that I know what he did."

"Jesus, Beth."

"Well, he did it to me first!"

The door opened without anyone knocking, and chills exploded like a rocket launching through her body. She felt herself lurching forward, ready and maybe even wanting to kill the intruder.

But it was just Sycamore, showing up with sitcom-worthy timing. "What was Five-O doing here?"

Sam caught Syc up while Beth sipped her macha and gathered herself.

"We need to do something drastic," said Syc once he was all caught up.

"Drastic like what?" Sam asked, knowing that she and her closest friend in Rush approached their problem solving in very different ways.

"You need to call the Feds on this shit." Sam could tell by his face that Syc was serious. "Just don't let them anywhere near Songbird."

"That's your big idea?" Sam laughed while shaking her head. "The Feds won't do anything."

"The cops here are bullshit. You won't be able to trust even one of them."

"He's right," Beth said.

"The authorities ignore rape, even when there are *credible* witnesses." Beth looked offended, so Sam added, "Between Beth's diagnoses and her overdose, there are legitimate grounds to dismiss her testimony. That's just the way it is. But to try and prove rape with someone who died almost thirty years ago *and* kidnapping or murder now…" Sam shook her head. "That's not just an uphill battle, it's impossible. Unless we have proof."

"But I *know* what he did." Beth protested. "Jenny told me."

"Isn't there a statute of limitations on rape?" Syc asked.

"Not if she was a minor, not any more at least," Sam said. "But that's not the problem. Jenny told you she *thought* it was Peter, and with her dead, there's no victim to testify. That's just a non-starter."

"We need else something on him. Either definitive evidence that he was holding Dorothy, or something else incriminating," Syc said.

"Like proof that he killed Dorothy?"

Beth whimpered, tears welling in her eyes.

Sam nodded. "So, if Peter had Dorothy, then where would he have kept her?"

Beth took a deep breath. "It would have to be on his boat."

"Fat chance." When no one laughed, Syc delivered his serious answer. "Not necessarily. He and his daddy own a bunch of commercial properties, several of them empty and sitting on the market. He could've kept her in any one of 'em."

"I can search for titles on his company website," Beth offered.

Syc shook his head. "That's a waste of time. If Wilder was keeping her in one of his places, then I'd bet all the grass in Songbird that it was somewhere off-book."

Sam held up a hand. "Look. This is not about finding where Dorothy *was*. We know where she is now. Sorry, Beth. This is about finding something that gets him off our backs. To do that, we just need something we can take to the Feds. If it's evidence that he kidnapped Dorothy, even better. Agreed?"

Syc and Beth nodded together.

"Great." Sam grinned. "Then I'll break into his boat."

"I should go with you," Syc offered.

Then Beth. "Me too."

"No." Sam shook her head. "It only takes one of us to find her, but we're fucked if all three of us get caught. Plus, I'm the only trained investigator." She turned to Beth. "If I do this, will you promise to go straight back to the hospital?"

Beth nodded, taking her medicine.

"So we're decided. I'm going to the boat, Beth is going

back to the hospital, and Syc will follow up on those lab tests for me. Right, Syc?"

"Tests?" Beth eyed the knowing look that passed between Sam and Syc.

"I'll tell you when I get the results," Sam told her.

"When are you searching the boat?" Syc sounded worried.

"Tonight," Sam said.

"How will you know that he's not *on* the boat?" Beth asked.

"Because I'm making another stop first."

THIRTY-FOUR

Sam

"WHAT DO you mean I can't come in?" Sam asked, knowing full well that she had a zero percent chance of getting any other answer.

"Like I said, the Kalamack is a *members-only* club."

"And like *I said*"—she hadn't—"I'm interested in becoming a member. How would one go about doing that if they were so inclined, which like I said, I most certainly am?"

Sam waited for the snooty blonde to answer. It was probably taking so long because her body was redirecting all available resources to the digestion of caviar.

"Membership isn't open right now," said the blonde.

"What if I had a bajillion dollars in my purse, or I handed you a check for a bajillion dollars and zero cents. I bet you'd let me join then."

"There's an application process in addition to the fee," explained the blonde, with a smile that belonged on a scarecrow.

"Do I have to like turrets?" Sam gestured up at the

grotesque fairytale-like exterior of the Kalamack club that kept tourists taking pics from dawn to dusk.

"Most of our members are multi-generational."

"Does that mean they've been members for generations?" Sam asked like she didn't know.

"Is there something I can help you with?"

"I bet Peter Wilder will vouch for me. He comes into the Back Bar all the time. That's where I work. You should come by some time. Everyone says I make the best mojitos."

"I don't think Mr. Wilder would appreciate being disturbed by a non-member while he's enjoying his membership."

"Fair point," Sam agreed with a nod. "Peter is a member, while alas I am not, but just one last thing before I go."

The blonde stared, waiting for her to continue.

"Do all the members have to work the front desk? Or just you? Or do you not have a membership?"

The blonde picked up her phone.

"You don't have to do that," Sam assured her with a smile, before turning around and leaving the Kalamack with exactly what she wanted.

She'd been to the Sequoia Lumber Company's head office just before closing, swung by the Back Bar, and now third time was the charm at the Kalamack Club. It was a relief, as her next stop would have been his family home, unlikely as it was that he'd be there. But now that she knew where Peter *was*, she also knew where he wasn't. On the Fat Chance.

Her heart was steady on the way to the marina, a good sign considering she didn't really know what she might be facing. It wasn't like Sam had a boat or had been invited to enjoy the experience even once while living in Rush, other than that one time she came back here with Peter. A time she'd rather forget.

Sam had no idea whether the area was patrolled by guards, video cameras, or drones — not that it would really be drones. As much as Sam had wanted to head out for some reconnaissance earlier, she didn't want to be spotted anywhere near the marina during daylight on account of her plans come nightfall.

She was ready to swim in the freezing water to reach the Fat Chance if that was her only option, but doing so sounded only slightly more alluring than a threesome with officers Reedus and Rue. Sam was putting all of her faith in finding a better way. She hated the *thought* of water, unless she was thinking about how much she wanted it to take her. She hadn't been in the water even once since Sophie had floated to shore.

That belief was rewarded with a marina that looked a lot like the best-case scenario she had been hoping for. Despite having a few families with bottomless pockets, and all of them harboring their boats in the same marina, Rush was one of California's most antiquated towns, and an area where the arrogance had thickened like a redwood's trunk over time.

There was a lone guard, but he was a man with no care for his job and therefore easy to maneuver around. Sam counted seven cameras, but considering how easy it was for her to avoid each one, she considered them "security theater" more than any actual security.

Boarding the deck was easier than expected. She crouched until a cramp forced her upright, but by then she felt certain that the boat was unoccupied.

Another several moments spent listening — some with her ear pressed to a porthole primed for any possible sound — yielded nothing.

Her heart pounded as she picked the lock. Until then, the shadows had fully obscured her, but Sam had no idea how long it would take to get through the cabin door, and she felt on display through every one of the seconds until then.

Some light pressure with her tension wrench as she pushed up the interior pins with her pick, then maybe a little extra wiggling and the lock should open…

But it wasn't happening.

It was easy to apply too much force to the tension wrench. Maybe she needed to ease up.

She looked left and right over her shoulder, ignoring the sweat all over her brow as she started over again, using a single finger for tension this time, investigating the pins with her pick, singling out the one that was accessible, then applying light but slowly increasing pressure to the pick until she could feel the springs finally giving away.

She swung the door open, dipped into the empty space, and closed the door as quietly as she could, looking out the window at a guard rounding the corner toward the Fat Chance five seconds behind a schedule that would've ended her.

But the guard kept walking, oblivious.

Sam did her best to ignore the claustrophobia that wanted to close in around her like a chloroform-soaked handkerchief. The rooms were even smaller than what she was used to in her Airstream. Hard not to feel like she was trapping herself inside a coffin bobbing on the water.

But such thoughts wouldn't get her anywhere, so Sam barred them from her mind as she searched the Fat Chance for any sign of Dorothy.

She looked through all the drawers and inspected every cabinet. She used the light on her phone to examine the floors. But if there had been any blood, then Peter or one of his underlings had cleaned it. And unlike when Sam was an MP, she didn't exactly have access to the kits that could test for any residual signs.

The bedroom contained multiple sets of clothing in the closet, a candle and lighter on the nightstand, and a drawer full of condoms. The perfect cheating pad for the modern wayward husband. She hadn't let Peter bring her in here six months ago, preferring the lack of intimacy provided by the floor of the main cabin. His office seemed barely used. A list of talking points scribbled onto the writing pad on his desk, no doubt for his upcoming mayoral debate. A drawer full of the typical pens, pencils, and stray rubber bands, and the file cabinet yawning empty. If Peter did any work, it wasn't here.

It could have been the claustrophobia, or the guard outside — even apathetic, the man was a threat. Either way, her instincts were screaming at Sam that she needed to leave. There was nothing to find here, and the risks of sticking around were steadily mounting.

Sam was about to get out of there when she realized something was off about the piece of paper on the desk she'd dismissed as unimportant. She picked it up again and reread the title of the list: *Little Pete's Talking Points.*

Everyone in Rush knew how much Peter hated people calling him Little Pete, so it seemed odd that he would ever write what he saw as a mild insult on a note to himself.

The points were all about bringing glory back to Rush by ensuring that the right kind of people were coming to town. It was a big job for the founding families. The message made it easy to see who had written the list, but the handwriting might as well have put it in neon. Sam had seen that pompously slanted text on every credit slip Big Pete had ever shoved back into her hands.

It hit Sam like a bottle smashing onto the counter.

Peter "Little Pete" Wilder was only a pawn. A weak, rapist, cowardly little pissant of a pawn, but a pawn nonetheless. The power is and always had been Big Pete. There it would stay until the giant of Rush was no longer breathing.

Big Pete had her followed. He had messed with her mind, sending cops to bother her and putting pills in her trailer.

Even if Sam were to find something that incriminated Peter, that wouldn't sever the head from this monster.

She crept back onto the deck, then hit the ground a beat after closing the door.

She heard the guard before she saw him.

"Hello?" The beam of his flashlight swung her way.

She swallowed hard but wouldn't surrender to panic. She would get out of this. She just needed to breathe. And think.

"Hello!" the guard called out again, now coming her way.

Sam lifted herself onto all fours and crawled to the other side of the boat, out of his line of sight. But he either saw or heard her anyway.

"Hey, you! STOP!" He sounded almost excited, like maybe she was providing him with a rare thrill in his otherwise monotonous job.

His footsteps got louder, clomping on the dock, uncomfortably close to the boat.

She looked over the side, drew a deep breath, and got ready to jump.

But she just couldn't do it. Sam was paralyzed, staring down into the inky black water. Half of her wanted to jump and let those depths drag her all the way to Sophie, but the rest of her couldn't budge an inch.

The guard boarded the boat, heavy feet suddenly pounding the deck.

"Hello!" One more time.

This was it. She had no other choice but to jump.

But Sam reminded herself of the fundamental truth that there was always a choice when she found herself still looking down into the water as the guard—

"Hey!" Now he had her.

Or he would have if Sam hadn't done something insane, crouching down, then leaping across the water and landing unsteadily on the bow of the next boat over, wobbly for a moment before she quickly recovered.

Sam looked back at the guard, both of them in shock at what she had done, then she did it again, launching herself across the water to the next boat, and then to the boat after that.

Her feet finally hit the concrete, and even though her ankles were throbbing, she was already racing toward the Jeep and its promise of escape.

She drove fast the whole way to Songbird, forgetting about the speed trap along the way.

But no cop came after her, only thoughts of swirling water and a small, bloated face following her through the night. The road narrowed as she approached Songbird, and Sam was forced to slow while navigating the curves where the path had to accommodate the ancient redwoods.

She lowered her windows and let the sounds and scents of the forest soothe her clanging nerves. She felt almost human by the time she stopped in front of her Airstream.

The two men she liked most in Rush were sitting side-by-side in front of the fire pit, passing a joint while laughing. Despite her feelings for each of them individually, Sam disliked the sight of them sitting together. Even with, or maybe especially because of, Dog wagging his tail in between them.

Syc had every right to be there. He owned all of Songbird Park, including the RV where she slept every night. *Alone.* Because even if she had slept with Chris enough times by now to have lost count, they had never done the deed in her bed. He'd never been to her home. Until she'd pulled up to this bullshit a moment ago, Sam had had every intention of keeping it that way.

Dog bounded toward the Jeep as she got out of it.

"Sorry you had to be with twice the number of assholes." Sam stroked his fur, enjoying the comfort of his shag. Then she looked at Chris and tried not to sound pissed. "What are you doing here?"

"I wanted to make sure you're okay."

Sam took out her phone, looked at the screen, and twisted her face into a puzzle. "Weird. I don't see any calls or texts from you."

Chris begged her with his eyes. "Come on, Sam."

"I'll leave you to it then," Syc said, standing from his chair and gesturing at the joint. "Take good care of her. That's the first Green Unicorn I've seen in a month." Then he waved his arm forward. "Come on, Dog."

Dog whined.

"He really hates you." The corners of Sam's mouth twitched with a smile, but she held it in.

"Come on, Dog." Syc started to walk backward. "It's *dinner time.*"

Dog loudly whined but followed.

"Sure. If you have to bribe him." She sat next to Chris.

"I'm sorry," he said after what felt like an appropriate pause, consisting of exactly one puff.

"Sorry for what?" Even if it made her an asshole, she wasn't about to make this easy for him.

"For just showing up." Chris puffed again. "But you ran out of my bar. Called me saying something about a crazy lady, and then you didn't show up today. I was worried."

She wanted a hit, but not enough to take it. "I've just had a lot going on."

"A lot that seems to involve Peter Wilder."

"In part." She pulled out her American Spirits and lit up.

"And you can't give me more than that."

Sam smiled. "Nope."

He took another puff, looking confused. "Are you sleeping with him?"

"Not at the moment."

He smiled. Sam hated how much she enjoyed seeing and feeling it, loathed the way he was worming in.

"That doesn't mean I'm not sleeping with anyone else."

"Right." He let the silence linger, twin plumes of smoke rising up into the void of trees and stars.

A bat swooped low, collecting an unfortunate insect from the air.

"I'm sick of you seeing me as some stray dog that you rescued with a job."

Chris laughed, but for some reason it wasn't infuriating. Maybe it was the boyish way he shook his head. "That's not how I see you at all." He took a final puff, then crushed the butt with his heel.

"How do you see me?" She wanted to know but shouldn't have asked.

"In as many ways as I can."

Cute. "I don't think we're on the same page."

"How can we get there?" he asked.

"That's the thing." Sam shook her head. "We can't."

"What is it we're not on the same page about?"

"This." She pointed from him to her, then back again.

"Us?"

She shook her head again. "There is no *us*."

"Come on, Sam."

"That's what you said when I arrived to an unexpected visitor."

Chris looked at her, clearly not knowing what to say.

"You were the unexpected visitor," she clarified.

"We have sex all the time."

"Fine. We have a sexual relationship. That's still not the kind of relationship you mean."

"I don't understand why you won't give anything more than that between us a chance."

"You're right. Maybe we shouldn't be fucking."

"That's not what I said." Now he was frustrated. "Of course I want what we have, if there really can't be anything more. I just wish…"

Chris didn't finish, or need to. They both knew it was her and not him. He did have the right to know why she kept refusing him. She just couldn't dig deep enough to have a discussion.

Sam was suffering an uncomfortable layer of déjà vu over everything. Chris and Ian were nothing alike, but the circumstances still felt eerily familiar.

Her relationship with Ian had also been a friends with benefits situation. Until she made the mistake of letting him get closer. Ian was a good time and had never left her anything less than satisfied in bed, but she should have left it there.

Sam had ruined her own life and eliminated her daughter's by letting Ian back into their lives. By thinking Sophie needed her father. He'd been so good with her. Sophie had even opened up to him a little, him so warm and so natural in a way that Sam hadn't seen her be with anyone else.

So she'd made the mistake of trusting him with the most precious thing in her world.

Then Sophie was taken away from her.

The math was simple yet unmistakable. If Sam hadn't opened up to him. If she hadn't gone back to bed with him. If she'd never heeded that splinter of connection and opened the door to temptation, then Sophie would never have wanted to spend any time with him.

And if Sophie hadn't wanted to spend any time with him, then she would still be alive today.

"It doesn't matter what you wish," Sam finally answered. "It's not possible. Not now, and not ever. We have a great time, and I'd like to keep on doing that. But I can't afford any complications in my life."

"Is this because of your sobriety?" He sounded scared to ask and determined to know.

"It's because I said so, and that has to be enough."

"I hear you." He nodded. "Friends with benefits it is." He leaned back in his chair and they inhaled the quiet together. But after a lingering spell, he broke their silence again. "Seeing as we're friends, do you want to tell me what's been going on?"

Sam knew what he meant, despite the lack of specifics. And it was a fair question, so she told him what she could, then ended her story confessing that she was worried sick about Beth.

"I have something first thing in the morning," he said, "but I'd be happy to go to the hospital with you and check on her if you'd like."

She shook her head. "I'd rather go alone."

More silence, but none of it awkward.

He made it easy with a prompt. "You want me to get out of here?"

She stood and started walking toward her Airstream. "I'd rather you get in there."

"Really?"

"There will be no snuggling, and you're not allowed to stay over." Sam opened her door, waited for Chris to enter, then came inside and closed it behind them. "I guess *mi casa es su casa* until you get outta here."

"Deal," he said.

But he was still there the next morning when Syc knocked on Sam's door to let her know that the lab results were in.

And the test was positive.

THIRTY-FIVE

Sam

SAM STARED AT THE NURSE, incredulous.

After spending the morning at a lab Syc wouldn't explain his access to and getting some deeply unfortunate but illuminating results, she wasn't in the mood to hear any more bad news.

But the nurse gave it to her anyway.

"I'm sorry." She shook her head again, more insistently so that this time Sam might actually hear her. "But Beth Garrick snuck out of here two nights ago and hasn't been seen since. I don't know what else to tell you."

"Thank you for your time." Sam gave her an anemic smile.

No longer in disbelief, Sam now felt furious. Beth flat out promised her that she would go back to the hospital and ended up lying right to her face.

Unless something happened to her.

The realization came with a piercing guilt. Her anger at Beth curled into a withering concern. She almost felt shrunken, now knowing just how bad this might get.

The lab results told an ugly tale, and Sam had yet to read the end of it.

The only thing that would stop her worrying now was information. She was on her way to Beth's, but in the meantime, she had a pair of calls to make. Starting with Chris.

"Hey there—"

"No." She cut him off. "I can already tell you're going to say something about how it's too bad we couldn't have French toast or a cuddle."

"You don't even—"

"I can hear it in your voice, Chris. You can flirt me with later, but only if you go out and start asking around about Beth. See if you can find anyone who's seen or heard from her in the last twenty-four hours."

"I'm on it. Let me know if there's anything else I can do."

"Thanks." Sam sighed, wanting French toast. "For everything."

"You can thank me later. And that doesn't count as flirting."

Chris hung up so Sam wouldn't have to. She called Syc next, asked him to do the same thing, but didn't say he could flirt with her later, and added that Dog probably needed the time away from him. Also that if he decided to bring Dog along with him, it would be a good idea to keep treats in his pocket so he didn't run away while trying to find her.

Sam broke and entered her way into the house through the same poorly patched, broken window, then searched the place from top to bottom. But her thorough rummaging revealed only more of the same mystery. Upstairs, under Beth's bed. The bag of bloody clothes, which hadn't been moved.

In the attic, Sam found two things of note. Gallons of water, canned food, and survival gear — she didn't think of the crazy sprite as much of a prepper, but Beth was apparently getting ready for the apocalypse.

The other thing was a horror show.

The unsettling narrative played out in full, the second Sam caught sight of that creepy old chair: the treasure chest sitting in front of it, with a long white-gown draped over its arm.

Sam didn't want to … but she had to open the chest.

She swallowed hard while lifting the lid, prepared to see anything, but in no way surprised by hairbrushes of all different sizes and shapes; belts with and without buckles; polished and unpolished canes; plus four shoes from high heels to oxfords, each of them missing its mate.

To the average person it would look like an assembly of old junk, but to someone who had seen plenty, its purpose was obvious: this was a collection of whipping devices. Its placement in front of the single wooden chair told a tale she already longed to unsee.

Sam couldn't stand the thought of touching a thing in that chest, but her gaze scraped every inch of the box, hovering over each implement of abuse several times before finally closing the lid and leaving an attic haunted by childhood trauma behind her.

The chills didn't really leave until she was halfway to Ruthie's.

Her time there was short. Ruthie refused to open the door for Sam and yelled from the other side that there weren't any more cookies. Sam told Ruthie that was cool because she already had cookies for breakfast. Ruthie compensated for not getting it by telling Sam to go away. Sam promised that she would leave Ruthie's porch immediately, if Ruthie could tell her the last time she had seen Beth.

"A couple of days ago," she answered, still through the closed door. "Not that it's any of your business!" Then Ruthie fell silent, before inexplicably opening the door and inviting Sam to come watch shows with her. Sam referred back to her promise to leave the porch immediately and left the old woman calling after her that she'd be willing to try "some of that Telemundo stuff."

Sam drove to Miller Bridge next. But still no luck.

Sam kept calling and calling a person that most of Rush saw as a crazy woman, until she finally felt like she might be going a little bonkers herself.

Finally, she started toward the bar, to check in with Chris and see if he had managed to get anything from the locals.

She swung into the parking lot, spotted Big Pete's Escalade claiming twice as many spaces as anybody else like it always was, and saw several shades of red.

She parked inches away from the monster-sized Cadillac, a hiccup away from crashing right into it.

Then she marched into the Back, instead of into the Rings like Chris would have wanted. And there, sitting at his usual table, Sam saw exactly what she expected to see: Big Pete and Rip, sharing a beer and tearing it up, laughing like lions dividing their pride, leering at another man's company.

Chris was in the background, standing behind the bar. He saw Sam's face and signaled to her: *Don't even think about it!*

The plea in his gaze was enough to relax her. For a beat, there was a spark of peace inside her, and that was enough to light her hesitation.

But then Big Pete turned his leer on her and whispered

something — filthy, Sam was certain — to Rip. The old farmer laughed, and she lost it.

Chris waved his hands, still silently beg Sam not to do what she was already doing.

She marched up to their table. "You got something to say to me?"

Big Pete raised an eyebrow at her. "Make me a mojito."

"I'm not on the clock."

"Then maybe you shouldn't be disturbing me."

"Why are you harassing me?" Sam demanded, then added, "And why did you sic the cops on me?"

Big Pete guffawed. Rip leaned back to enjoy the show.

"And what makes you think that?" Big Pete was still convinced that the conversation was his to control and an infuriating grin kept proving it.

"The same reason I know you're harassing a poor woman with mental health issues."

He grinned wider. "Are you referring to yourself?"

"Who told you about the pills? I'll give you a hint: It was someone from NA."

Now Chris was on his way over.

Big Pete looked at his watch, then back at Sam. "Mojito time."

"Where's Beth?" Sam asked. "What have you done with her?"

He laughed again. His loudest so far, and this one came with a slap on the table. "Sounds like the delusion is catching." Then the grin that made her want to throw a mojito in his face before she shattered the glass on his skull. "Not too surprising from someone like you…"

Big Pete let it dangle, knowing she'd take the bait.

Sam knew better. But fuck his racist bullshit. She could take whatever he said to her and make him look like the asshole he was for saying it, right in front of the entire bar, seeing as everyone was already watching.

"And what does that mean? *Someone like me?*"

She was ready for anything.

Except: "A mother bear who can't even protect her own cub."

Sam snapped.

Suddenly she was on him, her knees on the table and fists flying as Rip gave the brawl enough space to breathe. She pounded her fists into Big Pete like a mallet into meat, but he seemed impervious to her supposed beating.

Some nearby men — Sam couldn't see who in the confusion — rushed over to pull her off of him, but he waved them away, as if to say he enjoyed the tickling.

Then he threw Sam off of him and onto the ground.

Her body was a meteorite hitting the Earth. Every part of her throbbed as she stared up at his looming form, freshly grinning as he wiped spittle from his lips.

Chris got in between them, holding up his hands in placation. "Stop, Big Pete. She's had enough."

"You sure?" He laughed.

"She can't even breathe." Chris pointed to her body to prove it. She was curled into a broken comma, still trying to breathe.

"Hey, Nachito!" Big Pete shouted at her. "Can you hear me?"

"You can't call her that," Chris said, through gritted teeth.

Sam ignored Big Pete. In another few seconds she'd have all of her breath. Then she'd grab the first knife she could find and shove it into the nearest part of Big Pete.

"Hey, Nachito!" Big Pete came closer.

Exactly like she wanted.

Sam lunged—

But again Chris came between them.

"Step aside, son. It looks like this little Tijuana kitty cat thinks she can scratch me."

Big Pete's grin must have pissed Chris off same as Sam, because as soon as it flashed across his face, Chris' hand went flying toward his jaw.

But then Big Pete turned Chris into sausage.

Chris was big, but Big Pete was bigger in both weight and width.

The barkeep might have had the body of an MMA fighter, but he had a gentle heart. The Godfather of Rush was a giant, with a soul that was still paying for its bargain with Satan.

Chris went down hard and fast, but Big Pete wasn't done. He looked down at his opponent with his head cocked, then got down onto his knees carefully and laid an extra two hard blows to Chris's stomach before whispering in his ear, "You picked the wrong side, son."

Chris was curled in a ball, protecting his organs, and now doing worse than Sam.

Big Pete rose slowly and spit on the ground next to his fallen foe. "I'm done slumming it in this shithole."

He looked around the room before swaggering out with his knuckles dripping blood.

Rip followed.

Then half the bar after that.

THIRTY-SIX

Beth

BETH WAS SITTING in the most magnetically repellent place in all of Rush.

She had once had so many great memories inside the Mason cabin, from the time before life was determined to take more than it was willing to give her. The ruins offering comfort now were just the charred wooden bones of the cabin that had managed to avoid the ashen fate that had chewed through the roof and most of what remained of the now wet and rotting sides.

Long years had shown the ruins few kindnesses, but the forest showed its affection for making the cabin its home. She sat on a fallen log where she and Dorothy had once played with Jenny, now waiting for death to take her.

Beth didn't care how she went, only that it happened soon. An animal might eat her, or perhaps she would perish from the elements. A forest fire would be most appropriate. If she were to pass right here, eaten by flames in this place?

At least that would be poetic.

Painful, yes. But wasn't that exactly what she deserved?

She was the one who had murdered Dorothy.

Beth kept remembering the moment in an infinite loop. Her sister on a slab after a pair of scissors had turned her into a pincushion.

She couldn't stop picturing Dorothy's body, but she had no memory of hearing her sister screaming as she killed her. And somehow the silence was worse.

That's why she deserved this solitude now. Beth had never been more alone in her life, but at least that was where she was supposed to be. This was the only way to make everything right.

Beth couldn't tell Sam the truth in the Airstream, when she'd been speculating that perhaps Peter had killed Dorothy. She couldn't tell *anybody*. Instead she had to do what she would have done if Peter *had* been the murderer, instead of her own sister.

She would take herself out of the picture.

Even if she didn't have enough courage to pull the trigger herself, Beth could surrender to the forest and its will, doing nothing to halt her demise.

Beth was surprised to see Dorothy while waiting for death to claim her, suddenly sitting right beside her on the log.

She wasn't dead or even burned, and she for sure didn't seem in any way angry with Beth. This was the sweeter than a Fun Dip sixteen-year-old sister who loved her more than anything in the whole wide world, and told her so all the time.

"What are you doing?" Sweet Dorothy asked. Her glowing cheeks looked freshly scrubbed.

"I'm waiting to die."

"You don't have to die!" Dorothy laughed like Beth was being silly. "You just have to remember."

"How do I do that?" Beth asked her.

"Just close your eyes and let yourself go."

"Okay…" She swallowed and nodded, knowing she could do this.

Then she did.

And it was easy to remember after that.

THIRTY-SEVEN

Beth

1993 ...

BETH COULDN'T BELIEVE the words she kept hearing.

But Dorothy and Peter kept filling her ears with new ones anyway.

"I'm telling you, we could do it," he said, repeating his suggestion for the second time since Beth started spying on them talking just a few minutes ago.

"We can't just run away." Dorothy was repeating herself just as much as he was. "It looks like it's getting worse..."

Beth couldn't see her sister because Dorothy and Peter were in the living room and she was in the kitchen, crouched behind the counter at Peter's house, after following the two of them over and slipping in through the back door.

She imagined Dorothy touching Peter's skin around the black eye he'd confessed to getting from his father, just before announcing his intentions to run away with her.

"I can deal with a black eye. Big Pete has been walloping me since before I can remember. But I sure as hell don't wanna be going into the lumber business with him. And no matter what, my old man'll never let me be myself."

"But why now? Why all of a sudden? You've never talked about this before."

"I've told you that maybe I didn't think lumber was cool. A couple of times."

"Not like, enough to run away together…" Beth could picture her sister's bewilderment.

"He's had it with me 'being lazy.' And before I'm ready to inherit the business, which I don't even want to do, he's sending me to military school so I can learn some responsibility. I'm already enrolled. He just told me. I'm out of here in the morning if we're not gone *tonight*."

"And he hit you, just because you didn't want to go to military school?"

"You know I'm used to him hitting me. That's one of the reasons I want to leave. They'll probably hit me at military school, too. I'm through with being hit!" His voice cracked.

"Oh, sweetie!" Dorothy exclaimed. She was probably hugging him. A few long moments later she said, "Someone should confront him."

"That's the last thing you want to do."

"Someone needs to—"

"You know my dad, Dorothy. He destroys the people he decides to retaliate against. Believe me, you don't want him deciding that about you. It's bad enough that you're a Garrick. Do you want him to open those old wounds? Can you even imagine how pissed either of our dads would be if they found out we were dating? That's yet another one in the *let's get outta here* column."

"My dad already knows."

"Shit! Are you serious? What happened?"

A long pause during which Beth could hear only the beating of her heart, then Dorothy said, "*This.*"

The next pause was just as long. Maybe longer. Dorothy surely showing him the evidence of their father's corporal punishment.

"It's all along your ribcage…" He sounded aghast.

An uncomfortable laugh. "At least it only hurts when I take a breath."

"That's so terrible…" Peter started to cry. "*Please,* Dorothy. Let's run away together. Tonight. I don't understand why you won't."

"I could never leave Beth."

Her heart skipped a beat at the mention of her name. She almost gasped.

"Your sister doesn't need you," Peter argued.

"You don't know that. And even if she doesn't, I need her."

"You have me."

"She's my sister, Peter. It isn't the same."

"This is one of those moments. Like in the movies. Like when the Goonies make a choice to go after the treasure."

"This is nothing like that," Dorothy argued.

"It's a moment in life," he repeated. "Sometimes you have to choose to save who you can. Like in *The Land Before Time.*"

Beth was pretty sure that they stuck together in that movie, and that Dorothy knew it, but she didn't argue the point.

"Your sister is a survivor. She'll probably go and stay with your Aunt Ruthie."

"And where would we go?" Dorothy asked.

Beth's heart fell to the pit of her stomach, because now her sister sounded curious.

"Doesn't your other aunt live in Ukiah?"

"Yes. My Aunt Shelby."

"So we kick it with your Aunt Shelby."

"I'm not sure she'll be wanting us to 'kick it with her.' And that's not much of a plan. It's not like she's going to keep our being there a secret for us."

"She won't have to. At least not for long. Just a couple of days until we figure out our next move. I've got money. I'm just not sure how to get it, exactly. But you know me, I can talk anyone into anything. Me and Shelby'll be like this"—Peter did something that Beth couldn't see—"and then you and me'll be like this." He probably finished with something she didn't *want* to see.

They started whispering, and the sounds were too soft for Beth to hear much of anything. She perked her ears, pinching her listening for any possible morsel.

Soon the exchange changed to muffled dialogue, like they were talking into cotton, then Beth could hear Dorothy crying.

It lasted for several minutes, each one of which made Beth want to sob along with her.

Dorothy finally stopped crying and said, "I just need time to pack and prepare. But we can leave tonight."

Beth could barely breathe past the feeling of deep betrayal. The sister who promised to never leave, that they would always stay together, had broken every vow she had ever made. Now Beth would be totally alone.

Dorothy and Peter traded hurried goodbye-until-laters, then Beth emerged from her hiding place behind the counter. Dorothy had barely finished closing the door.

Peter leapt up from the couch, looking like there was an 18-wheeler roaring into his living room instead of a fourteen-year-old girl.

"Dorothy's not here," he said in protest.

Beth was sad and furious and confused, and there was no order to her emotions because she felt every one of them all at full blast. "I know Dorothy's not here, because she's at home packing, so that you can run away and take her with you!"

"I ... how long were you there? What did you hear?"

"You and Dorothy are running away!"

Then, when her lip was trembling too hard for Beth to make more words, he asked, "Are you okay?"

"No." It took everything she had not to cry.

"Are you sure?"

It was either tears or the truth. "I've been in love with you forever, okay! I thought that you would finally get my stupid sister out of your system one day and realize that you and me are supposed to be soulmates!"

Beth couldn't believe what had just come out of her mouth.

Or the expression still on Peter's face. There was surprise there for sure, but there was also ... something else. His posture changed, and so did his expression.

"I've never seen you that way, to be honest." Then he gave her the smile she sometimes pictured while falling asleep. "But who knows what the future holds. I guess we can never find out now that Jenny's about to ruin my life."

Beth swallowed. "Did you really rape her?"

"Of course I didn't! I'm not a *rapist*! She asked to have sex with me. I know it sucks to kiss and tell, but in this circumstance, I think I'm justified in telling you that she *begged me.*"

Just one summer ago, there was no way that Beth could have ever imagined Jenny wanting to ruin someone's life, let alone trying to. And yet both impossible things were obviously true.

"You have to convince Jenny to leave as planned.

Tomorrow. You're the only one who can stop Jenny from ruining everything. If Jenny's gone, then nobody else has to go anywhere … and who knows what might happen then?"

Beth was on the fence when he filled her with chills.

Peter said, "If you can't convince Jenny to go, then I'll just have to find some other way to get rid of her."

THIRTY-EIGHT

Beth

Beth opened her eyes.

Of course she saw the ruins, all that wet and rotting wood that had been swallowed by the forest. The ferns growing out of the once lively dining table. But for the first time she also saw the truth in all its bruised reality.

Beth had been wrong about everything.

Peter wasn't just a rapist. The monster was also a murderer. He had been the one to set the fire and burned the entire Mason family alive. To know them was to love them, and to lose them like she had was an atom bomb dropped on what had remained of her childhood.

Beth had always seen Jenny's parents as the perfect couple. The kind that did everything together and held hands even when they weren't in a picture. The twins were always arguing over who got the best coals when it came to marshmallow roasting time, but that might have been the only thing Beth had ever seen them quarrel about.

And Jenny. The best friend she'd ever had. Beth missed her every day. But the cancerous rot that had swallowed her body with the guilt over disregarding Jenny no longer lived like a tumor inside her.

Yes, she was to blame for her part. She'd been a terrible friend.

But Peter claimed her innocence, then her life.

Sweet Dorothy was back, sitting like an innocent on the log beside her.

"I remember," Beth told her.

Sweet Dorothy took her hand. "I know you do."

The comfort was immediate, even if Sweet Dorothy wasn't really there. "So what now?"

"We have unfinished business," said a voice coming from behind Beth.

She turned toward the newcomer and saw another Dorothy. Burned Dorothy, the apparition perforated from the scissors Beth had used to murder her.

"We have unfinished business." Her raspy voice made it sound like the vocal cords had been singed from Burned Dorothy's throat.

"We need to sort it out," added Sweet Dorothy.

Then a finer point from Burned Dorothy. "We need to find Peter."

A moaning came from the woods before Beth could answer either of them.

Ripples of fright filled her marrow, because Beth knew what she was going to see the second she heard those rolling wails, before their maker came drifting out from between a pair of gargantuan trunks.

Angry Dorothy, the worst one of all, the one who had showed up on her doorstep and started it all, slowly creeping out from the trees.

"The time has come!" Angry Dorothy ordered her. "And Peter must pay!"

The other two Dorothys disappeared, so Beth stood

and followed Angry Dorothy out of the woods, where the broken and tattered ghost laid out the steps for Beth to enact her revenge on the boy that had created this all in his selfishness.

The Wilder that had wrecked another generation of Garricks.

Beth knew where to go and what to do next. That's when Beth left all the Dorothys behind.

On her way to the Fat Chance.

To finally end it all.

Sam

———

WITH THE REDWOOD RINGS and the Back Bar both now empty and closed per the proprietor's demand, it was much easier to see how furious Chris actually was. Specifically, at her.

"Does that hurt?" Sam asked, tending to the wounds on his face. It was horrifying to imagine the bruises under his shirt.

He clenched his jaw and grunted.

"Everyone is gone. You don't have to act like a tough guy." She kept her voice light, almost playful despite the broken mood. But still, Chris refused to reply.

Sam kept dressing his wounds.

He finally shook his head with a low growl. "I can't believe that you would pick a fight with Big Pete."

"I—"

"And in *my* bar."

Sam swallowed and nodded. "I'm sorry."

"You've made it crystal clear on numerous occasions that we're not in any way together, and I am therefore entitled to zero opinions about how you live your life or what you do. So, fine. From here on out, I seriously don't give a shit what you do, but if you're going to act like a fucking lunatic, then you better keep the crazy someplace where it doesn't affect my livelihood."

"I'm sorry," she repeated.

He should have left it there. Instead Chris yanked himself away from her and stood from his barstool. "You should be."

Sam understood his anger, but she'd apologized twice now, and meant her *sorry* both of those times.

"You're the one who jumped in when he didn't need to and got yourself beat up!"

"What else was I supposed to do, Sam?"

"I don't know — STAY OUT OF IT?" She shook her head, her ire rising when she should be calming down. "I'm not some shrinking violet. I'm a grown-ass woman with more combat training than you'll ever have."

"You could have been seriously hurt."

"I'm not even bruised."

"I don't think you have any idea what you're getting into!" Chris snapped, loud but not yelling over her. "Big Pete could have you killed, or kill you himself if he felt like it, and we both know that Colton wouldn't do dick about it."

"I'll be fine." Her tone had finally relaxed with her posture. Softened now that she could see Chris wasn't really mad about his bar at all, but rather concerned for her safety.

"You haven't lived in Rush long enough to know that."

"I know more than you're giving me credit for."

Chris didn't argue the point. "Will you stay here tonight, upstairs?"

"No, Chris." Sam's air of finality was a closed door on that conversation.

"Then let me drive you home."

She shook her head. "I promise, that's really not necessary."

Then he insulted her. "You don't know what you're dealing with."

"Fuck you, Chris." Her ire was back, though she managed to keep her voice calm. "I've lived in Rush long enough to know that Big Pete is dangerous."

"Sure," he acknowledged, "but I still think you're missing the big picture here. You kicked the biggest hornet's nest in a hundred-mile radius and *right now* is when all of those wasps are most likely to start stinging. You made an enemy tonight, and I can promise you that Big Pete won't ever forget what happened here." He shook his head. "That's not good for either of us. But I got my beating, and you're the one who provoked him. So, like it or not, I'm not letting you stay alone tonight. It's either upstairs or your trailer."

She looked into his eyes, then she surveyed his wounds with a sigh. "But I want to sleep in my own bed tonight. And that doesn't mean together."

Chris nodded, no words necessary. Ten minutes later, after a hurried lockup, they were on their way to Songbird Park with Sam behind the wheel.

Syc and Dog were sitting in between their trailer and hers, with Syc staring up at the stars and Dog in Sphinx pose at his feet.

Until he heard the Jeep and looked up.

But Dog stayed by Syc's side like a good best friend as she gave them a wave and parked off to the side of her Airstream.

Then she and Chris were inside the trailer.

"Take your shirt off," she ordered.

"I don't know if I can do that tonight," he replied,

despite knowing what she meant. "And besides, you said you wanted your own bed, without me in it."

"Off," she repeated.

But Chris was already removing his shirt, and Sam was inspecting the damage. She was right about the bruising, though it wasn't quite as awful as she'd imagined. His body was built for the punishment and had obviously been taking abuse for a while. Not just with its bulging tightness and striated muscles, but every one of the tattoos that covered both of his arms must surely have hurt.

Sam rubbed an arnica salve across his wounds, then gently wrapped his abdomen. "Compression might help the swelling. But it won't do shit for your pain. You can put your shirt back on."

Chris complied, then said, "Your turn."

"I'm sorry?" Sam seriously had no idea whether he was coming onto her or not.

"You got knocked around too."

That was true, and his voice was a warm blanket more than an offer of lingerie, so she doffed her top and stood there in her bra, trying not to flush, even though Chris had seen her a lot more naked than that many times before.

He rubbed the same salve into Sam's skin, and she ignored the ripples of wanting that coursed through her, despite Chris clearly working hard to stay clinical.

That was hard, but it was even harder falling asleep in his arms. She agreed because at least they weren't having sex. But just as Sam was losing her battle to a heavy wave of oncoming sleep, she thought, *This is so much worse.*

And of course, they were both in her bed.

SAM SAT STRAIGHT UP and looked around the Airstream, inexplicably startled.

It was probably a few hours later, though hard to tell when she had been sleeping just a second ago.

"What is it?" Chris asked, now sitting up beside her.

"Are you asking because I'm awake, or because you heard something?"

"Both ... I think?"

CRASH!

"That came from the kitchen," Sam said.

Chris was already out of bed. Then Sam. Both of them creeping toward the kitchen as the crashing and clattering grew worse.

What do you think it is? she couldn't bring herself to ask.

"Ah!" Sam gasped like a girl and hated herself for it.

But of course Chris wouldn't think anything of it. By the look of things he'd nearly pissed himself when he saw the baby black bear sitting on the floor and staring up at them both.

Sam backed away to give it room.

"This little guy isn't the problem ..." Chris put his arm out in front of her. "I'm worried about where the mama bear is."

"Little Guy? I bet he weighs more than me."

"We need to get him out of here. Fast."

"You first." The bear began mewling and she turned to Chris. "What do you think it wants?"

He looked worried, but otherwise didn't respond.

Her answer came from outside. First another CRASH and then what had to be clawing at the Airstream.

The baby bear mewled even louder.

Chris finally replied, his answer now obvious. "It's the mother, trying to find a way in."

BOOM!

It sounded like thunder as the entire trailer shook with the force of Mama Bear throwing herself against it.

Another three *BOOMs* as Sam and Chris regained their balance and gathered their thoughts.

But the trailer was still rocking from the impact, and no one could voice any of those thoughts before claws ripped into the Airstream wall.

The still-shaking trailer couldn't take another attack from the angry bear outside. It finally tipped and spilled off of its foundation.

Chris grabbed Sam, curling his body around hers as they fell with the Airstream and landed on their side. She could already hear the mother bear sniffing around outside in search of her baby.

"We need to get up there." Chris pointed at the door, now on the ceiling.

"There's a bear outside."

"It'll be inside any second." A claw tore through the wall just five feet away as if to punctate his point. "We need to be ready—"

A gunshot tore through the night.

Then a bellow: "YOU GIT!"

"It's Syc," Sam explained, though of course he knew.

"Now!" Chris pointed to the ceiling again.

He dragged her shitty couch over to just under the door. Helped her up so she could peek through the opening and get a good look at things: Syc had managed to distract the bear, and it had fallen back several feet, but the colossus was quickly recovering, and clearly not leaving without her baby.

"We have to hurry," Sam said.

"Really?" Chris replied while helping her down. "Because I was planning on painting a mural."

The baby had plenty of chances to harm them, but despite its size, the bear was a lamb. Together they lifted it out of the hole, though doing so was more difficult than

Sam had imagined. Chris guesstimated that the bear weighed around a hundred fifty pounds. So, more than her.

She was outside, with Chris still in the trailer waiting his turn when Mama Bear was about to charge again. But then she saw her baby loping toward her.

That was the first distraction. The second came when Syc shot his rifle in the air again and Dog barked loudly behind him.

Then mama and baby escaped into the forest together.

"What am I missing?" Chris called from below, as Sam sagged and laughed in relief.

FORTY

Dorothy

1993 ...

DOROTHY WAS upstairs in her bedroom, packing for her new life. It hadn't been hard to convince Peter that Beth needed to be part of it. She'd simply told him in that there was no way she would leave her baby sister with their monster of a father. Even a hurried exchange had time for that.

It had taken some kissing and cajoling, but in the end, he agreed, and she ran home to call Shelby and pack for their escape.

Aunt Shelby wasn't exactly comfortable with harboring the girls and Dorothy's boyfriend, but Dorothy still hadn't needed Peter to help talk her into it. She understood. Said that she was young once, too. Dorothy thought Aunt Shelby's real reason for helping was because she knew how much of a monster their daddy actually was. And she hoped the knowledge would be enough to convince Aunt Shelby to take the sisters on more permanently. She had the bruises she could show if the situation required it.

If she and Beth were escaping an abusive home and

declaring the truth out loud for everyone to hear, then Shelby could gain custody of them. The Garrick sisters already knew how to live in a small town, and Ukiah was likely better than Rush. Dorothy just needed to get them both there.

Dorothy went downstairs to get a white rose from the garden — a symbol of their sibling love since forever. She found one with a perfectly lovely bloom, about two-thirds open. She snapped the stem with her fingers, then inhaled the rose while ascending the stairs, planning to give her sister the flower along with the good news. The reminder of why they desperately needed to escape.

The trudging of her footsteps was an ugly echo. She heard herself climbing stairs to the attic, on her way to yet another beating. A noise she desperately hoped she would never hear again.

But Dorothy felt suddenly icy when she looked up and saw Beth in the doorway. Something about her sister's pouting lips and aggressive posture put Dorothy on edge.

"I have good news," she said to soften it.

But Beth kept glaring at her. "I know what you're doing."

"What I'm doing?"

Anger was already radiating off of her, but something about Dorothy's question made it worse.

"You're going away and leaving me!"

"No!" Dorothy shook her head emphatically. "I would never do that!"

"Of course you would!" Now Beth was crying, this was all out of the blue and happening too fast. "I overheard you and Peter talking. I know all about your plan to go away."

"The plan includes you." Dorothy tried to give her sister a reassuring smile.

But Beth didn't want it. "I made sure that you can't go! And I'm gonna make sure that Jenny doesn't ruin Peter's life!"

"Jenny?" Dorothy repeated, feeling like she was missing something obvious. "What does Jenny have to do with any of this?"

"She's been making up lies about Peter!"

That didn't sound like Jenny. "What has she been saying?"

"Jenny said that Peter raped her."

"WHAT?"

"At the bonfire."

"She told you that?" Dorothy asked, still incredulous.

"I was the first one she started lying to about it. I think."

Dorothy fell back on the bed, in shock and needing a moment to collect her thoughts. Everything in her life shifted again in that moment. Because Dorothy knew, deep down, that Jenny hadn't lied.

Looking back on it all, Peter's excuse to run away had been so frail. This explained everything.

"How do you know she's lying?" Dorothy finally asked.

"Of course she's lying."

Dorothy was off of the bed again and pacing her room. What must Jenny be going through right now?

"Did she tell anyone else?" Then Dorothy said what she really meant: "Has Jenny gotten any help?"

"Why do you believe her?" Beth started to cry. "You didn't even hear her story and you believe her over me?"

"It's not about believing her over you!" Dorothy snapped, irritated at her immature and selfish princess of a sister. "Why would Jenny make that up?"

"Because she's jealous!"

"Jealous of *what?*"

"Of you. And me." Beth wasn't making sense. "Both of us."

"Did she seem upset when she told you? It's not like Jenny to joke about something like that."

"Peter told me she was lying. He said that she asked him to have sex."

"That sounds like something a boy would say when he's trying to get out of trouble."

Beth tried again. "He said that she practically begged him."

"That never happened," Dorothy said, now knowing the truth more than ever. "Peter—"

The door SLAMMED downstairs.

Dorothy's heart skipped a beat as she anticipated the deafening roar that often followed the slam.

"DOROTHY ELIZABETH GARRICK! YOU BETTER GET THE HELL DOWN HERE RIGHT NOW!"

Beth had gone frozen and pale.

"What did you do?" Dorothy whispered.

"I didn't want you to leave," she whimpered. "So I had to tell Daddy."

Dorothy grabbed the white rose still sitting on her bed, shoved it into Beth's hand, and pushed her across the hallway to her bedroom.

"HIDE!" she shout-whispered.

Old Jack was already stomping up the stairs, unwilling to wait, seeing as *RIGHT NOW* meant already. Dorothy almost made it back to her room, but—

He grabbed her by the hair a beat before she made it. Yanked her down to the floor before hauling her back up (still by a handful of hair) and throwing her hard against the hallway wall.

"You think you can leave me?" he growled in her face.

Dorothy didn't answer, just turned her head away from his breath.

"You don't *get* to leave me." His growl came closer, that breath now a fog of juniper. "I'll never let you. Just try and go, see what happens to you."

She turned back toward him. Stared at him, stoking his rage without ever uttering a word or crying, making him angrier on account of her stoicism.

Daring him to do his worst by doing nothing at all.

So he did.

With an almighty shove, her father sent Dorothy sailing down the stairs.

Even shallow and carpeted as they were, his eldest took one hell of a tumble. Her bones throbbed from the inside out as she lay sprawled at the bottom, pain piercing every inch of her, too new for her to know if anything was broken.

Dorothy worked for her breath, moaning in gasps as Old Jack came back down the stairs, looming larger with every step, until he finally stepped over her, then strode out into the evening.

Surely headed back to the bar.

The ensuing silence was brief but agonizing.

Beth finally broke it, pounding down the stairs to land on her knees at Dorothy's side.

"Can you sit up?"

Dorothy tried. Failed. Tried again and almost made it. The third time wasn't just the charm, Dorothy was also able to check herself for damage.

The pain was omnipresent and heavy but receding. No broken bones for sure, and apart from a twisted ankle, the fall a victory considering it could have been the end of her.

Dorothy stood to leave, then limped toward the door.

She only made it a step before Beth said, "Where are you going? Are you seriously still running away from Peter *now*? After all of this?"

"No. Of course not." Dorothy looked back at her sister in pity. "I'm going to do the right thing."

Sam

SAM STOOD NEXT TO CHRIS, Syc and Dog, all staring at the Airstream, now lying in ruins.

The trailer lay on its side in a pool of shattered glass and scattered debris. Her home was gone, along with all the countless hours Sam had poured into fixing it up and making it livable.

She sighed, wondering where she would be living next, and thinking that at least she didn't have a lot of shit to lose.

Syc finally broke the silence after a shrug. "Coulda been worse."

Sam looked over at him. "Not for Dog. Now he has no place to get away from you. It's the canine equivalent of being forced to live with your in-laws."

"So, back to my place?" Chris asked. Then he added, "For tonight."

"Syc probably has another empty trailer somewhere," Sam said. "Right, Syc?"

"A couple of 'em, actually. But even the best of those

makes that girl there"—he nodded at the ruins—"look like you were staying in the Four Seasons."

"Do you want to come with us?" Chris asked Syc. "My couch is comfier than it looks, and I think you'll agree that it looks pretty comfy."

"Nah." Syc shook his head. "Dog'n me'll stay here and keep watch. See if anyone is stupid enough to stick their fool head anywhere near this place now that I've got my eyes out for 'em."

Sam said, "Sorry, Dog."

Syc kept going. "It was smart, putting that baby bear in your trailer to piss its mama off. But now you've gone and poked the biggest bear of all. Much bigger than the one that overturned your trailer."

"It was your trailer." Sam hated how much she was being a burden on everyone. "I'm sorry for all of this."

"Are you kidding?" Syc laughed. "That was the most excitement I've seen in a while. I can take it. And I'll be ready for more." He glanced at his rifle. "I have that old DeVille we can get fixed up for you. Once the squirrels are all out of it, we'll have your new place looking like the Four Seasons in no time."

She looked over at the old blue and white trailer, smaller by half than her Airstream, tinged green with mold. "Or Motel 6."

Syc nodded. "Still for the bargain price of free."

"I'll take it." Sam nodded back as Dog started whining. "He asked if we could take him with us."

"I heard, *When the hell is she gonna get out of here?*" Syc said.

"Me too," Chris agreed.

And then they were off, with Sam tired enough to let Chris drive her Jeep. Good thing, because her phone started ringing about halfway back to the bar. The caller ID made her sit up straight in her seat.

"It's Beth," she told Chris as she answered. "Beth, where are you?"

"Angry Dorothy is here. She's here and she's mad, and she says that we have to do something about Peter."

"Slow down … What were you saying about Angry Dorothy?"

"We're going to the boat to finish things with Peter."

"Who?" She looked over to Chris and shrugged. "You and Angry Dorothy?"

"*Angry Dorothy*?" Chris repeated in a whisper.

"We're going to the boat to—"

"Finish things with Peter," Sam repeated. "I got that part. But can you tell me what it means?"

Chris again: "*Finish things with Peter*?"

"Please Beth, honey, I'm going to need you to help me—"

Sam stopped talking when she realized that the line had gone dead. She turned to Chris. "Turn around! Head to the marina — now!"

He followed directions immediately, no explanation required, swinging the Jeep onto a side road and racing toward the marina.

"I think that Beth is going to kill Peter on his boat."

"Holy shit. What makes you think that?"

"Hold on. I have to call the cops."

She got the number and dialed. They infuriated her immediately.

"I'm serious," Sam said, after a full minute of being laughed off. "Something bad is going to happen to Peter."

The guffawing got louder, and the insult sharpened. "Sounds like you might have stepped in some bear shit."

She gave Chris a look — *here's your explanation* — then

screamed, "BETH GARRICK IS NOT OKAY! She's on her way to the Fat Chance right now with every intention of killing Peter."

But still the officer laughed at her.

Sam tried one last time, shouting into the phone. "Little Pete is in trouble, and if you let something happen to him, it's not *me* you'll be answering to."

Then she killed the call so the chips could start falling.

FORTY-TWO

Beth

BETH PULLED up to the marina with the canister of gasoline that Dorothy's ghost had made her promise to buy, careful and observant as she stopped her car. She'd driven past three different gas stations, all with at least one person at a pump, and had finally found an empty one ten miles out of town, halfway to Scorpion Point.

She couldn't tolerate the sensation of eyes on her. Not anymore.

She almost felt prim as she parked. Her earlier hysteria would ruin everything now. Beth couldn't afford to draw attention her way.

So she walked from her car to the dock, gripping tight to the canister and with her back straight like she had every right to be there, straight to Peter's boat without looking over either shoulder, slowing only upon reaching the Fat Chance, then climbing aboard, dropping onto the deck and crouching low until she finally felt safe enough to make another move.

She'd made it through two steps of her dead sister's instructions. But the final step was surely the hardest. Her nose curled as she crouched and opened the canister. Fear was a current inside her already, and the reek of the gasoline rushed over her like a tsunami, tilting the world in a way that seemed … *off*.

She forced herself forward, like a ghost through the shadows, until she had drenched the deck. She stopped at a porthole and peered down into the cabin below.

Her heart skipped a beat and she fell back without meaning to. Crouched again, doubly scared now that everything was different than it had been a moment before.

Hallucinations were more regular for Beth than Big Pete's trips to the Kalamack Club. She needed another peek to be sure of what she saw.

But the second glance didn't change a thing. Neither did a third hard look.

Peter was cuffed to a bedpost with his ankles zip tied. A woman held a gun to his head, mouthing words she couldn't read.

The woman was burned. Scarred and furious. The rage on her face was something Beth had seen over and over and over, but always she had thought it was in her mind. Angry Dorothy.

And now, Angry Dorothy's ghost was holding a very real Peter Wilder at gun point. He was drenched in sweat and covered in bruises. She'd obviously been working on him for a while.

The stench of gasoline was now overwhelming, the scent like a bomb's ticking clock in her blood.

She needed to get out of there, but her body was frozen with indecision. So what if she died? Wasn't that a price she was willing to pay for her answers?

And if she lived in a world where enraged ghosts could capture, torture and kill people … wasn't Beth surely next on the list?

Before she could respond to her own question, Fate decided for her.

Angry Dorothy looked up, met Beth's gaze through the porthole, and smiled.

Beth swallowed hard, then did what she needed to do.

She wouldn't get far if she ran. The ghost had a gun, and if she didn't get her now, then she'd put a bullet into Beth's back soon enough. She had been staring death in the eye for a while, nursing untold versions of her escape from this life while crying herself to sleep.

This version was new, and better than most.

Beth entered the cabin to find Angry Dorothy aiming the gun at her heart, the spot where she'd been aching forever. Closer now, she recognized her own gun, the one that lived beneath her mattress.

"I want answers," the spirit said.

"Who are you?"

"Don't you know?" The ghost seemed to smirk.

"You're Dorothy, but you're not Dorothy." Beth took a breath. "I killed Dorothy."

"You always were a self-centered bitch. You don't even recognize your own *best friend*."

The world went frozen. For a moment, Beth was sure she could hear the sound of her own sweat glands, the sound of her churning mind as it finally saw the rest of this puzzle, and the sound of her gasping breath as she tried to collect it.

Shock had claimed both her voice and her oxygen. Beth could only stare at the truth.

Angry Dorothy wasn't a Dorothy at all. Nor was she a hallucination. She was Jenny.

Jenny Mason was very much alive. She and Dorothy had the same red hair, but Dorothy's mane was glossy and thick, like she only used salon shampoo, while Jenny's was matted and more like what you'd find on a scarecrow.

Their burns were different, too.

And of course the eyes, charred with a darkness Beth still remembered from their long-ago fight.

"I know you did it. And he confirmed it." Jenny gestured at Peter, cuffed and tied to the bed, yet surprisingly calm.

No. No. No. Beth kept repeating the refusal in her mind, because a bullet of truth had left the barrel and was already on its way to her brain. *No. No. No.*

"Did what?" Beth asked, after another hard swallow.

Memories in screams, the recall of whispers, a moaning remembrance as everything she had been dying to forget fell on top of her, its weight suddenly an unrelenting tempest inside her.

The truth had been percolating up from her rotten soil ever since its burial, but now it was bubbling up to the surface, about to spill out and cover everything.

"It's okay," Peter said, still calm and now nodding at Beth. "She just wants to know what happened."

"I don't know," Beth insisted.

"I don't believe you." Jenny came over, never moving her aim away from Beth's pounding heart.

"I don't know!" Beth cried out.

Jenny pressed the gun into Beth's chest, but it didn't scare her anywhere near as much as the anger in Jenny's burned and broken face.

"Just tell her." Now he sounded scared.

"TELL ME!" Jenny roared.

And Beth finally remembered.

FORTY-THREE

Beth

1993 ...

Beth had been hiding under her bed, time spent clutching Dorothy's rose tightly to her chest, for hours that felt like days now.

The encounter between her sister and Daddy had sounded so awful from inside her bedroom. Her heart had just about stopped when she came out and saw Dorothy all crumpled up on the floor. Then she left, and Beth just couldn't face the world even one moment longer.

So she had put on her nightgown and clambered under the bed, waiting for something else to happen.

That *something* came when she heard the sound of a car door slamming. She rolled out from under her bed and ran to the window, then peered outside, across the wide lawn at the Wilder house.

Peter was walking toward the house with his father.

Beth ran from her bedroom, downstairs and then outside, calling out to Peter as her white nighty flapped behind her.

"Peter!"

He turned around and saw Beth, then waved his father

into the house and walked over to the fence line. His features looked hard, like he forgot how to smile. A fresh bruise had bloomed on his cheek, even darker than the one that had darkened his eye.

"What happened?" Beth asked, startled to see the new injury.

"You told Dorothy. That's what happened."

"I didn't mean to." She gasped. "It was an accident. I thought she would believe that you didn't do it, just like…"

Beth stopped, seeing an expression flash across his face that made him question herself. Guilt or hesitation, maybe even something like irritation at the questioning. But it didn't sit right, whatever it was.

"Did you do it? Did you rape Jenny?"

Peter was still trying to keep his voice soft, but Beth could hear the edge behind his gritted teeth. "How many times do I have to tell you that not only did I not do what she's telling you I did, I *couldn't* have done it."

"Why not?" Beth needed to believe him, maybe more than she had ever needed to believe anything in her life. That might have been easy enough given her puppy love, but picturing Jenny's unflinching and anguished expression made her question him more than she wanted to.

"Because that's not me, Beth. *I didn't do shit.*" For the first time, Peter sounded angry. "Nobody raped Jenny. She's been trying to get on me all summer, and refused to take *no* for an answer, no matter how many times I keep telling her that it ain't gonna happen. You know how jealous she is of Dorothy."

Beth nodded — *everyone* was jealous of Dorothy.

"She kept trying to make me promise that I would break up with Dorothy so we could be together, and I kept telling her that I didn't like her in 'that way' and that I wasn't ever going to do that. Jenny finally threatened that she would accuse me of raping her if I refused to end things with Dorothy. I just never actually thought that she would actually do it."

There was a war inside her. She had no idea what to believe. Jenny was her best friend in the whole world, and she had never lied to Beth before.

Peter was always nice to her, but what he was saying right now didn't make sense. It felt a little like when her father said that he hadn't been drinking (and that it was none of her business if he had) when his breath smelled like liquor.

She thought about who Jenny really was. Her best friend every summer. Beth counted the months and weeks and days before Jenny would arrive to make her life a little better for a couple of months each year.

Dorothy had been right: Beth did know Jenny, and she knew that Jenny wouldn't have manufactured such a lie. She loved her friend *because* Jenny was always straight. She had taught Beth how to be direct more than anyone, and she didn't spew bullshit like everyone else in Rush. Including Peter.

And thinking about it now, Beth had heard him bullshit plenty.

She did her best not to gasp while slowly backing away from him.

"What?" Peter said, looking an awful lot like he wanted to snarl.

Beth felt like she could finally see Peter for the pathetic little boy he actually was. She should have listened to her bestie from the beginning, not this … *rapist.* "You did it."

"You really think that?" Anger warped his face. "Then *fuck you.*"

Peter swatted a hand at Beth. It didn't hit her, but still she was startled.

She fell another step back.

He stepped into it. "Fuck it. You can all have each other. Go ahead, get out of here! You and Dorothy can go be with Jenny, and the three of you can all ruin my life together. Good luck, you're sure as hell going to need it."

His anger was terrifying, but still Beth dared a question as she tried hard not to tremble. "Where's Dorothy?"

"Where do you think?" he scoffed. "She's with your precious friend Jenny right now."

But Beth shook her head. "Jenny is with her family on their goodbye tour. Every year they—"

"I know what they do every year!" Peter snapped. "And they *were* on their goodbye tour this year. Until Dorothy found the Masons at the Kalamack and they all went somewhere together. But don't worry, my dad has a plan."

"What do you mean?"

"I mean that we'll sink the Masons before they can touch me." He laughed. "They're probably all at that stupid, tiny cabin right now, planning my demise. Just wait until—"

"*The cabin?*" Beth repeated as panic climbed her esophagus. "Jenny and Dorothy are at the cabin?"

"The whole damn family is probably there," he smirked. "But not for long. My dad is going to run them out of town and—"

Beth could feel the blood rushing around her whole body. "Oh my god. They're going to die."

"Beth, what are you…"

But she turned and ran with all her might, out into the darkening woods.

She heard her name and ignored it, running even harder until she started to hurt, praying she was in time to save her sister and friend.

"BETH!"

She could barely breathe as she ran, but still she pushed herself, letting the day's events replay in her head as fuel to keep her body moving.

What might turn out to be the most disastrous day of her life had started out with a trip to the library, with Beth looking to figure out a way to cause a short in the wiring near the gas tank of the Mason cabin. Her father had been mouthing off for years about how easy it would be to set the Wilder place on fire if he wanted to, Beth was only missing the piece about how she might actually trigger the short. With that part handled, the rest of her plan was simple. Once she had the can of gas Daddy kept in the shed.

Before she knew the truth about Peter, Beth had wanted Jenny to leave. Now that she had her plan to destroy him, Jenny would never leave on her own. So Beth had to get the entire Mason family out of there.

Once Jenny's parents decided to leave and never come back, she wouldn't be able to ruin Peter's life, and Dorothy could stay with Beth here in Rush.

A fire at the family cabin would force the Masons to stay elsewhere, and without their cabin they wouldn't have a place to vacation next year.

The same thing had happened to the Fordes when Beth was only eight years old. She and Dorothy used to play with all three of the Forde children, two boys older than the Garrick sisters, and a five-year old girl, younger than all of them. The family cabin burned down, and Beth never saw any of those kids ever again.

The Mason place was supposed to go up in flames while the Masons were on the goodbye tour they always took their final night in Rush, spending time with each of the friends or prominent citizens whose opportunity for business or genuine company they enjoyed before bidding farewell until next summer.

But Beth's plan had backfired. Because Jenny and her lovely parents were probably at the family cabin right now, with her sweet twin sisters, plus Dorothy, all of them waiting to die.

And all because of her.

"BETH!"

She ignored Peter calling her name as she tore through the woods.

Tears streamed down her sweaty face as she panted, her feet crunching on dried twigs underfoot, then tripping on a root and spilling down to the forest floor — barely stopping herself from banging her chin on the ground by planting both palms in front of her.

She yelped as she scrambled back to her feet, ignoring the brush of what felt like a fern in her face and dripping blood on her right hand as she ran, on a determined flight in the darkness to reach her sister before it was too late.

The moon was full, but the canopy of branches was wide overhead, cast by an ancient family of redwoods. And the forest was a pall of darkness, blocking a full moon in a star-filled sky. The Goliath trees were gods of this forest, and it seemed like they wanted to punish her, slowing Beth from her mission, using the woods to stop her from reaching Dorothy.

She tripped on the underbrush again. And again, she quickly recovered, forcing her body to run faster than it wanted to.

"BETH!"

The voice was still behind her, louder now. She didn't know if that meant it was closer or angrier, but either way Beth felt the danger like heat on her skin, bristling with the warmth that comes before a fire.

She somehow managed to make her legs move even faster, focusing only on reaching the cabin in time. She ignored the sense of writhing danger all around her, the unreasonable yet overwhelming suspicion that the forest might swallow her whole. She also ignored the reek of gasoline in the air, telling herself that it was a different scent mingling with the slightly spicy and earthy sweet aroma of the redwoods.

"BETH!"

The voice was hoarse now.

But even if the enemy was right behind her, Beth had nearly reached her destination. She could see the cabin sitting like a portrait in the clearing ahead, illuminated by a strong wash of moonlight, no longer barred by the trees.

"BE—"

The cry was severed by a massive explosion, the sound drowned out behind her as the cabin became a fireball ahead.

And just like that, Beth lost her faith.

Salvation had been in front of her, but now all was lost.

She kept running toward the cabin, ignoring the first wave of furious heat rolling past her. Going ahead might spell the end of her, but staying back could mean something even worse.

The front door burst open and her sister came stumbling out of the cabin and onto the porch. Like a figure from a nightmare, she was a pillar of fire, screaming loudly enough to scald her lungs.

Beth looked past Dorothy, up to the second floor where a pair of burning children were pounding on the glass, begging for escape.

But Beth couldn't do anything. The cabin was already gone, and so was her sister.

She crumpled to her knees and sobbed on the ground.

FORTY-FOUR

Beth

BETH WANTED TO STOP WHIMPERING, but what else could she do now that all the memories were back? Now that she knew who she really was and what she had really done?

She had murdered her own sister, twice. And slaughtered an entire family.

Now that truth was as impossible to argue with as the gun in Jenny's hand.

Jenny moved her aim from Peter to Beth. "I'm going to need you to shut up."

But Beth kept crying. "*I'm so, so sorry!*"

Jenny put the gun to her temple and snarled, "Say you're sorry again and see what happens."

"It wasn't my fault." Beth shook her head and nodded at Peter. "He made me do it."

"You're kidding, right?" Peter laughed. "I asked you to *talk* to her. To tell her to leave me alone. Nobody asked you to set a fucking family on fire, you crazy bitch."

Beth violently shook her head. "He told me to get rid of you! He made me do it!"

"But you *did* do it, right?" Jenny glared at her.

She cowered back. "I didn't mean to … I never wanted to hurt anyone. You weren't even supposed to be there. Nobody was."

Jenny kept glaring at Beth. "What did you want then?"

"I just wanted the problem to go away."

"His problem"—Jenny waved the gun at Peter—"or mine?"

Beth whimpered without giving an answer.

Jenny turned the gun on her. "I knew you were helping him. That's why you pretended not to believe me when I told you what he did."

"I swear, I didn't know what was going to happen. It was only supposed to be a small fire."

"A small fire?" Jenny laughed without mirth. "So, just big enough to kill me and my family."

"NO!" Beth shook her head again. "It was only supposed to ruin the cabin so you'd go away! You were all supposed to be in Rush on your goodbye tour."

"So." Jenny turned both her gun and her rage onto Beth. "He raped me, then you murdered my family to shut me up."

Peter turned to Jenny and spoke in earnest. "She's a psycho and always has been. I'm guilty of what happened between us, and I'm really sorry about that, but I was willing to deal with the consequences then, same as now. But after you told Beth what happened, she couldn't stand the thought of her and I not being—"

"STOP LYING!"

"—together."

"NO!"

"*You did his dirty work for him.*" Jenny pressed the gun to her temple. "You're even more of a monster than he is."

"You're right! I am a monster. I deserve your hate. Please believe me, you have to know how sorry I am!"

"I remember when I begged you to believe me. Do you remember that, Beth?"

"Of course I do," she whimpered. "Can't you understand how sorry I am? How sorry I've always been?"

"Well, if you're sorry, then I can see how that makes everything else okay." A bitter laugh fell from her lips, but at least Jenny pulled the gun away. "You're so sorry that it's been nearly three decades without—"

"I didn't remember!" Beth exclaimed.

"Sure you didn't," Peter said.

"Another word and you'll be eating a bullet," Jenny promised. "You *both* left me for dead. And I might as well have been. My whole family was gone, and I was stuck in that goddamned institution. With only Dorothy to visit me once a week. You took my entire life from me. But at least I got far away from Rush and all of the assholes that live here."

"I'm so glad that you didn't die." It was dangerous to speak, but her truth deserved a voice, regardless of what Beth's captor might do.

"That sounds an awful lot like something someone who didn't want to die might say." Jenny stared, daring her to argue the point.

She didn't, so Jenny continued with a shrug. "I'm sure that one of you would've finished the job back then if you'd known there was still one to finish. I never planned on coming back here to this shithole. They wouldn't have let me anyway. Those nurses are jailers. But Dorothy brought that goddamned paper and I see Mr. Prom King himself, Little Fucking Pete, running for mayor and plastered all over it."

"*And you.*" She whirled on Beth. "You're even worse

than him. We both knew you set the fire. Always knew it. But I *thought* you were locked away in some institution. Somewhere worse than the one I was in. But NO!" She shook her head, manic. "Dorothy told me it was time to forgive. That you were here, in Rush living your life and making motherfucking cookies for the school bake sale. So while I was rotting away with only half a face, my would-be murderer and rapist were waltzing through life without a care in the world."

Peter said, "I'm sorry, Jenny. We were just kids."

Beth was sure she could hear the unbridled fear bubbling just under the surface of his voice.

"Just kids, huh? So that makes it okay that you raped me?"

"No!" He shook his head wildly back and forth. "Of course not. I really thought you wanted to … you didn't say no or try to stop until it was … you know, too late."

"*Too late*?" Jenny repeated. "I was asleep!"

"I thought you liked me."

"Any other bullshit rationalizations before we finally add *And then they lived happily never after* to the end of this story?"

"None of this was ever supposed to happen. Come on Jenny," Peter tried again, "there must be some way we can work this out. There must be something you need … something I can do for you."

"Or maybe something your family can do for me?" Jenny raised her eyebrows.

Peter made the mistake of seeing that as hope. "Sure! Of course."

Her expression curdled. "I'm so goddamned sick of rich people — *of rich men* — getting away with shit like this. They ruin people's lives without ever having to pay the consequences."

"I just offered to—"

"WITHOUT WRITING A CHECK!" Jenny roared.

Beth saw what might have been her only chance in the world and took it. "*Please, Jenny.* You're right about so much of this, but not everything. I'm sorry for letting him turn me into the monster that hurt you. I can never forgive myself, and I don't expect you to forgive me. I deserve all of this. *Of course* you can punish me. I destroyed the lives of everyone I ever cared about."

The next words stuck in her throat, forcing a pause for Beth to catch her breath before she could continue.

"And the worst part of it is that I did it for the one person in my life who wasn't worth caring about at all. It doesn't matter what happens to me … the world is better off without me in it. But the same is even more true for him." She gave Peter a nod. "And even though I know I don't deserve it, I was hoping that if you're going to kill us both anyway, maybe you could start with him so at least I can see Peter Wilder on his way to hell before me."

He chewed on his bottom lip, glaring at them both, surely considering his next move but unwilling to open his mouth and risk Jenny shutting it for good.

For the flicker of a moment, Beth almost felt hope.

But then Jenny pulled a zip tie out of her pocket and put it in Beth's hands with an order. "Tie yourself to the bed post."

Beth followed the order, terrified as Jenny continued to stare.

"Nice and tight." She checked Beth's work, then drew a box of matches from her pocket and shook them like a prize. "Now you're going to find out what it was like for me, and my whole family."

Beth wanted to beg for her life, but too much of her knew she had it coming.

Peter spat on her. "YOU CAN'T DO THIS, YOU FUCKING BITCH!"

Jenny was close enough that the glob landed on her burn-scarred face.

She swiped the smear away with a smile. "Watch me."

FORTY-FIVE

Sam

Sam peeked through the porthole and down into Peter Wilder's boat, barely able to believe her eyes, despite them confirming the worst-case scenario she kept turning in her mind while driving to the marina.

Beth and Peter were down there with the burned woman that could only be Jenny, prisoners of her gun. She looked furious enough to empty it into them both. Her attention was so fully on her captives, a world beyond the cabin didn't even exist.

Sam wished that she was armed with more than an empty mug that read *I'm sorry for what I said while docking the boat* that had been abandoned on deck. She would have paid a small fortune to have the weight of her taser in her hand, instead of the nearly useless ceramic mug. She gripped it tightly in one hand while pressing her phone to the porthole and recording the action below.

Jenny: "A small fire? So, just big enough to kill me and my family."

Beth: "It was only supposed to ruin the cabin so you'd go away..."

Moments later the gun was shoved against her head. "So, he raped me, then you murdered my family to shut me up."

Sam shifted her angle, assessing the access points to the room below.

Peter: "She's a psycho and always has been…"

Sam felt her upper lip curling back in anger: *Peter Wilder needed to die.*

Beth barely even tried to defend herself. She kept on apologizing while calling herself a monster and insisting that she didn't remember.

But Jenny wasn't having it. "That sounds an awful lot like something someone who didn't want to die might say."

She could pull the trigger any second now. Sam needed to make her move.

After Jenny's monologue:

"I'm sure that one of you would've finished the job back then if you'd known there was still one to finish…"

Sam tightened her grips on both the phone and the mug wondering when enough was enough.

"…Mr. Prom King himself, Little Fucking Pete, plastered all over it and running for mayor."

Peter made another stab at fleeing his responsibility, then Jenny kept looking angrier and angrier until she exploded enough for Sam to clearly see that it was about to be *now or never.*

"WITHOUT WRITING A CHECK!" Jenny's angry bellow cut Wilder off.

Beth started to beg, ending with a plea for Jenny to kill them both, starting with Peter.

Jenny had Beth zip-tie herself to the bed, telling Sam it was time to move. The box of matches in her hands said it all, even before she added words.

"Now you're going to find out what it was like for me and my whole family."

Sam could hear Peter's roar as she scrambled over to the cabin door.

"YOU CAN'T DO THIS, YOU FUCKING BITCH!"

"Watch me," Jenny said as Sam burst through the door, holding the sides of that mug like a baseball as she brought it crashing down onto the head of Beth's abductor.

Jenny cried out in surprise and fell back with Sam on top of her.

She tried to wrest the gun from Jenny's hand, but it wasn't easy despite the surprise attack. Jenny was running on pure rage, and managed to rake her nails across Sam's cheek and give her a swift punch to the gut before Sam's military training turned the advantage her way.

She flipped Jenny over and pressed her weight down, pinning the struggling woman to the ground.

She kicked and screamed and writhed beneath Sam, but she was a trapped animal and knew it.

She would have had to stop thrashing anyway, but Sam expedited Jenny's surrender by finally gaining control of the gun.

Sam stood, shoving the barrel into her ribs and hauling the burned woman to her feet, then used her own zip-tie on Jenny's hands and dragged her off of the boat.

Sam shoved her toward Chris, who stood at the end of the pier with a curt order to toss her into the backseat of the Jeep until the cops actually showed up.

She found Beth whimpering back at the Fat Chance. Peter kept glaring at her, surely knowing he was done for and likely calculating what he might possibly say or do to reverse his fortune.

Sam freed Beth first, cutting her ties while promising that everything would be okay. But Beth just kept shaking her head, still crying, muttering under her breath, barely audible, but still Sam heard the word *monster* and the phrase *deserve to die.*

Sam put a comforting hand on her shoulder and squeezed it, seeing the box of matches that had fallen on the floor and thinking about the family that had died, then deciding that she should leave this one to Meredith.

She freed Peter next. Sort of. He had just started rubbing his wrists when she yanked both hands behind his back and restrained them with another zip-tie.

"What the hell are you doing?" Peter demanded.

"I'm cuffing you for when the cops get here."

"I'm the victim here!"

"I'm sure you'll have a bullshit story all ready for the police. So you can go ahead and save it for them. But from what I've seen, and the evidence I recorded"—Sam pulled out her phone and let the implication sink in—"you're a rapist and an accessory to murder."

She was naive enough to think that might actually shut him up for a minute.

But Peter laughed instead, tipping his chin at Beth. "Do you really think that anyone is going to believe her? Everyone in Rush knows what a crazy bitch she is." He laughed again. "My father will post bail before breakfast, and our lawyer will take care of the rest by lunchtime."

Sam clenched her fists, flirting for a second with this asshole's murder. "I suggest you shut the fuck up before you make this any worse for yourself."

"I suggest you get the hell out of Dodge as soon as you can"—another nod at Beth—"before this bitch's crazy sticks to you."

"Rush is my town too," Sam snarled at him instead of emptying the gun into his face. "And I'm not going anywhere."

"You're—"

"Taking you to the cops." Sam shoved the barrel into his back. "That's right, asshole. March." The reek of the gasoline hit her nose again and she picked up the box of matches, dropping them into her pocket before turning back to Beth, already on her way to the door. "You're safe. Now, let's get you out of here."

But Beth didn't follow her.

FORTY-SIX

Beth

BETH WATCHED Sam while plotting out the rest of her very short life.

"I suggest you shut the fuck up before you make this any worse for yourself," Sam said, right before Peter called Beth a crazy bitch again.

But Sam wasn't having it. After slapping the asshole with a few choice words, she shoved the gun into his back and marched him toward the exit.

"You're safe," she said to Beth on her way. "Now, let's get you out of here."

Beth made it one step toward the door, but only so Sam would keep moving. She may have had the foresight to pick up the matches, but Beth had already spied a lighter behind the candle next to the bed.

Peter probably uses it to set the mood for his conquests.

She counted to ten, then went on deck, looking out to see how far Sam had made it with her prisoner. Sam shoved Peter into the Jeep, but she still hadn't looked back to check on Beth.

She drew a deep breath, reminded herself it was time,

then did the unthinkable, untying the boat so she could drift away from the dock and into a fate that had been overdue for too long.

It didn't matter what she could or couldn't remember, Beth was a murderer and that had been true for most of her life now. She hadn't just killed Dorothy — she had burned the Mason family alive.

That would have made her monster enough, but she had also helped to bury the rape of a best friend who needed Beth to believe her, more than she had needed anything else in the world that night.

But instead, Beth chose to believe the rapist … *and why?*

Because she liked him.

Because she was jealous of Dorothy and wanted what she had.

Because she was terrified of being left alone in that big pink and white monstrosity of a house. A fate she'd been subjected to anyway. Despite it all.

For all these years she had been haunted by everything that had happened without having any idea that it had only happened because of her.

She started the fire.

She burned a family alive.

She protected a monster by becoming one herself.

Beth was willing to betray both Jenny and Dorothy, all because a cute boy had asked for her help. And that had made her feel special — more than she was, or ever could be.

Now untied, the boat inched away from the dock and nearer to the end of her life. Even if this wasn't Beth's only way out, it was the only escape she wanted. It was too painful, to hate all that she was. She preferred a full departure from existence itself.

Death beat having to wake up every day for the rest of her life to the truth.

At least she wasn't alone. Beth was surrounded by her victims, all of them consumed by fire, the flames swallowing their bodies serving as a brutal reminder of what she still needed to do.

The Masons were with her. Jenny was still in the back of Sam's Jeep, but her parents and those two little girls were burning alive right in front of her, same as they had been for most of her life.

The scent of their barbecued flesh was both sickening and sweet.

And there was Dorothy right next to Beth, her body puckered and burned into a mockery of skin that looked more like desiccated fruit. But smiling. She wasn't the angry Dorothy anymore, but the sister who loved her. Despite it all.

Beth was ready to join them. She just needed to stir the last bit of courage inside her.

The reek of gasoline was still pungent in her nostrils. The hard work was already done. Beth just needed to flick the little wheel on the lighter.

She looked out across the water at Sam, now staring back at Beth, drawing her final few breaths on the deck.

"Make him pay."

It didn't matter that there wasn't any way for Sam to hear her. She somehow knew and bolted for the boat anyway.

But Beth couldn't wait another moment longer.

So she sparked the flame.

FORTY-SEVEN

Sam

SAM COULD SMELL what was happening moments before it actually did.

The overwhelming stench of gasoline should have kept her on her guard, but when she looked over at the Fat Chance floating out into the bay and saw Beth standing like a specter on the deck, she knew with every cell inside her that her friend was waiting to die.

Beth mouthed something from the deck and panic coursed through Sam, sending her in a hard sprint from the pier back to the boat.

But it was already too late.

Beth sparked the lighter and flicked it onto the deck.

The flames were immediate.

"RUN!" Sam screamed as she raced toward the Fat Chance, knowing that Beth would refuse her. "Jump into the water! You don't have to do this!"

But of course she just stood there, waiting to die as flames bloomed around her, higher and higher, obscuring Beth from sight.

A few hard slaps from her heels on the planks, then

Sam was flying off of the dock and splashing into the water.

She didn't stop to think about the inky black, or her daughter's mottled and bloated face. She didn't stop to think about how she hadn't been in a body of water in the two years since Sophie's death. She flew out over the water and crashed into the cold.

Several furious strokes, then she was at the ladder, climbing up onto the Fat Chance and into a wall of flames.

What the fuck are you doing, Sam? Do you want to die too?

Maybe she did.

"BETH!"

No answer, so Sam screamed again, coughing and choking as the acrid smoke conquered her nostrils as she shoved herself through the thickening rampart of smoldering fumes.

Sam finally got close enough to see the truth and fell back in retreat. It was too late for Beth.

"NO!" she cried out, whimpering, crawling backward, knowing that if she was going to survive this, she would have to jump back into the water.

With only seconds to make her decision.

Maybe this was where she deserved to be too. Maybe she could go out in the same blaze of glory as Beth. Peter and Jenny were restrained in her Jeep. Chris would turn them in. The cops would be here any second, and surely the Wilder Prince would get what was coming to him once a jury heard Jenny's testimony.

Beth's body had stopped writhing and was now a burned-out husk on the deck of Peter's boat. She was gone forever, so Sam couldn't look into her eyes.

And yet still she saw Sophie staring back at her, just like she always had when Sam abandoned her for duty abroad.

Now it was Sophie on fire, and Sam longing to join her.

She fell to her knees, sobbing, shredded from the inside by blades of guilt for everyone she had ever failed.

But then something in the cabin exploded and shocked her from that prison of recall. Already on her knees, Sam ducked lower, covering her head as she was pelted with fragments of flaming wood and pieces of metal, at last now finally realizing that she wanted to live.

Sam screamed again, inarticulate rage and grief turning her throat into pulp as she splashed back into the water, then swam for the dock with another failure burning behind her.

FORTY-EIGHT

Sam

RUTHIE WASN'T ANSWERING the door.

Sam pressed her ear to the wood, heard her TV, probably playing a daytime soap, and pounded harder.

"Who is it?" Ruthie finally said.

"Good morning, Ruthie. This is Sam."

"Who? I don't know you."

"Samantha. Salazar. I brought over some groceries."

"Oh! Beth's helper."

"Sure."

Ruthie opened the door and let Sam inside, eyeing her with suspicion as she entered. Or maybe that was only her paranoia, assuming Ruthie was just being Ruthie.

"So, I'm sure there's a reason you're here."

"I just wanted to say that I'm sorry for your loss."

Ruthie appeared downcast, but her shrug suggested that the loss wasn't exactly unexpected, or especially hard to take. "Beth was a very troubled girl, and I think she might be better off where she is now."

"Oh..." Sam was surprised to hear her say that. "Do you need any help with arrangements?"

Ruthie shrugged. "No point having a funeral now. They couldn't get me a body from the wreckage. And I'm not sure anyone in this town would want to come."

"I would come." It felt unbearably sad that even Ruthie wasn't mourning Beth.

"You've delivered your condolences. So now why are you here?"

"I imagine I have some answers if you're looking for them, and I was hoping you could fill in a few of the blanks for me."

"I suppose you'll want cookies," Ruthie said in reply, waving Sam to the sofa as she wandered off toward the kitchen. "I'll just be a minute."

Sam navigated through the monuments to Ruthie's hoarding, then sat alone in the living room until her host returned with a plate of cookies in a rainbow of colors.

"Jell-O cookies," Ruthie explained. "They're not very good."

"Oh." Sam wasn't sure if she should take one.

Ruthie grabbed two and bit into the orange cookie first. She made a face as she ate it. "Now that everyone is dead, I suppose there don't have to be any secrets. So, what do you want to know?"

"Can you tell me what happened back in 1993? After the fire?"

"You sure you don't want a cookie?"

Sam plucked a green one from the plate. Anything to get Ruthie talking. She popped it into her mouth and started chewing. She ignored the violent explosion of conflicting flavors and tried to hold her smile as Ruthie started her story.

"It was obvious straight away that Beth set the fire. The cops called in Big Pete like they always did, and they called me to come and collect her because Old Jack was down at the bar three sheets to the wind, and apparently also on the floor. Beth was hysterical when I got there, ranting and raving about setting the fire, and about Peter being a rapist and Dorothy being on fire. Seeing her like that…" Ruthie shook her head. "That might have been the worst part of it."

She seemed to shudder at the memory, but then reached for another cookie.

"Want to split this one?"

"No, thank you," Sam said, looking at the canary-yellow cookie.

"I know they're terrible." Ruthie made another face. "But I just can't stop eating them."

"You were talking about getting Beth after—"

"Right! Me and Big Pete made a deal. Dorothy and Jenny survived the fire, though both girls were badly burned. He would pay for them to get airlifted to Davis, if I would find somewhere for the girls to go and recover. I'd wanted to get Dorothy away from her father for a while, but now I also needed to worry about getting her away from Beth. So I agreed. Called my sister and asked her to take the girls in. Big Pete promised to pay for their care, and Shelby thought it was a good idea, seeing as she's always had trouble holding down a nine to five herself."

"So Big Pete just wanted both girls gone?"

"Exactly." Ruthie nodded. "And he left me with one hell of a threat."

Sam looked at her: *Go on…*

"Big Pete said that if Beth ever started talking about what Peter did, he'd make sure the truth about the fire came out, and that 'everyone from here to the San Joaquin Valley would know what Beth did.' So we told the town and especially Beth that the fire was just an accident."

Ruthie shrugged, "Wasn't hard. Between everyone talking about a gas leak and her trauma, Beth *wanted* to forget."

"What about Dorothy and Jenny?"

Ruthie mused before she answered, picking up a cookie and putting it back down again, seeming unsure of exactly how she should answer. Then finally:

"Well, Jenny never recovered enough for a normal life. Just too traumatized, I expect. She spent most of her years in Beacon Hill, just an hour from Shelby. Dorothy looked in on her but spent most of her time looking after my sister." Ruthie leaned back, looking like the story had finally defeated her. She shrugged. "But I have no idea what happened to make it all come out like it did."

"The sister!" Sam snapped her fingers, a final frustrating puzzle piece falling into place. "Shelby's neighbor thought she saw Beth, but it was really Jenny. She just didn't know her name."

Ruthie grabbed another cookie and tore right into it. "I wish Dorothy had come to see me first. We would have set it all straight."

"Or would you have told her to go back Ukiah and stay hidden."

Ruthie looked down at her half-eaten cookie without replying.

"She didn't get the chance to come and see you." Sam felt sorry for the aging woman, now all alone. "She was trying to find Jenny and sort everything out, but Peter fed her some bullshit story when she showed up at his boat party … about Jenny going up to the Mason's hometown in Oregon. She must have wasted days looking for her up there."

"How do you know that?" Ruthie asked.

"Peter spilled his guts after his arrest. Before Daddy arrived to shut him up."

"He's a Wilder." Ruthie snorted and shrugged. "No backbone."

Curiosity finally claimed Sam and she grabbed the other canary-yellow cookie. It was even grosser than the green one, but a bit more intriguing. Two chews in, she looked around the coffee table for a napkin, of course saw nothing, and swallowed the bite with a faltering smile.

Ruthie was waiting to hear something from Sam for the first time ever, and Sam was enjoying her anticipation.

"Beth wasn't as crazy as everyone thought," she finally started. "Turns out, Jenny had been living in the attic, for several weeks at least, slowly driving Beth insane. Poisoning her with manganese."

"What's that?" Ruthie asked.

"It's a mineral. You can find it in all kinds of foods. Like nuts and beans and seeds and stuff. It's not harmful in smaller quantities, but manganese toxicity can result in a neurological disorder called manganism."

"I've never heard of that."

"Well, Jenny was putting it down the well, enough to make Beth hallucinate. Then she would move things around at night, make a bunch of weird noises and try to freak Beth out, however she could. Beth thought it was Dorothy haunting her. She called her Angry Dorothy."

"Why would she do that?"

"Revenge." Sam shrugged. "Jenny didn't just want to kill Beth and Peter, she wanted to ruin their lives. She told the police she wanted them to suffer the kind of long-term agony that she had suffered herself."

Ruthie sat with the truth, looking like she wanted to grab another cookie.

"I will miss her," she finally said. "Beth was a good girl, despite it all. And such a help when it came to getting my groceries. I hope you're not dead set on ruining ice cream."

"Oh, I'm not—"

"I don't care if it's Ben & Jerry's or Safeway, but no tofu or whatever Beth was trying to poison me with last week."

"Poison?" Sam raised an eyebrow.

"Oops," Ruthie clapped a hand over her mouth. "I guess I can't joke about poison anymore."

Sam listened to a long list of preferences in regard to both flavors and brands — of course, Ruthie *did* care whether it was Ben & Jerry's or Safeway — realizing by the end that she had somehow agreed to be in charge of getting Ruthie her groceries.

Sam was surprised to find that, for now, it sounded nice.

FORTY-NINE

Sam

NOVEMBER ...

SAM WANTED to work the Redwood Rings side of the bar tonight, like she had every night since the boat fire. The Back Bar — once her quiet refuge from the barrage of tourists — was a painful reminder that Rush remained as unchanging as the tides.

Big Pete hadn't avoided the Back Bar after the fight with Chris and the bear in her trailer. Instead, he'd waltzed in the next night like he owned the place and told Chris that next time he interfered with Big Pete's "business," it would be his bar instead of his body paying the price.

Tonight would surely be the worst of all, because Little Peter Wilder had just won the election. Nina got the shift off, so Chris had Sam in the Back where she was forced to look at Big Pete and his buddies, all taking turns at his table leering at her in triumph.

Sam had spent most of the last hour weighing the consequences of dumping a pitcher of beer on the Big Pete's head, but she didn't want to find a rattlesnake in her freshly scrubbed DeVille. Plus, job hunting sucked, and while Chris gave her plenty of leeway most times, even a mile of it couldn't keep her from getting fired then.

Right around the time she was edging toward a sharp decision to fuck it all and proceed with the public soaking, Big Pete whipped his head toward the entrance as if expecting to see the very man who then came strolling through.

Big Pete smiled wide and slapped his hand on the table, whispering something to his buddies while unleashing a chorus of asshole-infused laughter.

Rush's new mayor kept strolling, straight to the bar without so much as a glance at Daddy's table. He held the grin during his approach, then widened it all the way while leaning across the bar.

"What can I get you?" Sam asked, instead of telling the asshole to fuck off and get eaten by one of the endangered species he probably kept trapped in a sequoia treehouse somewhere.

He smiled like a rapist pile of shit. "Surprise me."

She poured him a beer, then turned from the mirror with her back to Peter, so he couldn't see her spitting in it, even if he knew what she was up to.

She set the drink in front of him. "You here to *surprise me?* Make a point to show that you're still beloved, even though everyone knows what you did."

"I'm not sure everyone agrees on the facts of this particular matter." Peter shrugged like a rapist pile of shit. "Not that it matters. My lawyer has already settled with Ruthie. It's a good deal for her too. She gets compensation for the terrible accident that happened when Beth took the Fat Chance out into the water, *without my permission.* Stealing a boat is grand theft—"

"I'll press charges. I have everything recorded."

He laughed like a rapist pile of shit. "Go ahead and

spend whatever you've managed to scrounge from the tip jar. It won't do you any good. Because guess what the cops found when they tossed Beth's house?"

"Proof that you're a rapist pile of shit."

"That was fast," said the rapist pile of shit.

"I've been thinking it for a while."

He smiled and brought her that much closer to killing him. Because really, if Sam was willing to go, then why not take Peter Wilder with her?

She might even stay alive long enough to see Big Pete grieving and make him pay for everything he had done to turn an awful situation even worse.

"Your girlfriend had enough drugs to open a goddamned pharmacy." Peter leaned forward and whispered. "I didn't even have to plant them. Her bathroom made that bitch look like Heisenberg."

"That was blue meth, not pills, you fucking idiot. And Beth lifts right out of this. Jenny's accusations—"

Peter laughed again. This time, alongside his smile, the sound made Sam acutely uncomfortable. "Poor Jenny." He shook his head. "Her psych evaluation didn't go so well." A performative sigh. "Turns out she was suffering from severe PTSD leading to psychotic break." He made a face, as if this next idea disgusted him. "She was somehow *fixated on me.*"

He shrugged again. Sam pictured grabbing the nearest bottle and breaking it over his head.

"At least that's what her doctor says," he finished, with a smirk that deserved to be removed from his face with the most jagged shard she could possibly find.

"Her doctor? You mean, Meredith Graham?"

Peter made that face again. "Meredith Graham was treating Beth when she went all shithouse rat, so it doesn't seem prudent to trust her judgement in this matter now."

He grinned and Sam knew what was coming. "Reginald Jonas is treating her."

A retired good old boy. Drank himself into a stupor every other Thursday, came in jolly and left the bar looking like someone had dragged him behind a garbage truck. Sam had no clue about the particulars, but the man was obviously both miserable and living fat on Big Pete's payroll.

He was sitting with them now, and of course, they were all watching.

"You can't just make this all go away. Go ahead and hire a couple of bullshit witnesses, I bet a jury will still find Jenny's testimony interesting and—"

"Maybe that's how it works in Tostada Town, Salazar, but we have right-thinking juries here in Rush, especially when it comes to matters concerning the mayor. And such a jury could only rightly conclude that your 'recorded evidence' is nothing more than the deluded rantings of two mentally ill women, both of whom had loudly declared their vendettas against me."

Sam was seconds from clawing out his eyeballs.

"Better watch yourself, Salazar. You might not want to say anything you'll regret, because it wouldn't be all that hard to prove you were working with both Beth and Jenny. Phone records. Not just the calls you made, but wherever you went while the phone was on you." He shrugged. "Conclusions will be drawn…"

She chewed on her bottom lip while weighing her options. Whatever happened here, it wouldn't be tonight.

"Does it make me part of the vendetta conspiracy against you if I think you're a maggot who learned to talk?"

He leaned in again, this time with a lecherous smile. "This maggot made you come three times and shake your leg like a little doggie, so I guess you really do like it dirty." Then he took out his wallet, pulled out a hundred, and flicked it onto the bar. "Keep the change."

She fumed as Peter walked back toward his father's table.

He sat and they all started laughing, whispering to each other and making it obviously about her without ever looking over. The way she was breathing in and out like a dragon suddenly startled awake, nobody dared ask her for a drink. For once, Bill was doing all the work.

Sam had no idea how long she'd spent huffing and puffing when she finally felt a gentle hand on her shoulder. Tense as she was, she could have easily spun around and punched him in the gut. But she knew his feel despite her surprise.

"Not worth it," Chris said. "Believe me."

"Neither Beth nor Jenny deserve what happened to them."

"Who does? Life goes on."

"But not for them." Sam shook her head, staring daggers at Big Pete's table. "Beth is dead, and Jenny is back in Beacon Hill, probably on lockdown. They're gone, and those assholes are getting drunk and laughing about it. You don't know what I'm thinking, so how can you know whether it's worth it?"

"I have a pretty good idea what you're thinking."

Did Chris know she was thinking about dousing Big Pete's table with gasoline and lighting them all on fire, so she could watch those cackling assholes expire in some real-time hell just like what had happened to Beth?

Or did he have a pretty good idea that she was picturing herself opening Peter's throat while he slept, right after he finished fucking one of his little girlfriends?

Or maybe it was the most obvious among all of her

many possible thoughts: that Sam could do either of the above, or just about any other act of revenge if she wanted to, seeing as she really couldn't imagine sticking around in this godforsaken world much longer.

Dammit, she needed a drink.

"You have no idea what I'm thinking."

"Okay." He squeezed her shoulder, and it filled her with a warm chill.

"It's not like I'm stupid," Sam said, though Chris had given her no indication to suggest that he might have thought anything otherwise. "I know Beth wasn't exactly innocent. She killed her sister *and* set the fire. But shit, man, that asshole over there manipulated the hell out of her when she was just a girl, and then kept using her mental health as a weapon against her. What he did was worse, and still he gets to keep living and laughing and dropping hundies like singles: fuck him in all the ways."

Chris kept looking at Sam compassionately, letting her vent as he made eye contact with Bill, directing the flow of customers at the bar with his gaze for too long before Sam finally stopped letting all the self-loathing get the best of her.

"I'm done." She was disgusted that she wanted to hug him. "Thanks for listening to me."

"Of course." He nodded. "Want to trade places? It's pretty busy next door."

"I'll take a hundred JJs over one Peter Wilder right now."

"I've got it here." He nodded again, this time with a smile, then turned to the tiny line that was already forming.

Sam went next door, relieved to be away from the man who would for sure make her drink.

But the Redwood wasn't much better, and it wasn't

even JJ's fault. The bar had just as much alcohol, though really, a lone bottle was more than enough.

Sam was dying for a drink. Before, during, and after every customer exchange or interaction with the trippers, she would picture herself pouring a full glass, then do everything in her power to resist the temptation of turning an easy dream into her immediate reality.

What was wrong with her? Working in a bar while trying to stay sober. Just a shot or two of whiskey would dramatically improve her world.

She needed an NA meeting, but Sam hadn't been able to face the group since discovering that one of them had ratted her out to Big Pete. Not even after Meredith begged her to attend.

And again, what did it matter if she was on the way out? Fuck Peter, he wasn't worth her time. She could go home, take a handful of the pills his daddy so graciously gave her, maybe use the often-whetted paring knife in the tiny kitchenette drawer — either way she could see Sophie tonight.

Though the thoughts of killing herself weren't what they used to be. They were a pale shadow of the aching need they had once been.

And every time the consideration turned serious enough to unsteady her hand, Chris would come over to check on her. A quick exchange and then he'd be gone. Just enough and in no way overbearing. As if somehow he knew what she needed before she did, and that giving it too freely might be keeping her alive.

Despite her gratitude, Sam didn't want to see him after work. Whether or not she made it to the other side of the night, she needed to be alone either way. She ducked out a few minutes early, knowing it always took a little longer for

Chris to close shop next door, filled as it was with an even more entitled crowd.

But he was leaning against her Jeep before she got there. "Fancy meeting you here."

"Don't you have to close? Last man out and all that?"

"I closed the Back Bar early tonight."

"How'd you manage that?" Sam asked.

"I cited the old 'family emergency.'"

"And Big Pete didn't give you any shit about that?"

"He was already gone. They all were."

"Left as soon as they made their point, huh?"

He nodded. "They did."

"So you closed early to harass me?"

"I was hoping we could go to Hunter's Point. We don't have to talk. I just want to be with you and stare at the stars together."

Sam looked out across the lake while contemplating her answer. The waters were still dark and merciless, but framed by the redwoods that felt more like home now, the lake seemed somehow smaller than it had been.

"Okay. But no talking."

FIFTY

Syc

WHILE SYC WAS WORKING, Dog followed him around the campsite.

He didn't particularly enjoy the work, but Syc appreciated the solitude it provided, allowing him to tune out without becoming numb as he checked the park's electrical connections to ensure that nothing was sparking, while Dog wagged his tail right next to him. He weeded the grounds around the park, because people loved nature in the wild but expected it tame next to those places they paid for.

But this would be the last time Syc would be weeding for a while. Now that the trippers had all gone home, most of his work was about closing down for the winter. Clean up the fire pit and turn off the hot water in the communal showers. It was as simple as turning a dial since he and Sam each had their own now.

One advantage of losing the Airstream.

The ground around the fire pit was covered in ashes and soot, and the pit itself was filled with charred wood and embers. It wasn't much fun cleaning it, but Syc did feel good about having cleaned the pit thoroughly to end the season. He and Sam would have to stargaze from his front porch now.

Syc was grateful to have Sam nearby. It made the winters less cold and wet to have her around. The landscape remained a verdant region blanketed in ancient, towering redwood forests, but the air would soon turn cool and crisp. The loneliness always came. Less so since she moved into the park.

It was nice to have her company. Sam could be abrasive, but that was her nature, and Syc could say the same about his favorite loofa.

He wished she had pursued Chris more seriously. Between him and Dog, Sam seemed to finally be getting some of the help she needed.

Not to mention some resolution to the recent string of disturbing events.

"Come on, boy," Syc said as he walked away from the freshly scrubbed fire pit, deliberating whether he should mop the bathrooms or wait another spell for some more people to clear out.

Dog trailed Syc but came to a halt when his phone buzzed in his pocket and he paused to see who it could be.

Goddammit. Syc had a sinking feeling in his stomach the moment he felt the buzz, and he didn't even have a special ring for the number he recognized as the bad news he was certain it would be. Louis certainly wasn't calling to discuss the Golden State Warriors.

"Louis," Syc said as he answered. "How are you?"

"It's bad news."

Obviously. "Give it to me."

"I have some information on the Garrick case."

Syc swallowed — that case was closed, and it didn't

need to be opened up again for Sam's sake. "What kind of details?"

"A new body arrived at the morgue."

"Oh?"

"Dorothy Garrick," Louis said.

No. Shit was about to get started again, and right after the toilet got flushed.

Syc swallowed hard again, then reluctantly asked his buddy the question he had to get out, even though he was loathe to insult his friend's intelligence.

"Are you certain it was Dorothy Garrick?"

"Oh yeah," Louis said, "there's no doubt this is 100%, Grade A Dorothy."

"Where was the body found?"

"I have no idea. But wait, there's more."

Syc sighed. "Of course there is."

"There was something weird about the body."

Louis had assisted the medical examiner, so whatever this was, he'd almost certainly witnessed it firsthand. "Strangulation was the cause of death…"

"But?"

"There were also multiple stab wounds on the body, postmortem."

Syc sighed again as he processed the information, then thanked Louis and hung up the phone as Dog wailed in sympathy at his feet.

"You're damn right," Syc said as he patted Dog on the back.

He started walking back to his trailer — fuck mopping the bathroom for now — and thinking about his next best move.

This latest round of bad news most likely meant that Beth did not actually murder Dorothy as Sam believed, so there may be a bigger problem than he realized.

Syc was probably better off leaving this one alone and not telling Sam what he knew she'd want to know.

But Syc was determined to keep her safe. If she made the mistake of going after what she saw as the bad guys again, the Wilders would do far worse than a bear in her trailer.

So perhaps he needed to keep Sam from discovering the truth.

But he couldn't keep it from her forever.

Dog whined again.

"You're right," Syc said as he started to walk. "I, too, don't want to be inside."

No, he couldn't keep Sam from the truth forever, but his silence could buy her at least one more night of peace.

So, he and Dog took off for a walk through the rapidly darkening woods.

The End

About The Author

Lauren Street has always loved a mystery. As a kid growing up in bible belt country she devoured every whodunit book she could get her sticky little hands on and secretly investigated all of her (seemingly) normal boring neighbors. Sometimes their pets and farm animals too. All grown up now and living in the UK with her thoroughly unsuspicious (and often unsuspecting) husband, she writes domestic psychological thrillers about families torn apart by secrets and lies. And she sometimes still peers over garden walls to check up on the neighbors.

Also By Lauren Street

The Bishop Smoky Mountain Thrillers

Hide Me Away

Fuel To The Flame

Closer By The Hour

A Gamble Either Way

Calling My Children Home

Too Far Gone

Here You Come Again

Replaced with Nolon King

Replaced

In Her Place

Irreplaceable

The Salzar Red Wood Forest Thrillers

The Girl Who Couldn't Stop Dying

9 781629 553764